PRAISE FOR

Kismet

"Becky Chalsen's debut novel, *Kismet,* is the ultimate summer read. The Sharp sisters, Jo and Amy, are twins on the cusp of turning thirty. . . . The twins' future happiness is a lock until fate takes a turn and changes the course of their lives forever. *Kismet* is funny, poignant, and sexy, with enough surprises to delight and enthrall beach readers everywhere."

—Adriana Trigiani, *New York Times* bestselling author of
The Good Left Undone

" 'A wedding, a birthday, a holiday weekend. What could really go wrong?' Becky Chalsen's debut novel, *Kismet*, dishes up everything a reader could possibly crave: family drama, long-held secrets, and the what-ifs that can sometimes haunt even the most loving of unions—all set amid the sunset-soaked allure of Fire Island. Book clubs, take note: You've just found your next favorite read. Chalsen triumphs with her kindred literary voice, but especially in how she so beautifully, and wisely, illustrates the journey of healing and the subtle nuances of the heart. I loved this story, and I can't wait to see more from this new and promising voice in fiction."

—Sarah Jio, *New York Times* bestselling author of
With Love from London

"An atmospheric exploration of love, family, and sisterhood, *Kismet* is an utterly luscious debut. Keep this one in your beach bag for those sweltering summer days!"

—Sarah Grunder Ruiz, author of *Luck and Last Resorts*

"Intricate and heartfelt, Chalsen's *Kismet* is a moving meditation on how love changes and endures within a can't-look-away story of family, marriage, and complicated choices. With deeply sympathetic characters and rich, incisive writing, this gorgeous debut resonates on every page."

—Emily Wibberley and Austin Siegemund-Broka, authors of *The Roughest Draft*

"*Kismet* is a warm and wise beach read about marriage, sisterhood, loss, and life's biggest choices. Delightful yet deep, this novel is perfect for a summer weekend escape. It left me eager to book my own ferry ride out to Kismet, Fire Island! Chalsen's voice is filled with heart and hope, and I'm excited to read what she writes next. *Kismet* is a debut not to be missed."

—Elyssa Friedland, author of *Last Summer at the Golden Hotel* and *The Most Likely Club*

"*Kismet* takes place over only a few days but contains all the beautiful, visceral rituals of a lifetime of summer escape. Chalsen crafts an absorbing, layered story of sisterhood and secrets, mistakes and miscommunication. The Fire Island backdrop infuses every scene with the golden-hour feeling of beach sunsets, the constant balm of salt air, the distant pop of glittering fireworks; and Chalsen infuses her characters with a rare grace and warmth as they navigate the unreliable memories, temptations, and disappointments that arrive along with the end of their twenties."

—Katie Runde, author of *The Shore*

"With heart and tender insight, *Kismet* effortlessly captures the nostalgic radiance of summer on the seashore. Chalsen has crafted an absorbing story of sisterhood, friendship, and, ultimately, the unbreakable bonds that carry us through life. Readers will fall for the Sharp family in all its imperfect splendor. Like the very best of summer vacations, I didn't want this book to end!"

—Holly James, author of *Nothing But the Truth*

"A thoughtful exploration of love, sisterhood, and what happens after 'happily ever after,' *Kismet* is a beach read with a big heart. A sparkling debut."

—Lauryn Chamberlain, author of *Friends from Home*

"*Kismet* is a heartfelt tribute to the people and places that shape us, an ode to sisterhood and shared history, as well as a thoughtful exploration of a relatable question: Did we make the right choice? Are we on the right path?"

—Caitlin Barasch, author of *A Novel Obsession*

"Intense emotions, high stakes, characters pondering destiny—a truly enjoyable literary concoction. *Kismet* is the perfect beach read, a story of sisterhood, love, and loss that will have you thinking about fate and the sliding doors in your own life. I devoured it!"

—Kim Hooper, author of *Ways the World Could End*

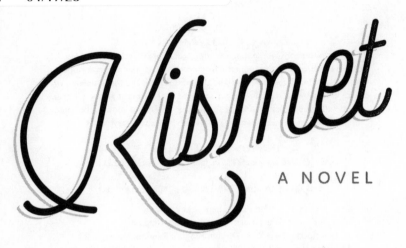

A NOVEL

BECKY CHALSEN

DUTTON

DUTTON
An imprint of Penguin Random House LLC
penguinrandomhouse.com

DUTTON and the D colophon are
registered trademarks of Penguin Random House LLC.

LIBRARY OF CONGRESS CATALOGING-IN-PUBLICATION DATA

Names: Chalsen, Becky, author.
Title: Kismet: a novel / Becky Chalsen.
Description: New York: Dutton, Penguin Random House, 2023.
Identifiers: LCCN 2022030994 (print) | LCCN 2022030995 (ebook) |
ISBN 9780593471500 (trade paperback) | ISBN 9780593471517 (ebook)
Subjects: LCGFT: Novels.
Classification: LCC PS3603.H336635 K56 2023 (print) |
LCC PS3603.H336635 (ebook) | DDC 813/.—dc23/eng/20220808
LC record available at https://lccn.loc.gov/2022030994
LC ebook record available at https://lccn.loc.gov/2022030995

I Want To Hold Your Hand
Words and Music by John Lennon and Paul McCartney
Copyright © 1963 NORTHERN SONGS LTD. and
MPL COMMUNICATIONS, INC.
Copyright Renewed
All Rights for NORTHERN SONGS LTD. in the United States Administered
by SONGS OF UNIVERSAL, INC.
All Rights Reserved. Used by Permission.
Reprinted by Permission of Hal Leonard LLC

Printed in the United States of America

1st Printing

BOOK DESIGN BY ASHLEY TUCKER

For my mom, who taught me to love books.

In memory of her mom, Grace Miller Roth,
and the sisters who lived in that large marble castle.
May their laughter live on.

Of all the gin joints in all the towns in all the world, she walks into mine.

—Casablanca

There are two things in life for which we are never truly prepared: twins.

—Josh Billings

Kismet

A CHAMPAGNE FLUTE FELL IN ONE FATEFUL BLOW. Glass pieces shattered all over the ground. Looking around, I knew: the scene was just one more sign of the damage I'd done.

The wedding I'd now singlehandedly destroyed.

Those fallen, misshapen specks were nothing compared to my sister's piercing glare. Oh, Jo. Her blue eyes soaked with tears, her pure bridal white a reminder of my own sins. She looked at me with so many questions, but I couldn't find the words to answer even one.

Next to her, Ben stood with his cheeks pale, fists clenched. My husband's wedding ring shone against the setting sky; each time it caught the light felt like a kick to my soul. A cry. The reflection of all my mistakes, painted like a sunset in his eyes.

I had devoted my entire life to these two relationships.

These two perfect people.

The introduction of a stranger had ruined them both.

Well, not quite a stranger. Not exactly.

I may have been born a half, a part of a pair, but I knew now that I'd have been better off alone.

Maybe we all would have been.

Together, it seemed like our only shared destiny was destruction.

Waves crashed, but the sounds around me muffled. My ears popped, my senses muted, as if the entire beach town had been submerged under the swirling, salt-filled ocean.

If we held our breath any longer, we'd surely drown.

'Til death do we part.

~ Welcome ~

Welcome to Joanna and Dave's Wedding Week!
We are so glad you have chosen to celebrate with us all week.
Below is a schedule of optional activities,
should you wish to partake in early wedding fun.

SUNDAY June 28	**7:00 P.M. · WELCOME DRINKS** Summer Wind, 17 Lighthouse Walk
MONDAY June 29	**4:00 P.M. · BEACH VOLLEYBALL** Oak Street Entrance

Bring gear!

TUESDAY June 30	**AFTERNOON CHOICE** **2:00 P.M. · Fishing Trip** Meet at Kismet Dock OR **2:00 P.M. · Lighthouse Tour** Meet at Summer Wind

Cash for Riley

WEDNESDAY July 1	**FREE DAY! ENJOY THE SUN** Kayak in the bay, tan on the beach, bike to Saltaire
THURSDAY July 2	**12:00 P.M. · FLOAT DECORATING** **6:00 P.M. · CLAM BAKE** Soiree at the Shoreline. Wear white!

**Note to self:
practice toast**

FRIDAY July 3	**7:00 P.M. · REHEARSAL DINNER** Le Dock, 60 Bay Walk, Fair Harbor **travel via golf cart from Summer Wind*

SATURDAY July 4	**11:00 A.M. · KISMET 4TH OF JULY** **PARADE & PARTY** Kismet Fire Department **5:00 P.M. · THE WEDDING** **6:15 P.M. · THE RECEPTION** The Out, 1 Bay Walk, Kismet

*Don't forget
the RINGS!*

SUNDAY July 5	**10:00 A.M. · FAREWELL BRUNCH** Summer Wind *Please see reverse side for ferry schedules home*

SUNDAY

SUNDAY

THE FERRY PULLED INTO THE FAMILIAR DOCK. THE one I'd come to associate with cold cheese pizza and sweet tea vodka sodas, bonfires in backyards and moon gazing on a starlit beach. Sand under fingernails, damp hair. Even the mosquito bites felt beautiful.

"You ready?" Ben asked me.

"I can hear the bells already."

My husband grabbed my hand and squeezed as the deck crew tied us in, a synchronized dance practiced to perfection. A gentle rock that might cause the uninitiated to lose balance if they weren't holding on to the paint-peeling handrail. For a moment, bliss.

And then reality crashed back full force like a tidal wave. Kids ran and parents scolded as passengers crowded their way down the just-too-steep staircase, disembarking with duffel bags and brightly colored coolers bursting with groceries that would somehow still need to be replenished before the end of the trip. Hosts greeted their arriving newcomers with hugs and red Solo cups—God forbid someone stay sober on the Island for the three-minute walk from the dock to the houses.

The Fourth of July weekend smelled the same every year.

As the chaos unfolded, I peered over the ferry's edge— we liked being the last ones off—and caught sight of Jo walking down the dock, wagon in tow. Her hair was golden from an early start to the summer sun. Jo had that inherent sense of style money couldn't buy, despite how hard one might try. She told me fashion was just in the hips, as if all attractiveness came from a confident walk and posture alone. Today, Jo was outfitted in an effortless wide-brimmed hat that I could never pull off and a midi white sundress billowing in the breeze.

The subtle glow of a bride-to-be.

"She's actually on time," I said with surprise.

Ben laughed. "Should we make a code word for the week? In case things get hard?"

"The only words I need to focus on are 'maid of honor,'" I said, as my gaze tracked north toward the beckoning town square. The Inn and the Out, the town's two adjacent restaurants, already filling with suntanned customers. The Red Wagon storefront overflowing with local crafts, the warmth of the Pizza Shack competing only with the constant rhythm of the sea.

These were the welcomes I craved, the dock arrivals that

had decorated my weekday daydreams ever since I was a little girl. Only this time, my hallmark homecomings seemed to stare back with a crooked smile. Somehow, they knew: despite the celebratory pretenses, summer contentment couldn't have felt further away.

I slipped the itinerary out of my tote bag with a sigh, the paper creased and folded. While Jo couldn't have cared less about potential crinkles in her invitation packet, I cursed my decision not to splurge for the laminator when I printed inserts at Staples all those weeks ago. Now my handwritten doodles danced back at me with derision.

"Don't you have that memorized already?" Ben said, elbow into my waistline, when he caught me rubbing the paper on my thigh as if my body were a human ironing board. Before I could retort, he stole the sheet straight from my clutches.

"Very funny," I said, my hand outstretched for the paper's return, but neither Ben nor his growing grin relented. I wasn't exactly in the mood for games, but I was even less in the mood for anything remotely resembling an argument.

Not after the way things had ended last night.

Fine. If Ben wanted to play, I'd play.

"'Welcome to Fire Island!'" I started to recite the lines from memory, my voice assuming a cheery octave like a docent rehearsing a script. "'We are so glad you have chosen to celebrate Joanna's wedding with us all week. Below is a schedule of optional activities should you wish to partake in early wedding fun. Please note: nothing else of import shall be happening over the next seven days, so, if by chance you think there's anything else the Sharp family is celebrating, you, my dear guest, are mistaken.'" I cleared my throat in conclusion. "How'd I do?"

"B-plus." Ben laughed. "It's 'Joanna and *Dave's* wedding'— your first mistake. How could you forget the groom?!"

"To my credit, it's barely been six months—"

"And I'm sorry to say, but the jury isn't seeing any of that last part on our answer key. Totally wrong."

"Ah, must have been thinking of an earlier draft. Pretty sure there was one that said: 'Happy thirtieth birthday, Amy and Jo! You made it! And oh yeah, Dave is here, too. Open bar all week!'"

Ben's smile remained, but I could see his eyes start to soften with concern. "Are you sure you're good, Ames?" he said, his tone lower. More serious. "We have time if you want to call Nina?"

"I'm fine." I swallowed, embarrassment growing alongside annoyance. I'd never have agreed to seeing a therapist if I'd known how often Ben would bring her up. "Seriously, I'm fine."

"Babe, you know you can always talk to me about—"

"Ben, I said I'm fine." Game over, I grabbed the itinerary out from his fingers and tucked it back into my bag. "We should get going anyway. Jo's waiting, and we have a ton to do at the house."

Ever since Jo had announced that she and Dave were to be married on our birthday this summer, the date had filled me with dread. Jo and I were born on July 4—two Cancers with every colored emotion to prove it, not just red, white, and blue. But this year, there'd be no need for stars and stripes, or the sun-faded birthday banner we always hung across the kitchen with care. It was wedding decorations only, whether I liked it or not. (And like it I did not, but being a twin meant sharing the spotlight, despite how one-sided the cause.)

The result? Our thirtieth birthday doomed to float by as a footnote.

"Can't believe the week's already here," I said now, my eyes once again looking down past the handrail and toward my twin sister. "Is it bad to say I sort of assumed she'd never get married?"

"Well, she's always been full of surprises." Ben smiled. "Consider this just one more."

"And, of course, she's literally glowing. I thought that was only in the movies."

"Hey, you glowed on our wedding day."

"Shone with sweat, is more like it."

"You were perfect. Our wedding was perfect," Ben said. "And everything is going to be perfect for Jo's, too. Surprising or not."

I nodded. If only I could believe that. A whirlwind engagement, a relative stranger now marrying my twin, all torpedoed by the fear of my own baggage taking center stage.

Perfect already felt like a broken promise.

As Ben hoisted our duffel bags higher up on his shoulders, I forced my stomach not to flutter at the flex in his biceps.

Any butterflies felt like a betrayal. He'd taken to weight training, a new lifting regimen recommended by his doctor. An outlet for all the added stress. *To help process.* I'd have been impressed, if I weren't the very reason for his needing an outlet in the first place. His muscles were now just another reminder of all that had gone wrong. All the ways I'd failed.

All the secrets we were still keeping.

One deep breath in to center myself. Nina's trick to silence the hamster wheel of worries running through my mind these days. I could do this. Whether I was ready or not, it was time to get off the ferry and run full force into Jo's Wedding Week Extravaganza.

I plastered on a smile and began the descent.

"A wedding, a birthday, a holiday weekend. What could really go wrong?" I said, hoping my voice now matched the breeze as we made our way down the ferry's steps.

"Nothing. But if something did, I'm sure one of your dozen color-coded planning binders would hold the solution," Ben said, without an ounce of malice in his voice. He always seemed to genuinely admire my organizational tendencies.

"First of all, there's only three binders," I said. "But fair."

"And look on the bright side: at least we'll never forget their anniversary."

"Ames! Benny! You're here!" my sister sang out, skipping over to us right as our toes touched the dock. Only Jo could make skipping look graceful at (almost) thirty.

"Wouldn't miss it for the world," I said, as she pulled Ben

and me both in for a group hug, each of us looped under one of her bangle-coated arms. She smelled like sunscreen and pencil lead. A writer on vacation.

"I seriously can't thank you guys enough for taking the earlier ferry," Jo said, her honeyed voice moving a mile a minute. "There's so much to finish, Dad's to-do list grows longer by the second. I swear, he's going to give me an ulcer before we even get to the damn aisle. That reminds me—we have to pick up more ice on the way to the house. We've been here less than twenty-four hours and we've gone through five bags already. We should've imported an igloo! What were we thinking? A wedding on an island? In July? Ha!"

In a millisecond, Jo's spiral subsided with a choke. Her eyes welled, and her face flushed as her lower lip quivered. "Look at me, a walking cliché. Pull it together, JoJo."

The Sharp family had a tendency toward the theatrical. Our grandpa cried so readily his nickname was Weeper. Jo and I both kept tissue boxes on all the coffee tables, a constant bracing for the inevitable heart-tugging commercial, and we'd taken many a stern look from strangers for crying "too loudly" during a Broadway show. We were suckers for a good cry, and weddings were especially dangerous territory.

Now, I took my sister by the shoulders, wiped a tear from her cheek. Whatever recent calendar grievances and marital strains clouded my brain instantly fell by the wayside. What mattered most stood right in front of me. "You, Joanna Sharp, couldn't be a cliché if you tried." Then Jo hiccupped out a sudden pitiful yet very loud sob, which made us both guffaw from the unexpected sound. It was just what we needed. A small relief that paved the way to belly laughs, a desperate break from all the tension that surrounded us both. The love language of our sisterhood had always been inexplicable, shoulder-shaking laughter. Once we started, we couldn't stop, and soon my own eyes blurred from surfacing tears.

"Do you guys need a minute, or can we get this show on the road? I think my forearms are burning," Ben said. He had dutifully reclaimed our checked baggage off the lower level of the ferry and loaded all the luggage onto the wagon. Suitcases and duffel bags threatened to topple over the edges.

"Yes, Benjamin, let us protect your pasty arms!" Jo laughed and grabbed my hand, leading the way even though it was equally as much my house as it was hers. Best to put aside protective claims to family ownership this week though, I thought. No good would come of that.

I turned over my shoulder and flashed Ben a grateful smile as he followed behind us lugging the wagon. Sure, last night ended in a rocky place, but that was marriage. Rough patches were par for the course, right? We would get through it; we always had. What mattered now was that we were here in Kismet. The weather forecast promised sun. My twin sister was getting married. And I was determined to be the best maid of honor the world had ever seen.

I could do this.

WITHIN SECONDS, IT WAS CLEAR THAT THE EN-
tire neighborhood had heard the news of Jo's wedding. Every neighbor we passed gave hugs and blew kisses,
offering best wishes for the bride and groom—and fingers
crossed for no rain on Saturday! When we bought ice at the
Kismet Market, the owner, Brian, even gave us a "bridal discount." "Redeemable all week," he said with a wink.

"It's like the town put your wedding date in the official
Kismet calendar." I groaned.

"Any press is good press." Jo laughed back.

I couldn't argue with that.

Despite the rushed arrangements, it wasn't surprising that
Jo decided to be married on Fire Island. So many of our firsts
took place in this town, the streets free of cars and cares alike.
Our first bike rides, our first sandcastle championships, my
first kiss at the Out (hers at the Inn), her first lobster roll at
the Inn (mine at the Out). Her first time having sex with her

high school boyfriend Zach. They snuck out to the beach in the middle of the night, under the moon, in line with the dunes. I asked her to spare me any further details. While we may never have had that sort of gossipy sister relationship like schoolyard girls, I'd never forget how she said the fireflies shone almost as brightly as his eyes.

Jo was always a romantic. Her stories had a poetic, profound quality since we were children. "The ocean sounds like it's telling a secret," she famously posited at age five. (Famous, in the sense that my dad would proudly repeat the line, endlessly retelling it to anyone who would listen.) Whereas I couldn't ever sit still long enough to finish reading a novel, Jo was eternally tucked in a book or writing plays for us to perform, the low and sturdy living room coffee table our renowned stage. It surprised no one when she began making a career out of her words, writing her way through the world.

Of course, Jo's starry-night retelling never seemed to include her eventual return, when she stubbed her toe against the bench in the darkened entryway and knocked over a lamp, sending it crashing. When the morning came and we assessed the wreckage, Jo blamed Rocky. But I don't think my mom ever believed that it was our twenty-pound cockapoo, and not her teenage daughter, still flush in her cheeks, skin sparkling with faded moonlight, responsible for the ruins.

Not that any of us would have ever hard-pressed Jo on the details of her stories, though. As much as we'd complain behind closed doors about her hazy view of the world, we always found ourselves subscribing to Jo's poetry.

Sometimes it felt like all our lives existed simply to service Jo's lyrics. We were the first-round readers and typo checkers, the front-row supporters at her performances and literary events, the quickly canceled plans when she was admitted to the Iowa Writers' Workshop. We were the never-bothered backups to her dreams. (Well, sometimes bothered—Forsythia still charged me fifty dollars per person when Jo made us reschedule our dad's birthday dinner at the last minute so that she could attend said fancy writers' workshop.)

Regardless, for Jo to now be married in Fire Island was just another fitting stanza, and I was ready to slip back into my role of adoring fan, grateful to bask in my sister's glow.

I fell behind as our trio made its way down Lighthouse Walk, slowing my steps to take in the views of my favorite street. No cars meant the roads were populated solely by bikini-clad pedestrians and bicyclists in flip-flops ringing bells and calling out, "On your left!"

Up ahead, Jo paused at the intersection of Lighthouse and Maple, pulling over the wagon to admire an unusual flower growing among a patch of wood and weeds. She slipped off her sandals and sunk her toes into the soil, nose pressed close to the petals to savor the scent. Ben crouched down after her, knees nearly touching his elbows as he angled out his phone to snap a picture.

"Come look at this one, Amy!"

"It's a stunner!"

"In these shoes? I can see it fine from here," I said, but

smiled nonetheless. I knew they'd scour the internet as soon as we got home, excited to determine the origin, unearth the flora. It felt like we were children again, the three of us walking to elementary school and jumping in puddles, inspecting every butterfly or mushroom sprouting along the way.

As we got older, I'd opted to watch the messier quests from the sidelines—manicures had always been more my speed than dirt and dust. I didn't mind it: I never took for granted how easily Ben and Jo got along all by themselves. How they'd managed to form their own separate, genuine friendship as strong as any best friends, let alone siblings-in-law. I never had to have that fateful moment of introducing my boyfriend to my sister, crossing my fingers under the table while gripping his hand, hoping she saw in him the potential for partnership, for a lifelong family entrance status, that I saw sparkling in his eyes.

Ben had passed Jo's test for approval the second our commuter carpool began. He'd known us—both of us, all of us—for a lifetime, essentially. Ben and I were kindergarten playmates turned high school sweethearts. For as long as I could remember, he was never farther than right next door.

After years of secret flirting, of holding hands or grazing elbows when we thought no one could see, Ben and I finally kissed in the ninth grade. His lips tasted just as I'd dreamed them.

When our families found out, they could have thrown us a parade or taken out an ad in the local gazette: the parental enthusiasm was that palpable for two neighbors in love.

Backyard adventures morphed into date-night car rides, belting to personalized mixtapes even though we were both tone deaf, fingers interlocked on the steering wheel or heavy on his thigh. Jokes falling from our mouths, desperate to make the other person laugh.

Even as we dipped our toes in teenage love, Ben always fit into my and Jo's twin-shaped puzzle. He and my sister would read outside for hours, spread on picnic blankets in our backyard, and I'd serve them pink lemonade made from Crystal Light packets during breaks. They'd make monthly trips to the Jacob Burns Film Center to watch Humphrey Bogart classics while I stayed back to study for honors math. Even though I'd never been one for old-timey films, I'd listen to their plot recaps and movie-star impressions with a smile in exchange for leftover popcorn. I loved that they had something just for them, that Jo cared about Ben enough to have a friendship with him of her own volition. Ben's navy JanSport was tattooed with the stains of smuggled salt and butter. It never failed to make me smile.

By senior year, Ben and I had both applied early decision to the University of Pennsylvania, Ben for engineering and me for business at Wharton. After months of silent stress and awaiting anguish, nervous for all the ways our future would change if my and Ben's collegiate chapters were in different books, we crossed our fingers and closed our eyes as Jo opened both of our admission letters at the exact same time. We nearly fainted when she read aloud not one but two acceptances. The three of us screamed and danced and cried, celebrating in a huddled circle. Jo would head to Bard and study English, while Ben and I would move to Philly. A destiny cemented.

After that, there was no question that Ben and I would end up together. In a way, we had been married our whole life before we ever moved out of our parents' homes. We learned everything together, growing around each other like plants that shared a sun. I had lost track years ago of where I stopped and he began, with Jo sprinkled throughout like a gently flowering vine. Never a fan of an individual flower, I always felt my best as part of a bouquet. Our bouquet. We were all more beautiful, together.

Or at least we had been.

Now, my entire body ached as I watched Jo and Ben brush the dirt off their legs and resume their pace down the street. The simplicity of our childhood puzzle had never felt further away. There was no denying that it had been many months since Ben, Jo, and I spent time like this together. Not to mention the looming addition of a new stranger, Jo's betrothed.

Would we ever be able to fit back into our old routine after all that had happened?

After all that we were still keeping hidden from Jo?

In that moment, I'd have traded anything to swap adulthood hurdles for schoolyard games, weddings and mortgages cashed in for arts and crafts.

Secrets for scavenger hunts.

Each step Ben took away from me made my heart wince. I knew I was lucky. Truly, I did. I had been handed a soulmate from the second I could even form sentences. Ben was funny and handsome and could complete *New York Times* crossword puzzles in record speed. He was the first one at any event or party but always the last one to leave. He was even awarded not one but two senior superlatives from our high school class: Most Likely to Succeed *and* Best Eyes. All with a kind and quiet aura that instantly put a crowded room at ease.

All with a smile that made me feel like I was the only person in the world.

Ben was a fairy tale, with the odds for "happily ever after" firmly in my favor. I was never going to risk that. Not again, at least. I had taken enough statistics classes to know that no possible reshuffle was worth losing the hand I already had. And yet, as I watched him walking away, his shape silhouetted by the blazing sun, a small part of me couldn't help but wonder. What we were going through would take a toll on any couple. Hopes turned to tears. Fights into resigned looks of exhaustion. Something had shifted, the fabric askew. While I hated to admit it, deep down, I was beginning to doubt if we'd ever be able to snap back in place.

Could our luck run out? Could mine?

The sound of crashing waves shook me out of my thoughts. We had made it to Summer Wind at last.

"It looks amazing out here, Mom!" I called, hoping she'd appreciate the compliment from whichever opened window the words might fly in and reach her through. When our parents had first bought the Fire Island house back in 1995, my mom was charmed to see a sketched engraving already

decorated on the post out front: "Summer Wind," it read.
"Now isn't this just *Kismet*!" my mom said, sweeping her
twins up in her arms and kissing our foreheads, alternating
faces in rapid-fire. "You two are the Winds beneath my
wings"—kiss, giggle, kiss, giggle—"and now we have a Summer house name to prove it!"

"What's 'kismet'?" we had shrieked, such a funny word
to four-year-old children. Our mom kneeled down to meet
our eyeline, as if this was the most important question we'd
yet to confront her with. "It means 'meant to be.' Like, you
two, Mommy and Daddy. We are each other's destiny. Now,
who wants to check out the beach?"

Ever since, the view of Summer Wind sent an electric
shock to my heart. Nestled right at the foot of the Atlantic, we
joined the line of beachfront houses with the type of ocean
views that made you pinch yourself, the brain not trusting
the eyes. Three stories tall, with brown mahogany walls that
seemed to climb right up to the sun. The house itself weaved
around a massive pool deck, the heart and soul of the prop-
erty, tucked right in the center. There were just enough hedges
and fencing to make it feel like we had been suddenly transported to our own private oasis, an island within an island,
but with enough crystal-clear views of the ocean to always
remind us exactly where we were: home.

The deck really needed no extra decorations, but the
nuptial details my mom had added today were effortlessly
transformative. White and blush roses on the patio tables.
Twinkling fairy lights strung along the trees like stardust.

No ring balloons or wedding signs or monogramed cocktail napkins needed, we still sensed right away that the stage was set for something extraordinary.

We opened the door and were immediately enveloped by the scent of eggs and browning bacon wafting down into the mudroom. Dropping our bags, we kicked off our shoes and made our way up the oak stairs two at a time. No matter how old, I always reverted to a kid on summer vacation right when I opened Summer Wind's door.

Nearly the entire second floor was comprised of one big open space with floor-to-ceiling windows looking out in all directions. The ocean-facing side of the room housed a sand-colored couch that could fit a record of twenty-seven of our closest friends and family. It wrapped around a large wooden coffee table, one that was always decorated with succulents and seashells and the latest fashionable volumes of nautical charts.

The other half of the room encompassed the kitchen. That's where all the magic happened. A Fire Island weekend wasn't complete without massive bagel spreads on Saturday mornings (whitefish salad a must), followed by sandwiches on the beach and then rounds and rounds of appetizers and cocktails until it was time for dinner at nine or ten o'clock. Late nights were the specialty, followed by late-morning hangovers. Cue the cycle beginning all over again with more schmear-laden bagels for breakfast.

My parents loved nothing more than to entertain, to squeeze in as many houseguests into a beach trip as physically possible. And the more bodies sleeping in every guest bed, nook, or cranny, the more bellies there were to be fed. This morning, we found my dad preparing to do just that.

Stationed at the commercial-grade stove, he looked up from his cast-iron skillet of scrambled egg whites and handfuls of spinach (wedding diet, etc.) with a grin. "Welcome home!" He wiped his hands on his apron, the words "Father of the Bride" embroidered on the front in cursive, before pulling us each into a hug.

While Jo headed to her room, needing to proofread the final edits on her debut short story collection before "clocking out" for the wedding week, Ben and I slid into the stools at the island counter.

"Really good to see you guys," my dad said, pouring us both heaping cups of coffee. Black for me, oat milk for Ben. (*What? It's creamy!* he'd always retort if I teased him for being too trendy.) I tried to hide my sudden frown: even thinking of Ben's habits now hurt my heart. "Sorry your parents couldn't make it out this week," my dad continued, "but we owe them big-time for the champagne."

"And Jo's honeymoon fund," I added with a grin. "Seriously, that was so sweet of them." Ben's parents had already booked a nonrefundable vacation to Greece for this week with a group of friends all celebrating their sixtieth birthdays. Flights purchased and hotels reserved all before Jo had announced her plan. They were naturally disappointed to miss Jo's wedding but sent their best wishes, a case of Veuve, and a hefty donation to Jo and Dave's post-wedding piggy bank with us in their stead. It wasn't a deal worth complaining about: if I'd added babysitting Ben's parents to this week's juggle, I feared I'd drop all the balls entirely.

"They definitely want to celebrate all together when they're back," Ben said.

"We'd love that. Feels like it's been forever since we've seen them. Feels like it's been forever since we've even seen you, too," my dad mused, as I reached for a knife and a cutting board to start chopping tomatoes, onions, and avocados for the bagels' sides.

"It hasn't been *that* long," I said.

"Your first trip out this whole summer," he countered.

I felt my body temperature rise. "Well, we've . . . we've been busy."

"The renovation has been all-consuming," Ben cut in, even though we both knew our new house in Irvington wasn't what had kept us away. "And work doesn't seem to quit."

"Don't have to tell me twice about workload," my dad said with sympathy, susceptible to the false excuse. He always said how his own late nights and weekends as a partner at his IP law firm were all worth it when he was able to retire after Jo and I graduated college. Ever since, our time in Fire Island had felt all the sweeter knowing he wasn't up in his office waiting for faxes or endlessly refreshing his email while we were playing volleyball on the beach. This week especially, we were grateful for our dad to once again just be our dad. Apron and all.

"How is that new project going, Benny?" my dad asked as he gave the egg scramble a stir.

"All good," he said with a humble shrug. "Can't complain."

"Such a modest man," I said, eager for the change in topic. "He's up for a promotion."

"No kidding? That's fantastic."

"The latest app we're developing is headed into review, and I think the board is going to vote to expand. If it goes well, they'd let me grow it out with a whole new team, launch a department and whatnot."

"That's incredible. I'm rooting for you, son."

"Thank you, yeah, it would be awesome. Just with everything going on, a promotion could really help." I could feel Ben trying to meet my gaze, but I stared straight down at my chopping. This conversation was beginning to feel like a haunted boomerang.

"Oh? What's on the radar?"

Slice. Slice. Slice.

Ben's eyes were about to laser-cut two holes into my downturned forehead when we were thankfully interrupted by a loud crash echoing through the house. "I'm okay!" Jo called out from her bedroom. My dad and I looked at each other and stifled chuckles fighting to break free. Jo had always been our clumsiest family member. A wedding wouldn't change that. In fact, the nerves might make matters worse.

For now, I was grateful. Jo had provided exactly the excuse I needed.

"I should check on her," I said quickly, volunteering myself up and off my stool while popping a fresh avocado slice into my mouth. "Nobody wants a bruised bride!" I called, exiting the kitchen faster than a blink. If Ben sensed my total avoidance of addressing that steer in conversation, he certainly didn't show it. Still, we both knew that those slivers of breakfast sides weren't the only things suddenly left on the table.

CHAPTER

3

K NOCK, KNOCK," I SAID, LETTING MYSELF INTO MY sister's bedroom. "All good in here?"

Jo was sitting on the floor, surrounded by boxes and magazines and books that had fallen from the top shelf. "I was trying to find a sweatshirt." So much for editing. I wasn't surprised, though. Jo always followed her ever-changing whims. The life of a creator: mood was everything.

"No need to tear the room down for a layer, Jo," I said. "Want to borrow one of mine?"

"I want that old navy one, from high school."

"Our senior class sweatshirt?" Ever since my parents sold our childhood house in Westchester a few years ago, they'd been splitting time between Fire Island and a condo on the Upper West Side. As a result, most of our childhood belongings and memorabilia were now tucked away in Summer Wind's closets. Sun and storage, best of both worlds.

"Yes, Sherlock. That sweatshirt," she said, pouting, and rummaging through the pile of boxes. None of the containers were clothing storage, that much was evident from the outset, but I still sat down and joined her on the doomed mission, not minding the excuse to journey down memory lane.

We pulled out yearbooks, *NSYNC HitClips we still refused to throw away, old textbooks and notebooks from college courses we insisted on preserving, now covered with thin lines of dust. Jo's worn librettos from *Our Town* and *A Midsummer Night's Dream*, the padfolio from my first accounting firm internship. Like road maps of our past, destinations verging as soon as we started deciding electives and hobbies for ourselves.

When Jo first put down her field hockey stick in exchange for fall play rehearsals in the seventh grade, it felt like a personal affront. An attack on our twinhood. I accused her of abandoning me. Of abandoning us. Field hockey was *both* of our sport, until Jo decided she was done. I cried, so Jo cried, too, and soon our mom was forcing us to talk through tears on opposite sides of the kitchen table. New was scary, our mom said, but new was also necessary sometimes. We just had to promise we'd support each other whenever one of us wanted to try something new; dreams separate but still a team. Always a team.

That fall, Jo practiced passing with me on weekends in the backyard. We rehearsed her Shakespearean lines in the living room at night, sometimes even in between brushing our teeth before bed. Jo cheered at every game she could attend, and I sat front-row center for all four of her performances as Hermia. I mouthed the words right along from the audience. *Methinks I see these things with parted eye, when everything seems double.* Different roles, but still together.

At least, we were back then.

Now, Jo tossed down her *Midsummer* script with a sigh. While the accounts of the past were plenty, there was nary a senior class sweatshirt in sight. "Ugh." She stood and flopped forward on her bed, her face in the pillows.

"Honestly, Jo, just take one of my sweatshirts," I said, shaking my head at how dramatic my sister could still be.

"I don't want yours. I want that one."

"It's probably covered in moth holes at this point."

"What's wrong with moth holes? I'm fine with moth holes." Jo kept her face pressed into the linens, her words coming out muffled after a beat. "How did you do this?"

"Do what? I didn't lose your sweatshirt!"

"Not the sweatshirt. The wedding. I need this week to end, and it's barely begun."

Ah.

"Weddings aren't so bad," I said, lying through my teeth. The entire industry was built on a lie agreed to among brides that getting married was the single most magical, blissful, wonderful experience that existed on earth. Flutes of champagne and happy family members at every turn. In reality, wedding planning was petty. It was passive-aggressive and pent-up anger and anxiety about conflicting priorities and taste in invitation styles. "Plus, I thought you loved being the center of attention," I teased.

"Ha-ha." Jo rolled her eyes as I pushed her over on the bed, freeing up space for me to climb in, too. As if by muscle memory, my bones seemed to remember that it had been months—longer?—since Jo and I had settled in like this, together. Only the two of us. This year so far had been filled with rescheduled hangouts due to Jo's writing gigs and deadlines, her burgeoning romance. My and Ben's house renovations and corporate climbs.

I tried not to remember the other reason why I'd put so much space between my sister and myself.

"It's just a lot," Jo said with a sigh, pulling my mind to her side. "Dave's parents are fine, I guess. They hate me, but it's fine."

"They do not hate you, Jo."

"His mother gives me death stares."

"Psh, yeah, right."

"Seriously!"

"Like how Ms. Gigi gave you 'death stares' in chorus and you still got the solo?"

"This is different. They're scary. I don't think his sister has ever smiled once."

"Don't be ridiculous. You're what daughter-in-law dreams are made of. Cute, smart, and not after his family's bank account," I said. Jo stuck her tongue out at me in protest. Internally, I tried not to harp on the fact that if Jo *had* spent more than six months getting to know her future husband before promising her hand, in-law drama might have dwarfed into a blip on a blissful horizon.

It wasn't that I didn't like Dave. He was pleasant enough the few times we'd met, and Jo's stories certainly painted him as a charming new beau. Recent distance or not, there was simply something inherently strange about Jo signing up for a life decision as big as this one without my sisterly stamp of approval. I couldn't assuage her fears about his family in good faith, considering I hadn't even been introduced to them yet. Instead, I had to simply hope that my sister's impressions were a by-product of rushed wedding planning stress and not something more substantial.

Knowing it was wise to keep such nags to myself though, I nestled my head on Jo's shoulder. So what if I wasn't there for the very beginning of her love story? I just had to play catch up. I owed Jo that much. No matter the distance, I'd try to be her teammate again. Even if I didn't understand her decisions. "Everything is going to be fine, Jo. I promise."

"I don't know. It's just, there's so many changes."

"And? You love change. You're the best at change. In fact, I think I remember a certain blond-haired twin shouting, 'Change is great!' my entire childhood. Does that ring any bells? I wonder what she's up to now—"

"Oh, hush." She laughed, nudging my arm. "I guess I just feel weird."

"Hate to break it to you, but it wouldn't be a Sharp event without something or someone feeling a little weird."

As if on cue, Jo's door creaked open and our mom walked

in, graying hair in a messy bun, with one hand propped on her hip. "Are my daughters calling me weird again?"

"Mom, come save Jo—she realized weddings are awful."

"That's not what I said!"

"Well, I love weddings," my mom said, coming to sit on the floor at the foot of the low bed. She rested her head on my leg, took Jo's hand in her own. Burrowed into her girls, it was like no time had passed. We were reunited again. "And I love you two. All shall be well, JoJo." My mom was a hippie, an artist. She loved free speech and free love and free everything. She was frustratingly optimistic, determined to see the best in even your worst enemies, which was a very annoying attribute for your mom to have when you were a teenager complaining about ex-boyfriends or the mean girls in your grade. But that was my mom: everything was an opportunity to rise.

"We're here to help," I said. "Want me on mother-in-law duty? I'm great with parents."

"I don't think even Amy Sharp can woo Mrs. Do-No-Wrong Valerie," Jo said.

"Be nice. She was lovely that night we met at L'Artusi," my mom said.

"She left early because the food was 'too salty'!" Jo cried. "Their food is perfect!"

"Well, I for one can't wait to meet them," I said. "And I'll make sure Dad doesn't salt any of their food."

"It's not funny. I think I might vomit my heart out," Jo said. "There's so much still to do, and Dave keeps disappearing the second I bring up any of the actual work. Like clockwork.

It's like he's allergic to wedding planning. Which means I have to plan. And I hate planning!"

Right as I was biting my tongue—once again trying my best not to point out how maybe the process would feel less overwhelming if they hadn't rushed into an engagement, if they hadn't forced a wedding during our sacred birthday weekend—our maternal tableau was interrupted by yet another untimely opening of Jo's bedroom door. I made a mental note to buy her a lock as the smell of sweat announced Dave's arrival before he even stepped through the frame, fresh from a long run in the summer heat. His usually pale and freckled face flushed red, his brown hair damp with perspiration. Dave did a frazzled double take when he saw us sprawled out on his fiancée's bed. He took out his ear pods, and the stifled rhythms of his running playlist automatically paused, causing me a silent sigh of relief that he hadn't overheard our gossipy complaints—I did not want to be blamed for any of Jo and Dave's wedding drama, especially not this early into the festivities.

"Didn't realize I was interrupting a party." Dave smiled through his shock. "Amy, so great to see you." He moved to give me a hug but thought better of it given his current moisture level. "Grace, can I help you with anything? I think Sam said about ten minutes 'til brunch."

"Thanks, dear. I just finished setting up your parents' guest room downstairs. They're still aiming for the three P.M. ferry?" My mom and I pulled ourselves up onto our feet, bones cracking, as Dave nodded in reply.

"Bobby and Mary are on that one, too, Mom." I had

been counting down the minutes until our cousins arrived. Close to us in age, Bobby had recently turned thirty-two, while Mary was clinging fast to twenty-seven the way we all do in our mid-to-late twenties. They were my uncle Greg's kids, my mom's only brother, and since they'd grown up in Manhattan, we'd been close in both proximity and personalities all our lives. Jo and I were elated when they accepted the wedding week invitation; most friends and family were trickling in closer to the actual wedding date on Saturday, but Bobby and Mary were not just any family. They were the most fun family members by far—wild and lively and *single*. They had an infectious energy, which we needed if we were going to get through this week intact.

"Fabulous," my mom said. "We'll greet them with the wagon and some cocktails when they arrive at the dock—"

"As if Bobby won't have a drink already?" I said.

"You mean a rum and Coke in his 'travel cup'?" Jo's loud, worry-free laugh was back as quickly as it had left.

Dave stood hovering by the door, needing to strip down and take a shower but not sure how to kick his future family out of the room. He pretended to busy himself by taking a clean shirt from the drawer and nervously refolding it over and over in his hands. I stared at him, polite but curious. Dave and I were still so new to each other, figuring out the other's quirks like a coworker who joined your pod of cubicles at the office. Who was this man marrying my sister?

"I forgot!" Jo jumped up from the bed. "Dave, show them what you did!"

"An early wedding present," he said, his face blushing as

he gently dropped the clean shirt and picked up a rectangular object off Jo's desk. I could immediately tell it was Jo's famous *New Yorker* article, accompanied by her very own black-and-white cartoons, shining behind the glass.

Their origin story, framed for eternity.

The same week of her article's publication, Jo had ventured to a poetry lecture in the Village, some author pontificating in a dim-lit bar with endless glasses of Merlot and wheels of Brie. By chance, Dave was there, too. He spied Jo from across the room, and like so many men before him, he was instantly captivated. There weren't many blond model types at these events, or so I imagined when I dreamed them up in my mind—unless Jo was performing, literary events were a scene I typically avoided, much preferring Pilates classes to anything with poems. Jo and Dave were frequent attendees though, and so they were immediately surprised by how long it had taken for their eventual crossing of paths. As soon as they got to chatting, it turned out that Dave was a fan of Jo's writing and had just finished reading her latest piece. In fact, he had it with him then. As he pulled that very paper out of his briefcase and shyly asked for her autograph, the world around them faded away.

Six months later, Jo moved into his faculty brownstone with a shiny vintage diamond nestled on her finger. Marrying the youngest-ever tenured professor at NYU and living off Washington Square Park—Jo's future had become a Nora Ephron film in Technicolor. All we needed to do was sort out the terrifying in-laws, and Jo was on her way to her very own happy ending.

Or so we hoped.

"That's so special, Dave," my mom said in adulation now, her hands pressed together. "Splendid!"

"Super sweet," I added, prompted by Jo's expectant eyes. "Well, lovebirds, you heard the man. Brunch in ten, so don't be late."

"Aye, aye, Lieutenant," my mom joked. My family's nickname when my punctuality steered toward bossiness. But in a family filled with freethinkers and head-in-the-cloud dreamers and just-five-more-minutes-of-work pleaders, who else was going to keep the Sharps in line? Especially with the fear of in-laws threatening to throw Jo's calm off-kilter, I knew it was going to fall on my shoulders to ensure that the Jo Sharp and Dave Beaumont Wedding Spectacular stayed exactly on schedule. While I was always allergic to the spotlight, at least I could confidently play the role of our family's timekeeper.

I grabbed my mom's hand and pulled her out of Jo's bedroom after me, but there was no hiding the groan we both heard as the door slammed shut behind us.

Dave's sudden exhale, audible against the wooden pane.

My mom looked at me with worried eyes, but I put my hand up to stop her.

"Everything is going to be fine. They're fine. Let's go greet the Beaumonts."

I T WASN'T UNTIL THE AFTERNOON ROLLED AROUND that I even had time to unpack. As maid of honor, I had led the charge from brunch cleanup to wedding chores to welcome committee at the dock. My feet were sore, and I hadn't even broken out the high heels yet.

"I don't remember Jo running around like this when it was your big day," Bobby said with a laugh as soon as he saw me, the nape of my neck already beady with sweat after piling suitcases onto the wagon.

"You think Amy would have trusted Jo with her planning?" Mary's voice chimed in.

"Please. I couldn't even get this one to use the wedding coordinator who came—*gratis*—with her venue," my mom said. "Trusts no one."

"Jeez, remind me not to plan any of *your* weddings." I frowned, though I was secretly pleased. There was nothing I loved more than a well-executed to-do list. For my own wedding, I wore the planning hat with pride. My only memory of the venue's in-house planner was a beet-faced man standing on the sidelines, back glued to the wall and (rightfully) nervous to interject amid the show I was conducting. Nominally, Jo of course donned the maid of honor mantle, but the only duties required of her were a smile and a toast. Easier for all of us—Jo wasn't exactly the most methodical, better with paragraphs than with plans.

"Oh, I'm never getting married. Such pomp. What's the point?" Bobby said now. "No offense. We're very happy to be here, Aunt Grace."

"Go, go. Get settled. I'll see you all tonight. And get ready, we're dancing!" My mom left our side with a flourish, as she headed to where Dave's parents were standing, arms crossed, in the single patch of shade. Despite the distance, I could see the shapes of their frowns. The Beaumonts hadn't even been in Kismet for fifteen minutes and their negativity was already shining on display.

Maybe Jo was right. Maybe this was more than a wedding-planning trope.

Maybe I did need to be worried about her future in-laws.

"Where do we start drinking?" Bobby's voice interrupted my thoughts. Thankfully and unsurprisingly, at least Bobby and Mary were already itching to start the party.

"Follow me," I said, leading my cousins to their home for the week. Our next-door neighbors had generously let us rent their house out for Jo's wedding guests—coincidentally, their son was also getting married this Fourth of July weekend, but up north in Warwick, Rhode Island, where the bride's family summered. Instead of putting their house on Vrbo and raking in a generous sum for a holiday rental, they let us borrow the space marked down with a neighborly discount and a promise to wash the linens and restock the vodka.

All the houses in Kismet had names. Some nautical, like Fanta Sea or Reel Paradise. Others were odes to the family living inside, like Lazy Bones, in which resided a chiropractor, or Murph's Inn, a nod to the dwelling's fierce and fiery Yorkie. Our neighbors' house was nicknamed Party of Five, and it was certainly shaping up to become the party house for the festivities ahead. The five bedrooms were to be occupied by Bobby and Mary, along with Dave's younger sister, Lila; his cousin Tyler; and his best friend/best man, El, the only guest Dave hadn't prepped us about during this morning's brunch. From the sound of Dave's stories though, they were all due to get along like a house on fire. Figuratively, we hoped.

Time-shares were a staple of Fire Island's history—my parents spent many summers young and drunk and sunburned, crammed into a rental in Ocean Beach with their best friends. Back when the thought of home ownership was but a kernel of a distant dream. They would charge their friends fifty dollars to sleep on the floor, sixty dollars for a couch cushion. Prices well worth the weekend's endless party. It was only fitting that Jo's wedding had our very own version of a time-share spectacle, although in this iteration, each guest was at least guaranteed a bed.

Dave's remaining guests were to arrive on the five-o'clock ferry, right in time for the seven-o'clock welcome drinks at our house. That meant Bobby and Mary had first pick of the rooms. But after touring them through every inch of the space and starting to load their groceries into the fridge, peeling off the Stop & Shop stickers from each banana, my cousins gently suggested that maybe Ben had something he needed my help with back home, and I should perhaps let them get settled on their own.

I hadn't even realized until that moment how much I had been avoiding my husband.

How grateful I'd been for any distraction.

I found Ben in our room. He had already finished transferring his clothing from his suitcase to the designated drawers, so he'd gone ahead and started unpacking my luggage, too. My silk travel slipcover was already pulled onto my pillow, my slew of matching toiletries already lined neatly on the dresser. It was a beyond-generous gesture, and any other day it would have given him a bonus boost on the husband scorecard. But this afternoon, when I was exhausted and sweaty and suddenly desperate for a quiet moment alone, it irked me. Ben was holding up a halter tank top, painfully focused on finding the proper way to hang it, when I walked in.

"I can do all that myself, you know."

His face fell ever so slightly. "Just figured I'd get started."

I took the hanger from him and finished the job. We

didn't have much time before we were due downstairs for setup, so my unpacking doubled as outfit selection for the evening. Bathing suits and cover-ups and underwear went straight to the drawers, but all dresses were tossed on the bed for a voting process.

A lavender dress flung from my suitcase to the comforter caught Ben's eye. "That new?"

"You've seen me wear this like three times." I knew I was being impatient, but I couldn't help it. "At Stone Barns? And then again for Connor's engagement party last month? You were there."

I zipped the now-empty suitcases closed, hauled them up, and shoved them in the top shelf of the closet.

"I could have done that. They're kind of heavy," Ben said.

"I'm fine."

"Is it okay to be lifting like that?"

"How many times do I have to say this? I'm fine."

He held up his hands in surrender and finished changing into khakis and a light blue short-sleeve button-down with small purple flowers. He smelled fresh and clean from his shower, something I'd missed the opportunity for during my afternoon of tasks. I resigned myself to an extra layer of perfume and dry shampoo instead, hoping it wouldn't result in the inevitable extra mosquito attention sure to follow.

"Well, my vote is for that purple one," Ben offered. "We'd match well."

I tempered, grateful for the olive branch after I thought I'd surely snapped it into pieces. Slipping out of my sundress, I turned my body away from Ben's direct eyeline. After years of intimacy, of studying and knowing and familiarizing ourselves with each other's skin, we had gotten to a point where our bodies were essentially functional operatives. A side effect of living in a tiny West Village studio apartment without central air-conditioning: you get used to each other's naked forms real quick.

But now there was an unspoken sense of vulnerability in the room. It wasn't shame or modesty, but I just didn't want him looking. Not yet. Hidden by the closet door, I swapped my strapless bra for sticky petal covers. The lavender dress was a short and breezy tank-style number, but with a deep V in both front and back, showing off the perfect amount of skin for a family gathering. Rushing, I rummaged through my travel-size jewelry box and pulled out a gold necklace with a tiny bear charm in the middle. An ode to my nickname for Ben: Bear.

I tried the clasp a few times until suddenly my hands started shaking. Right when I thought I was doing a good job of disguising my thoughts from my heart's anxiety, my body called my bluff. Fidgety hands and a slight headache were always the first alarm signals of my past catching up to the present. I could feel them coming in full force.

My closet was stuffed with beach clothes for all types of weather. My maid of honor dress was hanging safely, wrinkle free. Our schedule was going according to plan. Everything was as under control, as prepared, as it possibly could be. I was in charge. I was in my element.

So why was my body still riddled with doubt?

I knew the answer before I could even finish asking myself the question.

I motioned the necklace Ben's way. "Could you?"

He looked over at me from the other side of the room, and my heart caught in my throat. It had been a while since I had looked at Ben and felt so taken aback, so attracted. He wasn't doing anything special, planted in front of the mirror and finishing his own grooming routine, running his fingers through his smooth raven hair, dark like a wave at night. My husband was handsome. Handsome by every standard, but even beauty could grow mundane when given daily doses. It was like how you could stare at a word for too long, and soon the shapes looked unnatural by one another's side. You didn't even remember how the letters were supposed to sound.

I felt that way about Ben sometimes. I knew his body better than the back of my own hand, but still, there were moments when I closed my eyes and he morphed into a blur. I took his face for granted. One night, cuddled on the couch as teenagers, Ben asked what outfit he was wearing when I conjured him in my mind. I was so stunned by the specificity of his question, and so startled even then by the vacancy of my answer, that I brushed it off with an easy joke. "Nothing," I said with a wink, kissing him before he could protest any further, although the question gnawed at me for years. When I thought of my husband, my brain muddled the collection of old memories. An overlapping hodgepodge materialized: Ben at our high school cafeteria lunch table, snoring in bed, listening to a World War II podcast in the kitchen, sitting with legs crisscrossed on the couch. Ben, just being Ben. How to pick a singular moment out of a lifetime of togetherness, of mundanity?

For now, I took a mental picture of him for safekeeping— perhaps this could be the memory default—before moving to his side of the bed. When he placed my hips squarely in front of his own, I felt goose bumps explode from my toes to my fingertips. We hadn't stood this closely, this quietly, this alone, in a long time. Not since that awful night. Could it really have been that long? How had afternoons of avoidance turned into weeks? Now that I felt the heat of his breath on my neck, as he tightened the chain against my skin, I hadn't realized how much I had missed his warmth.

"Done." When he kissed the back of my head, I melted.

"Thanks, Bear."

He wrapped his arms around my stomach and pulled me in tighter against his body. His kisses moved from the top of my head, down my neck, and over to my shoulder. How much time did we have until we promised we'd be downstairs for setup? Surely enough for a quick break. I tried to steal a glance at the clock in the corner of the room, not wanting to interrupt this moment in the slightest, but I felt his head tilt in the direction of my gaze. And before his lips even formed the words, I knew he had misinterpreted my look.

"You know, your mom keeps dropping hints to me about how good a crib would look in that corner. I told her not to tell you that, but it made me smile a little."

My body filled with ice. I didn't want to have this conversation right now. He knew I didn't want to have this conversation right now. Why was he bringing up this conversation right now?

I pulled myself away.

"Can you go help my dad bring the folding tables up from the basement? Sorry, I totally forgot he asked me to send you down."

Ben frowned but recalibrated quickly.

"Sure. See you there?" He kissed my cheek and left me empty.

I was winded. We had promised this week would be different. Last night, he swore that we could leave the past in the past. Just for a few days. Just for a little while longer.

I slowed my breath like Nina had taught me. In out, in out.

It was over. Buried.

I couldn't go back there again.

I wouldn't.

THE STAGE WAS SET FOR A PERFECT EVENING. IT was a warm night, and the sky was that magnificent kaleidoscope of colors that melted right into the ocean. Summer Wind's pool deck had been transformed into a cocktail party scene, and a staff of blue-polo-clad bartenders and servers from the Out arrived to pour cocktails and pass hors d'oeuvres. This was the most intimate night of the week's activities, with only the bride, groom, parents, and closest friends and family members, so my mom and dad wanted to make it an extra-special welcome. We knew how much it meant to Jo and Dave that these guests were willing to take a week off from their lives to celebrate, so the festivity felt more like an earnest thank-you to the partygoers than a standard kickoff night for the bride and groom.

Even still, Jo and Dave opened the evening with a quick but lovely welcome speech. The first of many thank-yous to my parents for hosting, to the guests for making the multi-vehicular trip, to each other for being "the one." It seemed whatever flicker of annoyance Jo exhibited toward Dave's wedding-planning indifference had washed off faster than sunscreen in the ocean.

I might not have predicted Dave as Jo's first pick, considering her track record of Murray Hill boyfriends. Her past was filled with athletes and bankers who'd meet our parents and then meet the curb before we ever fully remembered their names. "Dating is like touring the whole world in just one city," Jo would say. Yet most of the times, she'd fly home alone. Jo loved romance but hated tethers more. She could barely stay in the same apartment for a year, and a steady relationship was even more terrifying than a fixed mailing address. After a shaky high school breakup, her romantic life fared no exception: the constant fear of being tied down kept Jo claustrophobically single.

Now, I raised my glass and sipped away my silent surprise. She shone. They both shone. Like a couple anchored in a long-lasting love.

I just hoped the rope wouldn't fray.

After their speech, I made my way over to where Dave was standing with his parents, eager, though slightly unnerved, to perform the sisterly duty of introducing myself to his frowning family at last. Dave looked a bit tense, not thrilled with something his mother, Valerie, was whispering into his ear. They were a glamorous but intimidating sight. From what Jo had told me, his parents were both academics like Dave. His father, Conrad, taught economics at Columbia, and Valerie had taught art history at Barnard before leaving to curate new exhibits at the Whitney Museum. Dave joked that he had been an accidental homework assignment for the young scholars, but no one risked mistaking it: his parents worshipped the ground on which he strode.

During the engagement period, Valerie had checked in regularly with my mom, volleying curt and perfunctory questions regarding the menu, the dress selection, the guest list. Everything, really. Offering opinions and criticism, welcome or not. Through it all, my mom swore (well, hoped) that they were well-meaning, just a bit rough around the edges. They were simply born-and-bred Manhattanites, emulating a particularity that could translate into haughtiness toward the unwarned.

Wooing them would be my personal challenge.

"Mr. and Mrs. Beaumont, so nice to finally meet you both," I sang, coating my voice with parent-charming sugar.

"This is Amy, Jo's twin sister," Dave added, after his parents remained uncomfortably silent. "She's an accountant." Crickets.

"Can I get anyone anything? Mrs. Beaumont, I love those pants," I chimed in again. Awkward silences wouldn't deter my attempts.

"Please, call me Valerie," she said at last, extending her hand in my direction. Her fingers felt frigid despite the still-setting sun.

"Your family did a wonderful job with the space out here. The furniture makes it look much bigger than it is," her husband, Conrad, finally added.

"Oh yes. And all those lanterns with the citronella are quite something. I didn't realize how buggy it was on Fire Island. I think I already have a bite on my elbow." Valerie outstretched her arm so I could inspect the nascent bump. "Shame. We're going to have to pick up some bug spray tomorrow, Conrad. This won't do."

I hoped my face wasn't as pale as it felt. "Can I refill your glasses?" I asked. "Rosé, maybe, or something stronger?"

"I'd take a tequila," Conrad said, but one quick, stern glare from Valerie prompted a new selection. "Actually, just another prosecco would be grand. Thanks, doll."

I headed to the bar, leaving the Beaumonts as quickly as I'd arrived. Jo was right: Dave's parents were something else. Especially Valerie. But weren't all mothers-in-law? Sure, I reasoned, there was a range of in-law characteristics, any combination of outwardly condemnatory or silently critical, vocally instigative or passively aggressive, controlling or too laissez-faire, that it made the bride doubt if she was even welcomed into her new family structure. Even Ben's mom was no exception, despite having known her for over two decades. Let's just say we had our fair share of "It's fine, I'm just disappointed" phone calls, when I announced that I wouldn't be changing my last name. This week, we would have to wait and see where Valerie would fall on the in-law-to-be spectrum.

At the end of the day, there were inherent growing pains

tied to a parent's realization that they were losing their front-row-center seats to a child's life. As soon as a son was engaged, his bride took on the role of a frazzled usher at a theater, awkwardly telling a guest they were sitting in the wrong row. *Apologies, we hate to do this, but would you mind standing up and coming into the aisle and moving to the back, please?* Scratch that: the bride was actually that smug audience member standing right *behind* the usher, grinning with the knowledge that they just scored the best view in the house, even if it meant kicking out the unfortunate souls settled there before them. How a mother-in-law handled the internalization of that transition could make or break a wedding-planning process. I wasn't saying it was right or wrong, just that mandatory therapy for all involved might not be such a bad idea.

I handed Conrad a bubbling glass of prosecco with a polite smile before excusing myself back to the party. I looked around and, for what felt like the first time all day, let myself relax. Jo was catching up with Bobby, while Mary and Ben were playing cornhole with Dave's sister, Lila, and cousin Tyler. We had also invited our closest family friends in Kismet, who were now making their way through the backyard, introducing themselves to the new faces while heaping hugs on the old. It finally began to feel like a holiday weekend, a wedding, a celebration. Not to mention a thirtieth birthday in a few days, provided anyone managed to remember it.

I made eye contact with Ben from across the pool, who smiled and mouthed, "Tequila shots?" Coming right up.

We could do this.

But when I turned to the bar, I felt my face turn white.

"Are you okay, Amy? You look like you've seen a ghost," the bartender said.

I had.

There, walking into our backyard with a hostess gift of Dom Pérignon in one hand and a card in the other, was a man I hadn't seen in almost ten years. A man whose existence I'd spent the past decade trying to forget. A man who was now staring directly at me. And smiling.

Emmett.

CHAPTER

6

WHO IS THAT GUY?" MY VOICE WAS FRANTIC, MY palms cold yet sweaty in the way that only dread combined with adrenaline can yield. "How do you know him?"

After I saw Emmett from across the yard, I panicked, downed both tequila shots, and ran to Jo. Pulling her off to the side of the party, I nearly pushed my sister into one of the light-strewn hedges. "Who is he?!"

Jo looked around and found the newcomer. "That's El, Dave's best man."

"El?" Confusion filled my frame as I glanced once more at the man standing by our entrance gate. A rub of my eyes only made his silhouette clearer.

"Well, that's his author name. E. L. Murphy. El's just Dave's nickname for him," Jo said, but the wheels in my head were already spinning so rapidly that they threatened to veer

off the tracks. "His real name is Emmett." I saw Jo's lips moving, but everything that came out of her mouth next sounded
like a mix of white noise and a horror movie soundtrack.
"Ames, are you all right?" Jo finally asked, grabbing my
shoulder and snapping me out of my trance. "Your face is,
like, four different colors right now."

"Actually, no." I needed to get out of there, fast. "Sorry,
I just got super nauseous. Vertigo or something. I should go
lie down. Don't hate me. I'll be back as soon as I can." I
skirted past her and up the stairs before she could get a word
in edgewise. Slamming the front door closed, I willed my
stomach to settle and my breath to catch. *In out, in out.* I
could hear Nina's voice in my head. My muscles rejected the
calming persuasion—they wanted to run.

Inside, in the air-conditioning and the quiet, my brain
started to reject the facts. To doubt my memory and my eyes.
It was dark outside, I figured. I wasn't wearing my glasses.
Sure, I *thought* Jo said "E. L. Murphy," but the music was
blasting, and we were standing right next to a pounding
speaker. I must have heard her wrong. There must be more
E. L. Murphys in the universe. Many more. After all, there
are three hundred million people in this country, almost
eight billion in the world. Statistically speaking, I would have
a better chance of accidentally taking a hallucinogenic drug
and fabricating what just happened. What I *thought* just
happened. Right?

Right?

The numbers made no sense. If anything, the numbers
themselves were proof: Emmett, my Emmett, was not here.

He couldn't be.

Even still, my heart itched. What if he was? Craving confirmation, I slowly eased my head toward the door's tiny window and dared myself to look. Peering out, I saw Jo whispering to Ben with a worried look on her face. As if sensing my gaze, Ben snapped his head up toward the doorway. I ducked quickly, desperate to hide. After a moment, my phone pinged with a new text message:

Ben: You okay?

My fingers froze, hovered above the keyboard, until finally punching out a reply.

Amy: Migraine, I think. Just need to lie down. Stay, enjoy the party. x

I bumped the back of my head against the door repeatedly, needing to feel something against my skin, some proof that the ground as I knew it was still solid. That I hadn't been transported to some alternate reality or living in a sudden simulation.

I needed to know, to determine if I could trust my eyes. If I could reenter the celebrations or be forced to resign and spend the rest of the week hiding in my room. Right now, I was grappling with the existence of both outcomes. My very own Schrödinger's cat—was Emmett here? Or was Emmett not here? I didn't dare let myself consider which outcome I'd secretly most prefer.

A quick peek was all it would take. When I poked my head back toward the window, my whole body went numb. There was no mistaking it.

Emmett was at Summer Wind.

I knew it was torture, but I couldn't tear my eyes away. He looked older, but his smile was frozen in time. He'd grown into his features, his large ears and square nose making more sense on his thirty-year-old face, still anchored by round glasses, often dirty enough that you could barely make out big, dark brown eyes underneath. Too lost in the vibrant world inside his mind to be concerned with wiping clean his lenses to see the regular one we mortals resided in. His graphic T-shirt and flannel warmed my soul. Hiding in the mudroom, I could sense he was exactly the same.

My charm morphed into fury as I watched Dave approach and begin to shepherd Emmett through the crowd. I internally screamed as he introduced Emmett, or "El," to my parents. During the emotional height of whatever it was that Emmett and I shared, I had sometimes let myself wonder what it might look like, that moment when Emmett met my family. Would they get along? Would they like one another? Now, I wanted to bang on the windows until the glass shattered, yell until my voice went hoarse.

My stomach churned, and I knew I'd seen enough. I needed to turn this off, to walk away, but my back just slid down the door until I was sitting on the floor, my knees hugging my chest and my head in my hands. I willed the rational part of my mind to make sense of the chaos. Was I dreaming? How was this happening? How was he here?

If Emmett was indeed Dave's best man, he must have read Jo's last name on the invitation. Hell, we were twins. Sure, we weren't identical, but we still looked like sisters! He must have met her, or at the very least seen her picture. To have pieced together by now that Jo and I were related. That this was my sister's wedding he was attending. In my family's beach town. Our home. Yes, we had promised zero communication. And yes, we had upheld that rather strictly. But that rule was mostly to prohibit drunk texts and distracting messages. I think a *Hey! So . . . your sister's marrying my best friend and I'm the best man at the wedding! See you there!* would have qualified for an exception.

He must have known I would be here, but he still came to Summer Wind anyway. Why?

I sat on the floor for what felt like an hour, too stunned to even cry. How was I going to explain this to Ben? To Jo? To everyone?

Then I remembered the notebook.

My heart dived straight to my stomach.

The notebook. Our story. Our past. It must have been in the storage container full of childhood and college memorabilia that Jo and I had gone through only hours before. That was exactly where I had left it after all that had happened. I raced back upstairs to Jo's room, where the yearbooks still laid scattered across her floor. Digging through the bin, I pulled a worn Moleskine covered in Philadelphia-themed decal stickers out from the bottom, covered in dust. How foolish, how ill-fated, that mere hours ago my fingers had come so close to grazing such a doomed omen for the evening.

I didn't open the notebook until I was safely back in my own bedroom. Perched on the edge of the mattress, I tuned out the sounds from the ongoing party, braced myself, and turned the page. If this was the week's future, I might as well embrace the past.

September 15

Dear Writing Seminar Journal,

     When I put down my deposit for Wharton, I assumed my first homework assignment would be a statistics problem set or an accounting exercise. Maybe a marketing research experiment if we were feeling bold. But a mandatory journal entry for a mandatory Freshman Writing Seminar? I guess this was the "well-rounded" part of the business school curriculum that perky tour guide gushed about.

     So far, all the business students seem to have that same energy coursing through their bodies. Is it a passion for finance, or have I just joined a cult? Either way, I do feel pretty grateful right now for my freshman seminar, and I'm not just saying that out of bias toward this current homework assignment and a paranoia that Professor Cleve might read this one day . . .

     !! Okay, I just checked my email! Lo and behold, Professor Cleve had posted on Blackboard asking us to please call her Kate and reassuring us that these journal entries will never be read by, quote unquote, ANYONE. We will only have to bring our journals in on the last day, quickly skim through to show her the ink-stained pages. All right, Kate. If you say so.

Our seminar is called "Mindfulness and Meditation," but I have never felt more distracted in my life than when I was in Fisher Room 303 today. I had come straight from a jam-packed morning of courses and meetings with my Wharton cohort. (A cohort is fancy business speak for classmates. (I know.)) Essentially every assignment in our fall semester is a group project with our cohort. And I've always hated group projects. In high school, I was usually paired with slackers who gave me the brunt (read: all) of the work and didn't even thank me when they got an easy A. I couldn't wait to graduate and leave that all behind me.

Journal, I had a plan. The Amy Sharp Plan.

Get into Penn with Ben—check.

Go to prom with Ben—check.

Graduate as valedictorian with Ben as salutatorian—check and check. Jo had won the English Department Prize, and we all came home from our senior ceremony with certificates and fancy cords, followed by celebratory Cold Stone sundaes on the porch. I spent the summer making trips to Bed Bath & Beyond, buying under-the-twin-bed storage and color-coded stapler sets. Creating checklists and crossing each task off with my lucky pen. I was ready.

Until I got to campus. Everything is so different from what I thought it would be. It's like, I'm trying on those old jeans in the back of my closet, and they don't quite stretch and flair like I remembered. My cohortmates are, well, intense. They want to schedule review sessions multiple times a day. They're obsessed with booking "GSR time" in group study rooms and joke about "moving in" to Huntsman Hall. I never thought I'd say this, but I miss the independence that comes with being the only academically passionate group member. A school full of valedictorians is way less fun than I imagined. Could I go back to being the only one who wanted to do the work, please? At least then I could be on my own schedule. (One that would never include intentionally sleeping in a class building . . .) Campus is beautiful, but I feel like a stranger on Locust Walk.

I'm living my life exactly as I planned it—so why does everything feel off?

That was what I was lamenting about internally as class began today.

And then, the door to the classroom opened. I'm not trying to sound dramatic, but, Journal, dramatic is the only way to put it. I met a boy. He wasn't in any particularly fashionable outfit, but from the second he walked in late, he changed the chemical makeup in the air. My heart nearly stopped beating when he moved toward the lone empty chair in our semicircle of seats. Right. Next. To. Me.

He tried to smile at me as he sat down, but I stared straight at my notebook. I could feel my face turning pink. One second of an adrenaline rush and it was like I was attacked by a blush-loving Sephora employee. Jo always said I had the inverse of a poker face.

I don't know why I got so nervous. It was like my body had a mind of its own. He seemed harmless enough, nice even. I tried to shift my focus back toward Kate, reviewing the latest reading assignments. But he kept trying to catch my eye. When I finally met his gaze, he leaned over and whispered, his voice barely audible, "Do you have a spare pen?"

I'm a terrible lip-reader, so I knew this wasn't going to end well. "An EpiPen?"

"Spare pen?" he repeated, miming using a writing utensil. Or I guess he thought he was miming? To me, it looked like his hand was cramping.

"Come again?" By this point, I was annoyed. I didn't want to get in trouble. He was the late one. He was unprepared. Don't bring me into your problems, stranger! But I guess he was annoyed, too, because he rolled his eyes and grabbed the pencil case perched on my desk. "Pen," he whispered again loudly, as he waved a newfound instrument in my face.

We must have been making too much noise, because Kate coughed in our direction, wordlessly telling us to quit the side whispers and pay attention. I was mortified. I never get in trouble (I'm still sorry, Kate!), and I didn't need this new guy looping me in with his drama. I spent the remaining hour and a half with my lips zipped tight, but all I could think about was NOT looking right at him.

I can't even believe I'm writing this. There's so much homework, and he was distracting enough in class. Why am I now writing about him IN my homework, too? College is wild.

I tried to call Jo to see what she thinks, but she hasn't picked up my last few calls. So, I'm here, turning to you. The truth is, Journal, I've never been in a situation like this before. I've only had one boyfriend— Ben, he's a freshman here, too. But three nights ago, we went to a frat party and had too much to drink, and I swear I don't remember suggesting this first, but apparently we are now thinking about maybe trying out a break.

A break.

Just until we're both settled. He doesn't want me to feel pressured or like I can't meet other people, he said. I don't know. I don't want to talk about it.

But . . . maybe that's why now I can't stop thinking about this new kid in class.

He said his name was Emmett.

MONDAY

CHAPTER

7

THERE WAS NO FEELING MORE PRECIOUS THAN when you woke up after a nightmare and realized it was only a dream. There was no murderer in the kitchen, no secretary in your husband's bed, no cancer in your sister's body. You breathed a sigh of relief so loud that you woke up your partner sleeping next to you. You laughed a little at how pessimistic your mind could be, how far-fetched from reality that nighttime horror really was. Thank God, you thought as you exhaled, it was just a dream.

Except it wasn't a dream. When I woke up on Monday morning, I realized my nightmare was only getting started.

After a REM-less sleep spent tossing and turning, my day began by discovering a lumpy object resting on my pillow. Opening my eyes, I saw the culprit: an ice pack, half melted and mushy. I pushed Ben awake, his head heavy on the pillow. "What's this? Are you okay?"

"Ah. Sorry," Ben whispered, dreams still on his tongue.

"Drunken me forgot that would warm by morning." My face must have remained wrinkled in confusion, because Ben yawned and then added, "For your migraine. I know they help sometimes."

Just like that, all my dread resurfaced. Emmett. The party. The fake migraine and the falsehoods still to come. "Oh" was all I could manage now. "Right."

"Sorry, just trying to help. How do you feel this morning?"

"Better," I lied. "Ice pack must have done the trick." Rolling over, I glanced at the time on my alarm clock. "Shit."

"I'm sure they'd understand if you're not up for it," Ben said.

"I can't just cancel. I promised Jo I'd be there," I snapped, wiping my cheeks awake.

"Jeez, sorry."

"You know I hate being late," I said, softening. "What are you up to this morning?"

"Mimosas. Mary's cooking up a boozy brunch over at the Party of Five house."

"No!" I shouted so suddenly that Ben sat up straight. The unexpected prospect of Emmett and Ben sharing morning cocktails made me physically sick. A horror I didn't realize could ever exist. I couldn't risk the two of them spending any more time together without my supervision. Not until I could figure out what was happening. How much Emmett knew.

Why he was here in the first place.

"Sorry," I spluttered, "I just remembered my mom actually asked if you could help her while we're out. Something about folding wedding programs? I'm sorry. Do you mind?" I lied.

"Oh sure, no problem," Ben said, but his look showcased a lingering suspicion.

"I'd be too jealous anyway. Save the mimosas for me," I pled.

"Fine." Ben shrugged, his head back on his pillow. "Weirdo." A few moments later, his eyes were closed, and his breathing rhythm signaled a return to sleep.

I wished that I could go back to sleep, too. Ignore realities and responsibilities and hide in a dream instead of this nightmare. But after a few breath cycles, I heard Summer Wind's floorboards creaking, a slipper-footed inhabitant walking in the hall. The echoes of another, awake and emptying the dishwasher in the kitchen. The clanging of glasses and the returning of silverware back in the drawer like an inherent alarm clock within the walls: it was time to wake up, whether I was ready or not.

I tried moving through my morning routine as quickly as I could, but by the time I met my dad and Jo at the Kismet dock, I was twenty minutes late. I couldn't believe it. Punctuality was part of my personality, and yet one glimpse of Emmett had me dusting off bad habits. A persona long buried away.

Now I filled the air with embarrassed apologies, tried to ignore the worried looks from Jo and my dad. Luckily, Captain Chris was a close family friend, and he took no issue with holding the water taxi in harbor until I was safely on board. We had arranged the private inter-island boat so that we wouldn't be limited by the less-frequent schedule of the larger ferry, and yet here I was already delaying the itinerary. Already making the day a disappointment.

I forced myself to snap out of it, to act normal. This was exactly what I needed: an escape from Kismet, albeit only for one morning. Couldn't my heart relax for a second?

Jo sparkled, tanned limbs shining, as we slid down into our seats. She was sandwiched between me and my dad, just like in so many of our favorite childhood adventures. When we took off and began to cruise along the waves, Jo squeezed both our hands in excitement. Still, I felt my face pale. A small sigh escaped my throat.

"You feeling okay, Amy?" my dad asked.

"Still sick from last night?" Jo's eyebrows were now raised.

"All good. Just a little seasick," I lied. Because what else could I say? *Actually, a man I never thought I'd see again just showed up for your wedding and now my stomach is in literal and figurative knots*?! Lies would have to do. "How was the rest of the party?"

"Magic. But we missed you," Jo said, wrapping her arm around my shoulders as my head fell heavy against hers with ease. If she didn't believe my words, she didn't show it. "Rest, rest," she said, patting my forehead, comforting my mind. "We need all seasickness gone before the tasting begins." I relented and closed my eyes.

Jo hummed a happy tune under her breath, leaning back

into the enthusiasm of the occasion, and I let my mind slowly ease. Let my stomach settle with each breath I took. In out, in out.

There could be a special clockwork with our sisterhood sometimes. The second that we were reunited, we'd feel like kids again. I always forgot how easy it was to be with Jo, how she could make it seem like everything was possible when my head was on her shoulder, when I was under her spell. A charm that memory alone couldn't always capture. As the boat rocked, my mind replayed the escapades we'd embarked on, just like this. I'd check the ferry schedule and she'd convince our parents to let us eat in Ocean Beach for dinner that night. Or I'd confirm the Metro-North train times while she'd entice our parents into taking us to the city and lining up at TKTS to see *Wicked* on Broadway.

We were the twins working in tandem, a double act taking on the world.

Now, at twenty-nine, we were the twins who had spent the better part of the year texting to cancel plans. What had happened to us? This week, I promised myself I'd lean in to Jo's magic. To let myself be tempted toward her spell, just like when we were kids.

When my eyelids blinked open once more, we were at the other end of Fire Island, easing into the dock and throwing lines onto the shore.

Sun beaming down on our hairlines, we stepped onto land and began our stroll down Ocean Beach's store-lined streets. Fire Island's buzzing metropolis. In the escapism of our simple errand, thoughts of Ben and Emmett somehow started to evaporate like morning dew, baked away by the sky. This was exactly what I needed. Finally, some fun.

My dad outstretched a free hand, camera open and angling toward our faces. "Smile!" We beamed on cue. "I'll have to send that to your mother; she's a bit jealous."

"Tell Mom we'll bring her back a slice of coffee cake," Jo said as we approached Rachel's storefront display, decorated with arrangements of baked goods so stunning and shiny that they looked more like props from a Mad Hatter tea party than something made here on Long Island.

Our entrance was announced with the ring of a bell.

"My favorite twins!" Rachel called out. Flour danced off her forehead as she stepped out from behind the counter and covered us in hugs. "Happy almost Fourth, happy almost birthday, happy almost wedding!" She endearingly grabbed my and Jo's faces, cheeks smashed in each hand like she used to when we were children. "Am I missing anything else?"

"We like to roll as many things into one weekend as we can," my dad said with a chuckle, but I avoided eye contact with anyone, a familiar heat resurfacing. After Jo and Dave announced their wedding date, she had sought sisterly affirmation. *Are you sure you're not mad? Can we throw a huge party next year instead? Thirty-one will feel equally as special!* I smiled and nodded, even though deep down I felt hurt, pushed aside. But what else could I really say?

Birthdays came and went. Even the big ones.

"Speaking of rolling . . ." Rachel snapped her fingers,

and one of her bakers rolled out a dreamy tray tottering with different cakes. "Sit, lovies, sit." She motioned us over to where a table was prepped with plates and prosecco.

"Rachel, you've outdone yourself," Jo said as we took our seats. "We'd be lost without you." Rachel's Bakery was as much a Fire Island necessity as sunscreen lotion or a hangover. As kids, Jo and I would beg our parents for weekend trips to Ocean Beach, eager to feast upon Rachel's treats. Now Rachel toured us through a dozen wedding cake flavor offerings for Jo and Dave's big day. Double chocolate, lemon sugar, salted caramel banana, cookies and cream, and more. Plates filled by the forkful, but that sense of childhood splendor felt somehow fresh out of stock. Even Jo seemed more stressed with each bite.

"What's wrong, Joanna? Are you not finding one you like?" Rachel asked.

"No, no, nothing's wrong," Jo said, swallowing, but I could tell her smile was forced. Her face suddenly looked tired, sad. Was something new bothering her? "They're all great, I guess. I just want to make sure I get this right."

"You know," my dad volunteered, a piece of red velvet cake fixed on his fork, "your mother and I didn't actually have a cake at our wedding. We did trays of cannolis instead."

"Ours was carrot, Ben's mom's favorite flavor. I don't think she even tried one, though," I remembered. "That woman was glued to the dance floor."

"Leftover cake may be against my scripture, but it's definitely a sign of a good wedding," Rachel said with a laugh.

"How can you ever pick just one?" Jo lamented, her eyes downcast. "Each has so much to offer. So much going for it."

"Does the groom have a preference?" Rachel asked.

My sister's sigh said it all: no help from Dave in sight.

"Ben didn't come to our tasting either," I jumped in. "Some work conflict he couldn't move," I heard myself saying, but suddenly my mind was busy wondering which flavor might have been Emmett's favorite in some alternate reality where he was the one waiting at my altar. Would he have sat by my side at the cake tasting, frosting on his teeth? Crumbs on his lips?

My body temperature started to rise.

"Men," Rachel hmphed.

"I wish Dave would have at least mentioned a preference. He just shrugged his shoulders and said, 'You pick.' Like always. But I hate picking. Amy, you pick for me? Like old times?"

Jo and I were a lifelong duo, our roles assigned from birth, and decisions were under my purview. For years, I picked the pattern and Jo colored between the lines. She brought the sparkle once I'd dictated the structure.

Part of me wanted to jump in and help Jo. To give direction, to be needed. Especially before Dave became her official decision-making partner in just a few short days. This might be one of my last opportunities where Jo was looking to me, and only me, for advice.

But at the same time, I could practically feel the sugar starting to mix with my anxiety from last night. Swirling up stress throughout my entire body. I couldn't bring myself to pick *anything*. Competing thoughts of Emmett and Ben tangled up and tangoed anew in my head.

A romantic errand based on decision-making was the very last thing I needed.

"You pick, Jo. It's your wedding" was all I could manage to reply, as the taste of vomit crawled up behind my molars. I just stared down at my plate and tried not to faint, all the while imagining what Emmett might say if he were here. Would he prefer a sea salt chocolate? Or maybe the cinnamon spice? Something new entirely?

Why couldn't I get his eyes out of my head?

"Well, who says you have to pick one?" my dad said, smoothing over the tension. A quick resolution followed: their reception would offer a table of cakes with varying styles, from strawberry to stracciatella. Rachel said she'd even throw in a few dozen cannolis as an ode to my parents' own wedding. It was in classic Jo fashion, to give each flavor a fair share at the spotlight and honor our family history, all at once. We exited with edible souvenirs, a decision made just in time.

Good thing, too, because it felt like my body would have exploded if we stayed another minute more.

With thoughts of Ben and Emmett again overtaking my brain, I was in no rush to return to Kismet. Back to all the distractions I needed to avoid. Instead, as we passed the bars, already filling with day drinkers and revelry makers, my mind flashed back to my own bachelorette weekend in Ocean Beach five summers ago. Whereas Jo had opted for a spa day at the Mandarin Oriental—she vetoed all events where "Bride-to-Be" sashes were the norm—I felt like I needed to perform the more traditional pre-wedding ritual of a girls' weekend getaway. Another custom crossed off my checklist.

"God, the sight of Sandbar alone gives me a headache," Jo said now, as we passed the lively bar and dance club. "Does that mean we're getting old?"

"Those bring back memories," my dad said with a chuckle, pointing toward a table outside that offered Rocket Fuel cocktail mixes to go. Coconut milk, pineapple juice, amaretto, and rum. A guaranteed good time, and perhaps now a potential solution to this week's problems? Everything seemed happier under the haze of a Rocket Fuel, and I could use the extra help.

"We're getting them," I announced. "My treat."

"No way," my sister protested. But her complaints fell on deaf ears.

"It's a Fire Island tradition!" I said, making my way to Sandbar's door. "You really can't get married here without it." I left out the other parts of my purchase reasoning:

That I needed to make this errand last as long as I could.

That I longed to rewind time, travel back to carefree nights out in Ocean Beach, when Jo and I would chase cocktails and dance for hours. When we'd take the very last water taxi back to Kismet, hair flying in the wind.

That I craved a way of escaping the nights now spent fighting with my husband. Restocking the wine fridge. Lying to his face each time I said "I'm fine."

That I knew I'd need a shield of liquid courage if I was ever going to face Emmett and our history head-on.

I thanked the cashier and grabbed the goods. This would be a perfect party trick. A festive cocktail for a fun night later this week. A celebration, I promised myself.

It had to be.

"All aboard!" Captain Chris called, helping us onto the taxi one arm at a time.

As we resumed our seats, Rocket Fuel ingredients in tow, I watched Jo's face darken. Suddenly, another memory trickled in. Jo outside Sandbar, tears running down her face, rum-induced sobs escaping her throat. The midst of a traumatic breakup. The whiplash of a cheating ex-boyfriend.

Devastation.

I shivered, shoving the memory down and away into its previous locked-up depths. When Jo's face hadn't resumed its normal coloring by the time we reached Kismet's shores, I prayed I hadn't triggered the same faded scene in her brain as well.

Walking down Kismet's streets, I told myself Jo's shift in mood was only in my head.

CHAPTER

8

I HOPED THAT THE MAN (BECAUSE OF COURSE IT
was a man) who invented the phrase "ignorance is bliss"
was living somewhere in a mansion off the Pacific Coast
Highway in Malibu. Or an estate in Hawaii. A private island in Bora Bora. Ignorance was the only way I was getting
through this week, and for the past few hours, boy, it was
working.

After Jo's nauseating cake tasting, I rushed back to my
bedroom. I couldn't risk dallying outside Summer Wind's
borders and potentially crossing paths with Emmett on the
street.

Not yet, at least.

Ben was out for a run, so I checked in with my office.
My assistant Margaret's chipper greeting was better than a
Xanax, so anxious was my bloodstream for a normal re-

prieve. In times of chaos, I craved routine. A coffee on the 7:20 A.M. Hudson line train into the city, and a second coffee and everything bagel with cream cheese from the Zaro's at Track 34 in Grand Central Terminal. I'd race the twelve blocks to my office on Park and Fifty-Fourth, needing to be moving faster than any other pedestrian, huffing as I passed commuters even though I was never in jeopardy of being late. A quiet floor as I settled into my office and turned on my computer. One moment of peace before the private equity fund where I worked flushed to life.

Margaret was eager for the wedding scoop. In your early twenties, weddings meant open bars and beautiful dresses, catching the bouquet, or locking eyes with a groomsman. She didn't realize the budgets or the breakdowns that accompanied the forging of a marital bond.

"How is it?! I want pictures!" Margaret's voice was practically singing, an octave shriller than any person's voice ought to be carried.

"It's one day in. Nothing has even happened yet."

"Well, there must be drama if you're calling me. You said you were going off the grid this week. Speaking of—how's Ben?"

I took a deep breath and tried to channel my latest lesson from Nina. The idea was to analyze the trigger moments and find a way to control them instead of letting them control me. What was the trigger in Margaret's sentence? The wedding, the drama, or Ben? Normally I got a kick out of Margaret's outspoken, presumptuous nature. Now, I found myself cursing the ground on which Gen Z walked. Was it possible to remotely put in a request with HR for a new assistant?

I rolled my eyes and moved on. "Any calls, Margaret?"

"Just Gordon again, asking for an update on the audit. I reminded him that it's not due until end of month and that you are on it like avocado on toast."

"Ugh, thank you. Gordon's the worst."

"Other than that, we're all caught up."

"Really?" I deflated with the sinking realization that work wouldn't distract me for long.

"Yup!"

"Great." I rested my head in my hand. "Well, I better get going. Brides, you know—"

"Have fun! I'll text you if there's an emergency."

"Email works, too, Margaret."

"But texting is faster—"

I ended the call and fell back on the bed, my head heavy on my pillows. Was it too early to go to sleep, start again tomorrow? I let my eyelids shut for a second, one moment of beautiful quiet, until a knock on the door jolted me back awake.

"Amy! I didn't realize you guys were back. Sorry, honey, were you sleeping?" My mom had a laundry basket perched on her hip.

"I'm up, I'm up." I smoothed out my shorts, which had crumpled during my bed dive.

"Any whites you need washed? I'm starting a load." Her voice said one thing, but her gaze was riddled with maternal subtext.

"All good, thanks." I checked my phone. The screen showed no new emails, no new distractions.

My mom sat down next to me on the bed. The subtlety never lasted long. "Are you feeling okay? I saw you head in early last night. Stress can manifest within the body in countless ways. Jo's wedding, your birthday, it's perfectly reasonable—"

"I'm good, Mom. Seriously. Too much to drink too quickly, or something." I got up and moved to the door, ending our heart-to-heart before it could even begin. "I've gotta get ready anyway. The game starts soon."

My mom gave me a half smile. "Okay, dear. See you out there."

I locked the door behind her. No more interruptions, especially not as I approached another aspect of the week that I had been dreading, one that arrived delicately wrapped up in a bikini-size box. When had I become such a pessimist?

Oh. Right.

I hid from my own reflection as I changed into my bikini, a ribbed black bottom paired with a matching longline triangle top. Sleek, sexy, and who couldn't get behind the high-waisted bathing suit trend? I shuddered thinking back to the days of low-rise bottoms hanging by literal strings. Afternoons spent upright in my beach chair, angled just so, my belly tucked in, and afraid to loosen my shoulders in case I revealed any unseemly cellulite. Down the beach, boys our age twisted their bodies with reckless abandon to nail a Spikeball shot or jumped to catch a football pass. I'd look on longingly but breathe in tighter.

Now I turned to check out my reflection and add some mascara, but suddenly my body seized. My blood went cold, threatening to sink me like an iceberg. My breath caught, and my vision blurred, tears forming as I grabbed the closet door for balance.

As I forced a memory not to form.

My confidence evaporated into thin air.

Don't do this, Amy, I willed myself.

Not now.

This week isn't about you.

My breath slowed, in and out, until my mind paused.

In control of my body again, I stripped out of my bikini and threw on a pair of Lululemon bike shorts and a flowy tank. Athleisure would have to do. Twisting my hair into a top bun, I forced myself to stare into the mirror this time and smile, cheeks hurting, until my expression went from pained to joyful. Much better.

Grabbing my beach bag, I poked my head into the kitchen on my way out, hoping to grab an iced coffee. Instead, I froze when I saw Ben, back from his run and making a green smoothie at the island counter. I couldn't handle my husband right now. It had felt like we were on a collision course even before Emmett's untimely appearance. Now there were only more secrets in the space between us.

We needed to unpack them, but where to even begin?

I tried to pivot quickly, but Ben saw the tail strands of a topknot whipping around the corner.

"Hey, babe, want one?" he called out after me. Busted. I

backtracked once more toward the entryway, giving my husband a fake smile that withered my insides. Why did I have to make everything so hard?

"Better not or I'll cramp up during my serve."

"What are you serving, dearie?" a voice croaked out from somewhere deeper in the kitchen. "Hopefully a tequila soda?"

"Conrad, give it a rest."

I stepped farther into the room and saw Dave's parents seated at the breakfast nook reading the morning paper. Two signature Ben smoothies sat nearly finished by their plates.

"Five o'clock somewhere," Conrad said with a wink. Valerie's lips pursed into an even tighter line.

"You know what they say: 'No Rules on the Island,'" I offered. "My dad always puts his watch away the second he steps off the ferry."

"Island Time," Ben added from the kitchen.

"I like the sound of that." Conrad toasted with his smoothie and finished off the remaining green liquid in one gulp. "Maybe we can add a little something to these tomorrow?"

"Well, it is a wedding week," I said with a fake smile.

"A lot to celebrate," Ben said.

"Is there?" Valerie said under her breath while slowly sipping the last of her smoothie.

"It's a whirlwind wedding, Val. Might as well go for a whirl!" Conrad said, his voice loose.

"I don't whirl," Valerie whispered harshly before standing up and leaving the room.

Conrad sighed. "I keep telling her to look on the bright side. A child getting married is one step closer toward retirement. Forget college. The real empty nest is when they're finally financially obligated to someone else. We've been dreaming about this day since she gave birth!"

"I'm glad it's finally here then," Ben said with a forced chuckle before starting to clear Valerie's and Conrad's breakfast dishes off the table. Ben was always prepping snacks or picking up after people, helping in the tiny ways that went unnoticed. Most of the time, he'd never even get a thank-you, but he wasn't asking for any gratitude or favors. He just genuinely liked to help. It was one of my favorite things about him.

I hated that I couldn't let myself fall back in love with him right now. Watching Ben clear the Beaumonts' dishes and laugh at their bad jokes made my head want to explode. The cartoon Amy would have steam puffing out of her ears right about now. It was all too much. I needed to get out of there, fast.

"What about you guys?" Conrad's voice filled the room again, and I knew I didn't want to hear the rest of his sentence. "Some baby-size financial dependents claiming your livelihood anytime soon?"

"We certainly hope—" Ben started.

"Who knows? You do make that empty nest sound pretty appealing, Mr. Beaumont," I said, cutting Ben off with a sharp smile. "Well, I better go. See you guys later." I waved from across the room and raced out of the kitchen before

Ben could react. I hadn't planned the words, but maybe Conrad's empty nest had some merit to it. It *was* appealing, in quiet moments, the idea of no kids, no responsibilities. No future weddings to plan, no tuitions to pay for, no in-laws to make nice with for the rest of eternity. What was the point of all the time and work and effort of child-rearing if the allegedly real rest, the "retirement," only came once it was all over? Could a nest start empty and still be just as beautiful?

After all that had happened . . .

I shuddered. I knew what Ben's answer would be. What our plan had laid out in black and white, what we'd promised. I knew he'd be annoyed by my response, but I also knew he'd be busy the rest of the day helping my dad build Jo and Dave's wedding arch. A task I'd purposefully assigned for him this afternoon, to secretly schedule in some time for us to be apart.

There was safety in silence, but my heart still panged with guilt. Avoidance via itinerary planning was a new low, but my anxiety was approaching an all-time high. Desperate times.

I just hoped my desperate measures would work.

As my fingertips grasped the front door handle, I heard Ben's voice call out after me, "Good luck!" His second warning was at a lower volume, and while his voice was threatening to be drowned out by the ambient street noise, I knew exactly what he said. Practically the only thing he ever said anymore. Always accompanied with a pitiful look befitting a porcelain doll.

A warning that had taken on a new layer of weight, ever since Emmett's arrival yesterday.

A fresh threat of which my husband didn't even know to be wary.

Ben's words echoed through the stairwell.

"Be careful."

WHEN MY PARENTS SUGGESTED A WEDDING week beach volleyball game, it was my request not to split up the teams along the typical "guys vs. girls" assignments. Yes, it felt tired and heteronormative, but more than that, I selfishly wanted to be on the same team as my cousin Bobby. We were the undefeated Sharp Family Beach Volleyball Champions for the summers of 2014 and 2015. Jo and Ben gave us some tough competition those summers, but we always hoped that if the cousin-wide tournament occurred again, Bobby and I would surely cement our three-peat destiny.

Now, I was cursing my steadfast loyalty to Bobby and his championship-winning serve. The sweet taste of potential victory turned sour by the fear of a particular male player who might be added to my team. Bracing myself as I arrived at the beach's entrance stairs, I let my eyes scan over the crowd of attendees already gathered around the net. For now, I could breathe: no sign of Emmett.

"What's up, party people!" I said as I jogged over toward the net. I felt like I was playing the part of Amy the Fun Sister as I juggled a volleyball in one hand and raised a tote bag up to the sky. "Your uniforms await." I rummaged through the bag and pulled out a fistful of wedding-themed athletic headbands. They were tacky but in an endearing fashion, with sparkly, loud letters declaring "Team Bride" in white or "Team Groom" in black.

"For the groom," I said as I handed the pile of black headbands to Dave. Unnervingly, the recipient of the white headbands wasn't standing by his side. "Wait, where's Jo?" I asked. "She said she'd come play." Jo had promised to captain Team Bride, to kick off the week's beachside games in her honor. Now she was nowhere to be seen. Had something happened after we'd gotten back from Ocean Beach?

I willed the flashing Rocket Fuel memory out of my mind again.

"Cold feet already?" Tyler, Dave's cousin, teased.

For a brief moment, Dave's mouth tightened into a worried frown. To anyone blind to the behind the scenes of their wedding planning, it might have been imperceptible, but what I saw was a clear flicker of concern: Jo was acting strange, and he knew it, too.

To his credit, my sister's fiancé recovered quickly. "She just doesn't want to risk any injuries before Saturday," he said, plastering an easy grin back on his face. "Plus, I don't need Godzilla spiking the ball into her teeth, asshole."

"That was one time! In the third grade!" Tyler protested. When Mary laughed a little too quickly, my eyebrows arched toward Bobby. Could *that* be a thing already? From his subtle groan, I had a feeling it might be. I spent one night in hiding and romance was already brewing at the Party of Five house.

"She said to go on without her, that Amy could handle her captain duties," Dave continued. "And that she'll meet us all on the deck afterward for a drink." I wasn't entirely convinced, but Dave's steadied eyes told me to try to believe him. He was her new half now—Jo hadn't even texted me to say she was bailing on the game.

I guess I'd have to start trusting Dave sometime.

"Sure," I relented. "But, Dave, since it's your wedding and I'm just the lowly maid of honor, I'll let you get first pick."

"Oh, man," Dave said, as he assessed the crowd. In addition to Mary, Bobby, and Tyler, the volleyball participants included Dave's little sister, Lila, and my mom, the latter of whom was wearing a long flowy skirt with seashells sown throughout. She never quite grasped the concept of activewear on the beach.

"This was always the worst part of gym class, wasn't it?" Dave said.

"Sounds like someone who didn't win a lot in gym class," Bobby joked.

"Then do *not* pick me," my mom called out. "I won't help you change that record."

"I'm having flashbacks of locker rooms and oily skin and bullies tying my Reeboks together," Dave said, and my heart warmed a bit. Middle school Dave could have used the middle school Sharp twins as allies. "I think I can smell the dirty gym clothes and toxic masculinity from here—"

"Get on with it, dude!" Tyler pled.

"Okay, fine." Dave sighed. "My first pick is . . ." After pausing for a moment of suspense, Dave then tried to drum-roll with his tongue for dramatic flair. Instead, he produced a terrible gurgling sound that sent everyone into hysterics. This must have been the side of Dave that Jo had fallen in love with. "I pick Grace!" he announced.

"Yippee!" my mom said with childlike wonder. "I don't think I've ever been picked first before! My new favorite son-in-law. Sorry, Benjamin!" She shouted the last part toward our house in case Ben could hear.

"Suck-up," Bobby faux-coughed under his breath.

"All right, all right," I said with a laugh. "My first pick is Bobby." He jogged over and slapped my palm with a high five. The rest of the assignments proceeded smoothly. Dave selected Tyler, and in an effort to mix up the families, I picked Lila. Jo hadn't told us much about her future sister-in-law other than the fact that she was unsmiling and shy (which too often Jo used as a code word for haughty) and worked in design. That didn't explain the blasé look she always wore, but I tried to shrug that off as introversion and nothing more.

Since we had an odd number of players, Mary was given the choice to pick her team. Unsurprisingly, she shimmied over to Team Groom, where Tyler was already bouncing the volleyball between his objectively muscular arms. I couldn't blame her—the man was toned.

As we assumed our positions—I always played middle blocker, right at the net, whereas Bobby stayed back, ready to return with perfectly controlled sets—Dave cleared his throat to make a quick pregame toast.

"Friends, family, countrymen," Dave began, using his exaggerated professor voice. "In life, there will be ups and downs, wins and losses. But if we score in love, we will always come out on top. Play ball!"

"I think love is just in tennis, man," Bobby said.

"And 'play ball' is for baseball," Tyler said, laughing.

"You should probably stick to textbooks, brother." Even Lila had joined in.

"Whatever, I'm starting." Dave smiled and threw the ball high in the air. When it fell toward his face, he slammed it with his right palm and the ball soared above the sand until it crashed loudly right into the net. "That didn't count."

The game continued back and forth in similar fashion. Bobby, Tyler, and I tried our best to keep a gentle rally, but our teammates were rusty. Even still, my abs were sore after ten minutes from laughing so hard. I only wished Jo were here to see it. I resolved to not let her miss out on any more of the fun, even if I had to physically pull her from her bedroom. Throw her pencils out the window, like I'd always threatened when we were kids and she wanted to write in her room instead of playing Monopoly or dress-up games with me.

Every so often in between volleys, I'd look over my shoulder at the ocean waves, the crashing melody a soundtrack in my mind. The sun was beginning its descent in the sky, bringing along with it a cascade of pinks and soft yellows. The heat on my arms and legs felt like an embrace. These were the moments I clung to all year, waiting for the summer days in Fire Island, toes covered in sand and my mind at ease. Gratitude exploded through my veins.

This was my favorite place in the world. This was my peace.

But my calm vanished like a wave smashing a sandcastle when I noticed a figure at the top of the stairs. Contentment evaporated in a moment's notice. It took everything in me not to laugh out loud, to shake my head at my own naivety. Of course this harmony wasn't meant to last. Had I forgotten everything that happened last night? Everything I still had to face head-on?

Bliss wasn't deserved—the worst had yet to come.

"El! You made it!" Dave shouted out to the figure on the stairs, having noticed his best man's approach a split second after I had. The ghost of my past somehow was now speed-walking toward the net in red board shorts and a T-shirt that read "Rough Draft" above a cartoon pint glass. I scolded myself for even beginning to smile at the way he waved toward Dave, like he was a cast member on some sort of intellectual spinoff of *Baywatch*. Maybe Dave and I had more in common than I thought, if he'd also found his way toward Emmett's friendship orbit.

I stopped myself. Emmett and I weren't friends anymore; we couldn't be.

Certainly not here.

"Finally, my cornhole partner has arrived!" Bobby exclaimed. "Join our team—we're one player short and could use a boost of last night's mojo." If looks could kill, Bobby would have been eviscerated. I stood there frozen until Bobby prodded me, my futile glare toppling over his head. "Amy, give the man a headband! Welcome to the squad. I think we're winning, but it's kind of hard to tell."

"So glad you could join us, Em," my mom called over the net, and my anger tripled. Were they already on a nickname basis? My stomach flipped thinking of how much I had missed—no, inadvertently allowed—by wallowing away in my room last night. Hiding, while Emmett waltzed in and charmed my family. From now on, I resolved, any Emmett–Sharp interaction would be strictly under my supervision. It had to be.

Swallowing my pride, I grabbed a headband and offered it out to Emmett, but my vision stayed fixed on the ground. It would have been easier to count every single grain of sand up and down the Atlantic's shoreline than to look directly at his eyes, his nose. His face. It was like staring at an eclipse; the memories were blinding.

Emmett nodded his thanks, and I couldn't help but

wonder if his throat was suddenly as dry as mine was. If words felt impossible for him, too. When our fingertips came together, touching for a brief moment with the fabric's exchange, I whipped my hand instinctively back to my side.

"So sorry I'm late," Emmett said to the rest of the group once his headband was secured. "My alarm went off hours ago, I swear. I just have the worst internal clock when I'm working."

"The life of a writer," Mary teased, "clocks be damned." *Et tu, Mary?*

"More like deadlines be damned," Emmett said, "but I've kept you waiting enough already. Sorry, again. Please, pretend I've been here all along. Play on, play on."

The game resumed, but my mind couldn't connect anymore with my body. I couldn't pretend what was happening was normal. Emmett in a shorthand with my closest cousins. Joking with my mom. Playing volleyball in Fire Island with my future brother-in-law.

Just an arm's length away.

Of course he showed up late. Always so late. His hair was a mess, his shirt characteristically wrinkled. Some things never changed. But none of that stopped my pulse from quickening when I heard his laugh again. None of that stopped my cheeks from filling with pink.

I willed myself to channel this adrenaline into sport, but with each move, it felt like my entire being was shifting more and more out of sync, the dial turning irreversibly far. Bobby didn't seem to mind as I missed shot after shot. None of us were playing at a professional level anyway. But I felt consumed with mortification. Was there nothing I could do right?

If Emmett noticed my lackluster performance, he didn't say so. In fact, we upheld our implicit code of silence to such an overt degree that I feared my family members might actually pick up on the truth; even strangers wouldn't naturally ignore one another the way we were. As the rounds played out, I felt Emmett trying to catch my eye, his vision a focused beam of heat boring into my back or along the side of my face. His attention so strong it could have given me a sunburn. I didn't want my rudeness to provoke suspicion, but I still couldn't look at him. I couldn't smile at his jokes or cheer when he scored a point. If I so much as opened my mouth, I couldn't promise what I'd say. It was a risk I wasn't willing, wasn't ready, to take.

In the end, the first word Emmett and I exchanged after a decade of willful silence was not a word but rather a scream: "Ow!" It had happened in a blur: Tyler announced he was serving up a "killer" as he tossed the ball and ricocheted it over to our side. All I needed was Tyler's taunt to kick my competitive nature into overdrive. My eyes were glued to the spinning ball, but I knew it was going to land right behind where I had been standing. "Mine!" I called as I stepped back, my head still to the sky. Or at least, I thought I called it. The next thing I knew, it felt like a brick wall had careered out of its foundation and toppled onto my shoulder. I yelped in pain and fell backward onto the sand. The sound of the volleyball plopping behind me echoed my defeat.

I heard footsteps and a "Woof, guys, are you okay?" and

then an embarrassed, deep-voice reply: "Amy, I'm so sorry." Emmett was on the ground next to me, clutching his head in one hand and rubbing an already protruding bump on his forehead with the other. Despite trying to avoid each other, our paths collided for all to see.

"I'm the one who should be apologizing. It was totally in your part of the court."

"It really was a killer, Tyler. Great job," Emmett joked.

"That obviously wasn't supposed to happen. Can I try again?"

A chorus of nos resounded.

"Are you sure you're okay?" Emmett asked me. With five words, the beach was gone. We were in our old world, freshman year all over again. Locust Walk suddenly surrounded us, a historic brick pathway sprouting in all directions. Leaves turning brown and yellow overtook the sky, tucked in a secret universe. In my mind, we sat on College Green and ran our fingers through the fresh grass. Hidden in a memory.

"I'm fine, thanks," I said. "Your forehead is telling a different story."

"I can feel a mountain growing," Emmett said. "This will be cute in wedding photos."

"A hat, perhaps? They're all the rage."

"Alas, I can't risk outshining the bride."

"Maybe just an ice pack and some Advil?"

"Yes, please."

"Coming right up," I said as I extended my hand. Just as

his fingers touched my palms, the beach crashed back to life around us. Reality was gaping relatives and rosy foreheads, ripe with sweat. "I'll be right back. Stay here and try not to get another injury."

"I think I've had enough athletics for the year. I'll come with," Emmett said, but then turned his phrase into a question: "If that's all right?"

I hoped no one noticed my cheeks once again swirling with color. "Of course."

"Amy, I put all the pain meds in the downstairs bathroom. There should be some compression bandages for the swelling in the cabinet down there, too," my mom said.

"Last one here and first one to leave. I'm so sorry, guys, I should've just sat this one out," Emmett said.

"Don't even sweat it." Dave clapped his best man on the back. "But seriously, go put some ice on that thing before it doubles in size. I don't have time to find a new best man."

One hundred steps from the shoreline to my front door. I'd walked the short trek over a thousand times. And yet, as I made my way back to the house with Emmett, I felt like a stranger in my own body. Self-conscious and unsure, I didn't recognize my footsteps. My soles were heavy, my mind confused. If my house had been any farther, I would have gotten lost.

Emmett broke the silence first. "This place is beautiful."

"Thanks," I said, grateful to have arrived at Summer Wind in one piece. "Bathroom is straight through here." I led him down the lower level's hallway, passing a den along with the guest room where Dave's parents were staying. In the quiet, I could make out the steady rhythm of what I assumed was Conrad snoring away. I rolled my eyes: glad he was getting some afternoon rest while Ben and my dad were sweating out back, constructing Jo's arch in eighty-five-degree heat.

In the bathroom, I rummaged through the medicine cabinet, grazing past the jars of aloe lotion, insect repellent, and anti-itch creams. A lifetime of summer scars sped through my mind, like the year I went through an entire box of Band-Aids to keep myself from scratching off mosquito bite scabs. The tan lines from those Mickey Mouse–shaped bandages took until Christmas to fade away.

First aid kit in hand, I closed the cabinet door and was startled by my own reflection. The woman looking back felt so different from the young, carefree, Band-Aid-covered girl I was busy remembering. My eyes looked exhausted, my face flushed and puffy. Cheeks weighed down by stress. By secrets. Like the very existence of the man standing next to me.

Emmett.

We made eye contact through the mirror. He offered a smile, and it set my pores on fire. A bonfire in my bones, first a subtle glow and then a roaring flame. It was charming and sweet and terrifying all at once. The two of us in one small room. The air felt like it was a hundred degrees. Suddenly, everything exploded within me and I spun around, a scowl on my face, my voice at a whisper but with the intensity of a scream.

"How are you here, Emmett? *Why* are you here?"

"I know, I know—"

"Did you, though? Did you know this was my twin sister's wedding? My house?"

"Of course."

I sat down on the toilet seat lid, rubbing my forehead. "'Of course,' he says."

"I know. I wanted to call. I almost did maybe forty times. But what would have changed? Dave is like a brother."

"Well, Jo is my actual sister. My twin."

"Would you have asked me to stay home? Miss my best friend's wedding?"

"Yes," I said. But then I softened. Would I have? I wasn't sure. "Maybe."

He was silent for a few moments. "It doesn't matter, though. You're right. I should've called. Or texted. I tried to DM you on Instagram, but I think you blocked me." He wasn't wrong. I had blocked Emmett on every form of social media, every type of digital chat. Even if he had called, I never would have answered. We had promised no communication, and this was the wildly unintended consequence.

Emmett slid down the wall until he was sitting on the floor, his knees to his chest. He looked like a kid again, that same unusual friend I met in those early days of college. Back then, he was pimply yet full of promise. Now his skin was clear, and he was more handsome than I ever could have predicted. Still, his dreams shone the same. Blindingly bright, always sparkling from the corners of his eyes. It took everything in me not to want to share in the warmth.

He laughed to break the silence. "I feel like a stalker. I don't know what I was expecting. It sounds stupid, but I guess I thought it would all just be okay?"

"This isn't okay." Typical Emmett, I thought. No preparedness, never a plan.

"I should just leave. I'll tell Dave something came up for the book." Of course there was a book. There was always a book, a project, a deadline. A dream. With Jo's own debut short story collection coming out this fall and Dave's latest academic paper winning awards, it had started to feel like my body was a magnet, attracting a sphere of these literary minds. Creating a creative club around myself from which I'd forever be barred entry.

I took a deep breath in, praying I wouldn't come to regret the words leaving my mouth. "You can stay. You should stay."

"Are you sure?"

"I'm sure." I kept my eyes on the floor but could hear his smile. "What should we tell people?"

He considered it. "Nothing, I guess. I haven't told Dave about . . . us. And I don't tell most people that I went to Penn anyway. It's a mouthful to mention I was only there for a semester," he said, and my fury was tempered by gratitude, even just momentarily. The only thing worse than exactly what was happening would be if Emmett had already gossiped to Dave all about our history, our past. If our truth had to come out, it would be on my terms.

"I guess it's a good thing I was away for most of their engagement," Emmett continued. "I only even met Jo briefly, when I was home in between a few international retreats this spring. We kept small talk to a minimum, but I knew who she was right away."

"Oh yeah?"

"Has anyone ever told you that you two have the exact same smile?"

My ears started to burn. "Well, she will never smile again if she ever finds out the truth. Jo will seriously lose her shit."

Emmett cracked a grin, piecing my words together. "So, you told her about me?"

"It may have come up once or twice." I didn't want to give him the satisfaction of knowing that he was the subject of multiple late-night voicemails that fall of freshman year, asking—no, begging—for sisterly advice. I had tried to avoid incriminating details when I could, ashamed that I had even been contemplating the existence of feelings for anyone other than Ben. Jo was always Ben's biggest fan, even then. So, for one of the first times in our sisterhood, I spared the truth to circumvent the guilt trip from Jo, a surefire lecture about how I was letting our best friend and an objectively amazing boyfriend slip through my fingers. I never told Jo, never told anyone, that Ben and I had been fighting. That we decided to take a break that first fall term. All she knew was that there was the possibility of a new boy, a new friend. A super-smart student in my writing seminar forever dubbed "Brainy Guy." If Jo knew that Dave's best man was the same face behind the "Brainy Guy" moniker, she'd never unsee it. Shattered glass can't be saved, not even with tape and glue. The happiest week of her life would be defined by my betrayal and my past.

What other secrets would she realize I'd been keeping?

Emmett had already threatened to send my course crashing once before. To upend the plan that I had meticulously crafted. I couldn't, I wouldn't, let him do it again. No matter the fire his smile stoked within me, like friendly flames lapping up my spine.

"I guess we just pretend like we're meeting for the first time," I said.

Emmett exhaled a sigh of relief. We could make this work. The trip was just one week. How hard could it be? To protect our loved ones, we had to lie to their faces.

"Thank you. Seriously."

"It's fine," I said. "Just don't mess up."

He held out his hand. "Emmett Murphy. Nice to meet you."

I kept my hands clenched tight into fists. It wouldn't work.

"Groom's side or bride's side?" He was grinning now even wider.

I rolled my eyes, fought off his charm.

"I'm guessing bride's side. As the best man, I'd know if you were one of Dave's friends. That man can *chat*. So, how do you know Jo?"

"Stop."

"You actually look pretty similar to her. A cousin, perhaps?"

Nope. I stood up, moving toward the bathroom door to get on with my evening. Surely the volleyball game had ended by now, or Jo needed help with a wedding task. Ben was probably wondering where I was. My dad would need a hand cooking dinner. There wasn't time for games with Emmett in the basement, even if a part of me wanted to stay right here.

But right as my hand grasped the doorknob, Emmett playfully grabbed hold of my ankle. The contact sent a shock through my lower body. Still sitting cross-legged on the floor, he looked up at me with a boyish smirk.

"Maybe let's try just ignoring each other instead?" I offered.

"Now who's messing it up?" He clucked his tongue, which only made it harder to avoid thinking about his mouth, his lips, his teeth.

"You are so annoying," I said, but I could feel my face morphing into a smile.

"Emmett Murphy," he said again, palm once again outstretched in greeting.

I relented. "Amy Sharp," I said. "Sister of the bride." Emmett waved his hand in my direction with a satisfied grin.

Still outstretched, he was now waiting for a handshake as well as some help up off the tiled floor.

"All right, all right." I tucked my hand in his and pulled him up, shaking my head all the while. "Time to go." Yet Emmett kept hold of my fingers even once he was standing, our eyes now face-to-face, noses almost touching. My breath caught, my world silenced. All I could think was how he smelled exactly the same. Cinnamon and fire. Ready to explode.

"Very nice to meet you," he said.

I forced a swallow down my dry throat. It burned.

"So, how about that ice pack?"

TUESDAY

N OW GIVE ME FIVE FLYING WARRIORS," MY FA-
vorite yoga instructor guided in a singsong voice
through my ear pods. Over the past few years, I'd picked up
a rather obsessive Melissa Wood Health yoga and Pilates
practice. Nothing cleared my mind more than a flow, and
this morning, I woke up more desperate than ever to unroll
my mat. A virtual MWH yoga class set against the ocean
background seemed like the single most necessary start to
the day.

Thankfully, the remainder of last night's evening had
progressed with relative ease after Emmett went off to rest
with his ice pack. He had a draft due at the end of the
month, he said, and he needed to write whenever he felt inspired. I tried not to let my heart wonder if it was the time
with me, or simply an injury to the head, that did the creative trick. Regardless, I didn't question his methods: an
Emmett-free night was a relief. The volleyball players had

trickled in from the beach, and we all gazed on the deck as the sunset faded along with the day. Even Jo seemed more herself.

As the group gathered around the pool, some guests dipping their toes into the water, Ben and I shared a lounge chair and I let myself lean back into his chest. A rare pose for us these days. Folded between his arms, I shivered as his hands traced my hip bone. His scruff had grown to my favorite length; three days without a razor and he had the beard of a surfing champion. Or, at the very least, an engineer on PTO. Either way, I enjoyed the view.

"How'd the game go?" Ben asked once I'd settled in.

"We lost, but Bobby is pretending to be a good sport about it." I laughed.

"Well, it sure sounded fun. We could hear your laughter all the way at the house."

"Sorry you're getting stuck with the manual labor." At first, I had felt guilty ensuring Ben would miss out on the volleyball match. Now I was relieved that he hadn't been there to witness my and Emmett's fateful crash. I needed to keep them in separate spheres for as long as I possibly could.

"Happy to help," Ben said. We'd been married long enough that I knew he meant it.

As the sky shifted, champagne was poured, and slices of my dad's handmade pizza were passed around the pool. Jo and Dave were seated in the center, anchored by their loved ones. On the surface, it was perfect. And if I hadn't spent so much of the day on edge, or the past weeks analyzing my own behavior with my husband, I might not have noticed the small signs of irritation that bubbled under the group's skin. The way Valerie avoided Lila's eyes during a story about a family vacation, or my own mom's silence when my dad regaled the group about his glory years and epic cases before retirement. Crediting it to weary travelers who'd had too much to drink, I tried to let each signal roll right by. Willed myself to stop being so sensitive to other couples' problems. To stop trying to fix things I knew nothing about. To stop projecting my own instability onto an otherwise peaceful scene.

Even still, I couldn't help feeling acutely aware that something else was strangely amiss.

Moving through pigeon pose now, I stretched my torso onto my thigh and let my forehead touch the mat. Inhale, exhale, repeat. My yoga instructor, Melissa, always ended with a reflection of gratitude, a moment of positivity. Even though her voice was nestled in my ear, I couldn't feel further from her morning message. Anxiety had always chased me. Especially in moments of happiness, when most people could sit back and soak in the joy of a moment, I always found myself worrying about the negativity sure to follow. If I had a lucky week, I'd fear the weekend. After a strong performance review at work, I feared a nonexistent firing. Superstitious and paranoid, I was convinced failure hid behind each corner. I lived with an unsettled feeling in my bones.

That's probably why when I felt a tap on my shoulder, I screamed.

The morning sun may have silhouetted the newcomer's face into a dark blot, but I knew from the pitch of the startled laughter that it was Emmett. My teacher's final prayer was replaced by his apologies as I pulled my headphones out one ear at a time.

"Note to self: check for headphones before disturbing a yogi," Emmett said.

"Very funny. Why are you here?" I asked, fighting off a smile from forming. Normally, I hated when Ben interrupted my practice, walking past my mat on his way to the kitchen always right as I'd settled into a final vinyasa flow. Yet here with Emmett, the irritation usually accompanied by an interruption seemed to vanish. The annoyance nowhere to be found.

"Is that an existential question this time?"

"The beach." I checked my iPhone's clock; it was barely 8:00 A.M.

"Early riser. Plus, I don't sleep much, night or morning." That was new, I thought. There were weekends in college when he'd sleep so late, he'd snooze right through our Saturday study sessions. Two o'clock would roll around with apologies and a fresh round of vanilla skim lattes. "Anxiety, insomnia, all of the above," he added.

"Me too," I said.

"I remembered." He smiled. "Had a feeling you'd be here."

I had to distract myself from his face. "Well, welcome to the insomniac's silver lining," I said, motioning toward the beach. It was nearly empty, save for an elderly woman reading a worn book in a beach chair and a family of birds trotting nearby. The lighting in the morning was transcendent, the sun cemented directly overhead in the eastward sky, dancing off the waves in a way it never quite seemed to replicate as the day progressed. A secret treat for the early risers, one I usually enjoyed alone.

Surprisingly, I didn't mind the newfound company.

"Just the inspiration I needed." He held up a small spiral notebook in one hand, a pen in the other. "My best man speech won't write itself."

I groaned. The idea of public speaking was a terror in and of itself. But to deliver a speech in front of two—now three—of the smartest writers I'd ever met was a particular form of self-loathing. A task I was in no rush to perform. "I was hoping Dave's mysterious best man would be illiterate like me. Tell stories of drunken college days and reckless nights. Not quote Kant."

Emmett guffawed. "Why would I quote Kant?" I simultaneously shrugged and cringed. Emmett was the first person I met who was a natural scholar. He retained everything he read, from ancient philosophy and modern economic principles to every player of the Giants lineup. He swore it wasn't a photographic memory, and I believed him. He had no interest in reciting facts. Rather, he seemed to absorb them straight into his being, into his bloodstream, the way one does with any other lived experience. I remembered learning to ride a bike the way Emmett remembered the plot of

Dante's *Inferno*. Infuriating, but undeniable. He uninten-
tionally alienated others because of it, but I had found it
inspiring to be around—even if I caught myself more fre-
quently spell-checking (and rechecking) my texts to him
before pressing send, just in case I said something he'd find
an error in. Like with Kant.

"You know what I mean."

"I promise I won't quote Kant."

"Stop saying Kant." If Ben were here, I'd point out the
pun—I *Kant* stop saying Kant. But Emmett always made it
clear he hated puns. *The B-movies of the English language.* I'd
have to make a note to tell Ben later. Then of course I remembered: I couldn't tell Ben.

More secrets were rolling in with the tide.

"Can I borrow that?" He pointed to my yoga mat. I
obliged, repositioning myself directly on the sand. "Thanks,"
he said, as he started stretching. "Besides, what if I did want
to tell drunken college stories? Would that be so unfathom-
able?"

"Yes, because you two didn't go to college together."

"Well, we met *at* a college. The workshop was technically sponsored by NYU. I'd deem that close enough." It
didn't surprise me that Emmett and Dave had overlapped
early on in the city's academic scene. After transferring out
of Penn our freshman year, Emmett quickly became Columbia's writing wunderkind, his talent unprecedented. He completed a dual BA-MFA degree in record time, graduating
with both a two-book deal and a TA position in the creative

writing program. The latter gig he secured for both the expendable income it would cover and the continued access to Butler, Columbia's oldest library and his favorite place to write.

At least, that was how he'd always explained it in the interviews he gave. I'd secretly followed Emmett's career over the years, hating myself as my fingers seemed to google his name of their own accord. Reading his press Q&As, watching as he bounced his way up the bestseller list. Secretly cheering along as his spy fiction trilogy was optioned by Paramount, as he wrote and recorded its companion podcast all by himself. When he turned thirty last spring, he was honored with a profile in the *New York Times*' Arts section. I may or may not have read it a dozen times. Always while Ben was in the shower, safe from peering over at my phone screen.

Now, the writer extraordinaire was blabbing away about the irony of wedding speeches while folding himself up and over, from downward dog into a plank into a headstand.

"I just don't understand what I—a thirty-year-old single man who has never even kept a girlfriend for more than a year—could possibly advise to a newly married couple. What do I have to offer them besides a handful of 'What Not to Dos' and a mild case of envy?" His legs hovered in a pretzel above his head as his shirt billowed in the ocean breeze, revealing the hint of a six-pack. *That* was a new side of Emmett. The Emmett I had known was allergic to the gym, partial instead to cheesesteaks from Jim's and late-night Wawa runs.

"Well, I've been married for almost five years. So, I guess you'll just have to be okay with having the worse speech." I was teasing, but I could see his muscles tightening.

"Wow, five years, huh? Congrats, by the way." Whether spurred by the idea of matrimony or the idea of Ben in particular, Emmett's face seemed to darken slightly in its shade.

"Thank you—"

"Right on schedule."

My heart felt winded. Like I had been punched in the gut. A callback to conversations I had once wiped away.

I went to change the topic, to salvage the morning's flavor, but I felt my phone buzz in my hand before I could retort. A lifeline. The screen displayed a new text:

Jo: A! She's early! Where are you?!

"A bride in need." I showed him my phone screen by way of an apology. "Duty calls. I better get going."

Emmett toppled down from his headstand, wiped the sand off his legs. "Thanks for the mat. Juices are flowing already," he said with a smile, smaller than before but just as annoyingly charming.

"I wouldn't worry too much. Pro tip: no one really pays much attention after the open bar begins."

"God, the human attention span is depressing. But valid." He laughed before pulling a miniature spiral notebook out of his pocket and turning to a clean page. Seeing Emmett again, pen in hand and ink-stained fingers, sent my mind straight back to our writing seminar days.

Our friendship that threatened to become something more.

I had gone from never wanting to speak to him again to never wanting our impromptu beachside yoga session to end.

Walking toward Summer Wind, I fought every urge to turn my head over my shoulder and take one more look at that strange man who had stumbled back into my life. And I couldn't help but hope he was thinking the same thing.

In that moment, I felt a surge in gratitude toward my yoga practice. If one thing had become strikingly evident this week, it was that we would both need to be increasingly flexible.

CHAPTER

11

I YELPED AS THE PIN PRICKED MY SKIN.

"Sorry, sorry!" Josette said, adjusting her hold on the fabric around my waist. I winced at my overreaction, but Jo's question had sent my body shaking.

"Helloooo? Can you hear me out there?" my sister's voice called from beyond the closed bathroom door. Standing on the other side of my parents' en suite dressing room, I could hear her perfectly fine. I just wished her words were different. "I *said*," she continued, her voice somehow simultaneously light and loud, "what do you think of El? Of Emmett?"

"He seems nice," I finally managed back, my mouth parched.

"He's amazing, right?"

I felt my neck starting to sweat. A sticky moisture growing.

"It's funny, I had pegged him as Mary's type, but Dave

said there's something with her and Tyler. Already!" She laughed. "I guess I'm wrong, but I just thought the whole 'intellectual dreamboat' shtick felt very Mary. Scholarly and sculpted, incredibly successful—"

"Well, Tyler's way hotter," I interjected, trying to digress from all things Emmett.

"Easy, Ames." Jo laughed. "You already have a husband."

"A very handsome one, if I might add," Josette chimed in with a gracious smile. She must have picked up on the rising heat in my body temperature and thrown me a life preserver.

Josette was a legendary seamstress in the city but had a fondness for our family ever since she and my mom lived in apartments next door to each other in the '80s. A struggling artist and an aspiring dressmaker, the two immediately bonded over that shared hustling, scrappy energy that came with having a Big Dream but no Big Paycheck. Ever since, any important Sharp outfit had her fingerprints all over it, even if that meant adding a task to my maid of honor checklist: arrange a Tommy's Taxi car service to bring Josette from Manhattan to the ferry on Tuesday morning, right in time to finish Jo's wedding alterations.

"Feels like just yesterday it was your big day, Amy," Josette said now, smoothing over the final stitches on my dress's hem.

"I can't believe it'll be five years in September." My mind flashed back to my own tailoring sessions all those years ago, when Josette perfectly altered my Vera Wang satin white ball gown. It was an A-line with a full skirt, traditional and timeless. "Classic" became the theme of the event. From the venue (the New-York Historical Society) to the food (steak and salmon), we followed practically every tradition in the guidebook. A seated dinner, then dancing. My diamond earrings were a borrowed family heirloom, my garter "something blue." Even now, years after our engagement, it felt like every piece of wedding etiquette remained branded in my brain, memorized for eternity.

"Well, you were still one of the most beautiful brides I ever saw," Josette gushed.

"Thank you." I smiled, but what I really wanted to say was how that bride felt like a different person these days. Scream from the rooftops about how that version of myself felt like something from a dream. Cloudy, and always out of reach.

I looked at myself in the mirror and forced a smile. "I love this color at least. Jo picked well, that's for sure." Unsurprisingly, Jo didn't want anything traditional or stuffy, so my maid of honor dress was a trendy midi slip dress. I smoothed my hands over the dusty-rose fabric, thwarting the rising memory of a secondary dress still hanging in the closet at home. Same color, slightly different shape.

"Can someone zip me?" Jo called out from the master bathroom, snapping me out of my thoughts. "Wait, Ames, not you! I want you to see the grand reveal!"

"Coming!" Josette said, as I silently swallowed the reminder: I had missed all of Jo's earlier dress shopping appointments. I tried to block out the thoughts of all that I'd done instead.

Growing up, I had fantasized about Jo's wedding day almost as much as my own. Visions of white dresses and handsome grooms and ornate decorations filled our heads as we'd playact our big days in the background. Handfuls of grass assumed the role of flower petals, which we'd toss as we twirled down a faux aisle demarcated by soccer cones or beach toys we grabbed from the garage. I would declare a wedding must-have—"mac and cheese for dinner!"—and in classic twin fashion, Jo would nod her head and parrot for the same.

In the early years, if I had something, then Jo wanted it, too, and vice versa. My parents would try to deter this tendency, thinking it childhood selfishness, but in reality, our brains just worked the same way. Our preferences in line, Jo's choices matched my own. As we got older, the parroting stopped, morphing instead into a three-legged race as Jo veered left and I veered right. New friends, new clubs, new tables at lunch. Bunk beds exchanged for separate rooms, each painted in a different color (mine blue, Jo's pink). My hair even settled into a deep oak shade, contrasted with Jo's light blond. Twinhood meant walking in lockstep while testing out new rhythms.

Our weddings were another three-legged race. The core was the same, two limbs glued together: we were each other's maids of honors with no other bridesmaids, the father-daughter dances were both to Bob Dylan, and the last song was Frank Sinatra's "New York, New York." After that, one might never guess the brides were cousins, let alone twins. I had a six-course dinner menu, while Jo will have a buffet. My three hundred guests to her sixty. That was the beauty of sisterhood. I had a formal fairy tale but would live vicariously through Jo's intimate beachside ceremony. I followed every rule, while Jo threw out the guidebook, followed mandates set only by her whims, her heart. Twins were a perpetual study in comparisons and contrasts. Matrimony style was no exception.

Now, I leaned toward my reflection and nearly screamed.

Blinking did nothing. Gray hair still shone back with a sinister song.

"Ta-da!" Jo strutted into the dressing wing, but I couldn't take my eyes off the newfound discovery in the mirror. "Amy?" Her voice softened.

I turned to my sister and tried to hide my worry. Jo looked breathtaking. Her heels a clear block, silver earrings cuffed her lobes, a slim silver bracelet hugged her wrist. Delicate accessories for a showstopper of a bridal jumpsuit, white silk pants that morphed into a one-shoulder neckline, her tan, toned arms on display.

But instead of a wedding smile, her face just stared with concern. "What's wrong?"

"It's . . . it's stupid, forget it," I stuttered. "You look perfect."

"Amy."

I sighed and pointed to my scalp.

Instead of sympathy, laughter bubbled out from my sister's belly.

"It's not funny," I insisted, but my voice broke, and tears started falling from my eyes. I could feel my cheeks turning red, my breath staccato gasps. I wanted to pull myself together, to take charge, but I couldn't. It was like my brain was malfunctioning. "I'm sorry." I hiccuped.

"I'll give you two a minute," Josette said, excusing herself, off no doubt to find my mom, to collectively roll their eyes about the dramatic Sharp twins, now with gray hairs included.

"It's okay, Ames, I have them, too. You get used to it, I promise," Jo consoled, squeezing my arm after taking a closer look at the light gray speckles decorating my part. "Is it weird that I kind of love mine? Distinguished." She grinned.

"More like a dinosaur," I groaned, plopping onto the nearby vanity chair, and dabbed my face dry. I knew it was silly, but the discovery hit me like a hurricane. Conclusive proof that I was always getting older. Life was speeding up, and even though I was headed in that very same direction I had always dreamed about, I still somehow felt so lost. Like I needed to stop the car and jump out. Pause, reverse, rewind. Instead, I was faced with silver hair on a silver platter—a sardonic thirtieth birthday present hand-delivered by Father Time.

Jo settled down on the chair next to me, pulling me into a hug. "We can handle grays. Grays are decorative." It was something our mom always said.

"I know, I know," I said resolutely, wiping my face dry and balancing my breath. "I shouldn't give them such power over me. I need to reclaim that power to use for myself." Nina's voice already on loop in my head.

Jo gave me a puzzling look, not expecting a therapist's reply. "Are you all right, Amy?"

I wanted to give Jo an honest answer. That nothing was right anymore. That when Ben looked at me, he saw damage. And even if he said he didn't, whenever I saw Ben looking at me, all I could think about was how he must be thinking of all that we lost. We had fallen so deep in a mind game that we couldn't find the way out of the maze.

A maze in which now Emmett had somehow appeared, dredging up even more pain.

It was all too much. If I dared tell Jo, she would just be yanked into the labyrinth with me. It would swallow everyone up, and the wedding would be filled with subtext, with hidden looks of concern. Regret. I couldn't do that to Jo, not this week, not until after the wedding. Not until I had found the emergency exit for myself.

"All good, just tired. And now, gray." I tried to laugh my misery away.

"I can't believe I forgot to tell you about mine. Feels like months since it's been just the two of us."

"Way too long," I agreed.

"I've really missed you. Missed Benny, too. You guys still owe us a double date, by the way. No rescheduling this time. You're all out of reschedule cards."

"Hey, you are, too, Ms. Paris for Presidents' Day." I forced a laugh, but my heart slipped at the reminder. There were so many reasons behind our rescheduling. Yes, everything with Ben in recent history, but the distance with Jo, too. Her upcoming debut required a new level of attention, a focus on edits and press and publicity alike. Her new beau demanded date nights, an exploration of their chemistry that filled her already limited free time.

This year so far was busy, but it had been happening for a while now. These past few months just shone a light on how each year we lived put yards between us. How quickly we were becoming busy, distant adults.

After graduating college, we thought it would be easy. Like winning the lottery, being back in the same city. But as I moved in with Ben instead of Jo (two incomes for one bedroom just made more financial sense), she pushed away. She insisted it wasn't personal, that her work was based on "research," and sometimes "research" meant canceling plans to revise with her writers' group or sequestering to write for four weeks alone in a pool house in Palm Springs. Or even jetsetting away with a new date on a random Tuesday if she thought she could turn it into a poem. It meant valuing her ideas over calendar items. Even this past February, Jo bailed on our sister weekend in the Catskills for a solo trip to Paris to work on her collection. To *more honestly record the sound of the Seine*. (That's actually what she said.)

To write about life, Jo needed to *live* life, and Sunday-night dinners with me, Ben, and our favorite Chinese takeout didn't cut it. Conversations about accounting and bosses and mortgages weren't always inspiration enough for Jo's prose.

I tried not to mind it. Truly. I loved my career, my life with Ben. It was enough for us.

At least, it had been. Until it wasn't. Until our rescheduling transformed into a new reason for secrecy. The excitement and the potential. Then the absence and the tears.

The entire point of that Catskills trip was to fill Jo in on what we were thinking. What we were dreaming. But she canceled, and then I canceled the reschedule, and then I simply couldn't find the words. The song changed and the story was over before I had sung a single note.

I had to stop. All of this was in the past. We had moved on. Hadn't we?

"Double date, wherever you want. I promise," I told Jo, forcing myself out of my thoughts. "Pick a date and we'll be there. As soon as you get back from the honeymoon."

"Honeymoon. *Honeymoon.*" Jo shuddered. "It sounds so strange when I say it. Like the words don't fit in my mouth." Jo sighed, her face growing an ever-so-slight shade of somber. "You know, it's starting to feel hard to come back here. To Fire Island."

"What do you mean?" I asked.

"It's hard to explain, but sometimes I just want to squeeze back into the body of the girl who used to spend entire summers out here. Naive and blissed-out on sun and nothing else." She smiled at the memory. "Sweet seventeen."

I could taste those same summers on my lips. Before new cities and new apartments, new jobs and new responsibilities. Before our twinhood had been bumped down in priority. Before our sisterhood sunk under the weight of adulthood's corporate ladders and calendar conflicts, not to mention the never-ending cycle of weddings and bridal showers and bachelorette parties (and repeat) that filled our weekends with RSVP cards and societal courtesies. Before the world tore off our eyelids and woke us up to its realities that adolescence was the Eden we took for granted.

"Every time we come here, that summer feels further away," Jo said. "It gets, I guess, hazy in my mind. Foggy. It's probably just nostalgia."

I squeezed Jo's hand as my heart filled with guilt. Was I imagining things, or could my own melancholy be contagious? Was this standard wedding anxiety, or something worse? Because Jo's trembling voice made one thing clear: something serious seemed to be stirring in my sister.

And no matter what happened, no matter what I was dealing with, I would do anything to prevent her from wallowing, too.

Reminiscence pricked my arms with goose bumps, budding excitement spreading like magic. We were back in Fire Island, in our favorite home. Why couldn't we fall back in time? Why couldn't we cast our own spell, wrap ourselves up in our favorite twinhood charms the way we always used to?

I pulled her up to stand, newfound resolve rushing out along with the words. "Let's go back then. For the rest of the week, let's pretend we're seventeen. The only job we have is to get you to the altar in one piece." I smoothed out the wrinkle now apparent on her pant leg, an indent from the chair. "We'll steam that. But I mean it: no worries, no deadlines. Just sun, love, and booze."

Jo burst out laughing. "God, that's so cheesy, my ears are bleeding!"

"You know what I mean." I laughed back. It felt so good to laugh. "Pretend that sounded poetic. I'm not good with words."

"Seventeen?"

"Seventeen," I promised.

"Why not? Seventeen." Jo grinned, her smile electric.

Looking at our reflection in the mirror, I just hoped we wouldn't regret it.

CHAPTER

12

WHILE LBJ DIDN'T SIGN THE BILL THAT WOULD create the Fire Island National Seashore until 1964, these sandy lands have been enjoyed by man since the 1600s. Seventeen official towns make up the Fire Island seashore, but you folks are lucky, because Kismet is my favorite one."

Riley's steady voice was a welcome distraction. Between his flowy sun-kissed hair, freckle-spotted face, and giant aviator sunglasses, Riley embodied the best part of Fire Island: total relaxation. He was a local who lived on the island the entire year. Even when the temperatures dipped and the ferry schedules shrunk to one boat ride per day, Riley could be found walking the beach every morning and filling his schedule with an assortment of entrepreneurial beach-style gigs. From lifeguard duty, to shifts on the register at the market, to hosting Saturday movie screenings at the firehouse, or organizing nature stargazing sessions at night, Riley was an omnipresent force in Kismet. Our local everyman. Today's role as Fire Island tour guide was just another well-versed offering in his repertoire.

The itinerary for this afternoon gave wedding guests a choice: a fishing trip or a walk to the Fire Island Lighthouse. The lighthouse was iconic, its black and white stripes a symbol of safe harbor, of home. I never missed an opportunity to remind myself of its magic. Plus, my mom suffered from a fairly reliable case of motion sickness. After a rough batch of nausea during a sailing trip in her early childhood, she had resigned herself to a lifetime on land. Seaborne was not her strong suit (the only worthwhile exception being, ironically, the Kismet-bound ferry). Whereas Jo and my dad itched to drift away, to sail into deep waters until the shoreline was but a minuscule illusion, my mom and I always stuck together as the land-bound pair. I preferred anything stable, day trips included.

"Now, does anyone have a guess as to why they named this here stretch of land beneath our feet 'Fire Island' in the first place?" Riley surveyed the crowd.

"Surely Grace knows the answer to this one, considering how many years she's owned out here?" Valerie asked, her nose crinkling up toward her forehead. All morning, Valerie had seemed different. Colder even than usual, her face frozen in a permanent scowl. Her criticisms were more frequent and made at a higher volume—disdain for the slow internet, for the afternoon clouds, for the browning avocado left over

from breakfast. Nothing seemed up to her standards. Lila
had a similarly morose aura, but she had never been anything but reticent from the moment we had met. I silently
prayed that Jo had nothing to do with her future in-laws'
unshakably sour moods.

"You know, after almost forty years, I don't think I've ever
asked myself that," my mom replied. "If I had to guess . . ."
She paused, giving the question an artist's thought. "Maybe
it has something to do with the sunset? The sun has a way
of looking like it's been set on fire when it descends into
the bay."

"My favorite view," Riley said with a smile. "But not
quite, Mrs. Sharp. Anyone else?"

Valerie shrugged her shoulders while Lila kept her face
in her phone.

"Maybe in honor of the trees? Burnt leaves like fire, and
all that?" I volunteered, determined to not let Valerie's and
Lila's standoffishness spoil the mood.

"This might be completely off, but can I take a guess?" a
familiar voice cut in, and it made me want to hold my breath.
"I remember once reading how, in the early days of settlements, pirates would cast fires to lure travelers to the shores,
hijacking ships and stealing supplies once the seamen reached
the sand. I imagine the hopeful settlers would look out from
sea, mesmerized by the balls of fire reflecting off the waves,
beckoning them closer and closer. Unknowingly putting
themselves right into the pirates' greedy hands. Hence, fire
island?"

"What? Yes! Right on, my dude! No one's ever answered correctly before. What's your name again?"

"Emmett."

Well, that confirmed it.

Hearing his name could still make my heart skip.

"Exactly, Emmett! Well done!" Riley said, before explaining the order in which the Island's towns were settled. I could feel Emmett hoping to meet my gaze, stifling a spreading self-congratulatory pride, but I refused to look at him head-on. I hadn't yet accepted the reality that he was even on this walk in the first place.

Ten digits had lived buried in my heart for years. Locked and hidden away. Last night, I texted them. Fingers shaking, I typed out a draft. Deleted words, rearranged phrases, and then rearranged them again. All as my heart pounded to the beat of a once-forgotten song. The words were fuzzy, but just like that radio hit of youth, I still knew the exact right key. Was it wrong to try to sing along?

One deep breath as my hand hovered, and then pressed send.

> **@Emmett:** Tmrw, are you walking or boat? Let's
> split up.

After watching Emmett's typing bubble appear and disappear for what felt like an eternity, the three dots mocking me with bated breath, filling my mind with regrets and admonishments and anxiety, my phone had pinged with his response.

Emmett: Sure. What do you want?

Amy: Walk.

Again, the typing bubble flickered back and forth like a light bulb about to extinguish.

Emmett has liked your message "Walk."

So much for a symphony. The internationally acclaimed writer couldn't even string together an actual text back. Instead, the passive, lazy thumbs-up reply. I groaned and deleted our entire text exchange.

When two o'clock rolled around and I saw Emmett sitting by the pool, his feet up on a lounge chair at the designated meeting point for the lighthouse crew, I could barely hide my irritation.

"Are you purposefully trying to make this harder for me?" When Emmett's jaw dropped, his surprise matching my own, I realized there must have been some sort of miscommunication.

"You told me to walk!" he whisper-yelled back. "So, I'm walking!"

"I said *I* was walking!"

Emmett pulled up his phone and reread the messages. When he looked up a moment later, his eyes practically sang with apology. "I thought you meant that I should walk, so *you* could go on the boat."

"For a writer, you're not the best at reading texts."

Emmett checked his watch. "If I sprint, I think I can make it to the dock in time."

"They'll have left by now. My dad's been dreaming about this ride all week."

"Shit. Plus, I already told Dave I was Team Lighthouse. It's not like they'd just wait around in case I changed my mind." Emmett looked at me in earnest. "Want me to hang back?"

"It's fine." Anger wasn't going to make the situation any easier to live through, and more important, if Emmett skipped both the lighthouse walk and the boat trip, someone might start to wonder if there was a larger reason behind his attendance issues. "But if you're planning on stalking me the rest of this week, just be honest about it, okay?"

"As if," he tossed back.

"And delete those texts while you're at it. You'd be a terrible spy, you know."

I'd be lying if I said a small part of me wasn't a bit excited about the mix-up. Well-read and an animated storyteller, Emmett was always a reliable conversation buffer.

I just needed to resist the growing urge to sit or stand any closer to him.

Luckily, Emmett had spent most of the mile walk up ahead with Riley. After he had answered the titular origin story question, the two history buffs babbled away at the front of the group, sharing factoids about early New York settlements and geographic land shifts. Tangential anecdotes that most forgot the second their brains learned them. Not Emmett.

My mom and I lingered a few steps behind the men, but she caught me smiling when I overheard Emmett telling an extraordinarily niche but well-meaning story about early boating machinery gone wrong.

"Dave attracts such interesting people, don't you think?" my mom asked, her bright blue eyes fixed on the back of Emmett's brown hair. Lila and Valerie had fallen behind, safely out of earshot.

"Academics, I guess." I shrugged, not wanting to get into it much more. Silence was safer.

My mom continued nonetheless. "With Ben's family, it never felt like a huge change. Friends first, in-laws second. But it feels kind of funny now, knowing we're gaining a whole new community. It's tickling in a strange, new way."

We walked quietly a few steps more, but I could sense my mom had more bubbling on her tongue. "Just say it. What's wrong?"

"Nothing's wrong." Even when my mom tried to backtrack, she could never keep her lips shut for long. "I'm worried for Jo is all. She's so pure. Gentlehearted. I don't want her to get lost."

"Jo's an adult, Mom. She'll be fine," I said, but I knew what my mom was implying. Valerie and Lila were city women. Tough, opinionated, even when it came across as cruel. Jo was a drifter, a dreamer. She was the quiet cobblestone street with sprawling ivy and a rusted reading bench, hidden from the chaos and concrete. It was hard to envision her at holidays with the Beaumonts or folding into their family to watch television on the couch. They were all angles and hard edges, whereas Jo was all softness and warmth.

My mom bit her lip, remaining unconvinced. "Emmett?" she called out suddenly. I grabbed her hand with my fist.

"What are you doing?!" I yelped. When she looked at me like I had three heads popping out of my neck, I had no choice but to release my mom's fingers from my clammy clenches. "Sorry, you're just clearly interrupting their conversation," I scrambled. "It's pretty rude."

But it was too late. Emmett had already excused himself from Riley's attention and slowed his steps, falling back to stand on the other side of my mom. As we walked in the direction of the lighthouse, I kept my vision straight ahead, refusing to meet Emmett's eyes. I knew he was thinking the same thing that I was: so much for keeping our distance.

My mom lowered her voice before saying, "Emmett, I hate to even ask you this. But you know Dave, his family. Do you think they'll welcome Jo? Treat her well?"

"Ah, so you've seen the harsher side of the Beaumonts," he said with a knowing smile.

"They aren't exactly chatty." My mom's voice was coated with such vulnerability and fear, I wanted to wrap her up in a hug. She was strangers' biggest champion. The first to see the best in anyone. If my mom was venturing toward gossip right now, she had to be exceptionally concerned.

"Well, from my experience, and from what Dave has

told me about his childhood, I wouldn't be too worried," Emmett said. "Sure, they're strong-minded. But they're loyal. And when they care about something, it just sort of drives everything they do. Family first. Not unlike the Sharps, from what I've seen so far."

I felt my cheeks blushing but refused to move my gaze.

"That's good," my mom murmured. Yet after a few steps, her musings picked up again. "I just feel like I'm missing something. There's a change in energy I can't quite put my finger on. Something feels very off. Very wrong." Chills exploded along my spine.

Could my mom's anxiety have nothing to do with Dave and his family? Could she be picking up on the very lie she was currently sandwiched between instead? It wouldn't be the first time she'd used this tactic, to send maternal worry in as a Trojan horse to confirm a suspicion.

"It's probably nothing . . ." Her voice trailed off, but anyone could tell she didn't mean it.

Emmett cleared his throat. "Dave would kill me for saying this, but what can I do? Your peace of mind is worth irritating the groom." He winked. "Dave's parents can be intense, yes. But Dave is not his parents. He's naturally shy, so he can sometimes be perceived—wrongly—as judgmental. A prick, if you will. But he is the kindest, funniest, smartest man I've ever met. I know Jo sees that part of him, too.

"And it might sound cliché, but he is head over heels about your daughter. Whenever they're together, and I've seen it countless times already here in Kismet, Dave wants to be right by Jo's side. And if he can't be right by her, holding her hand, he spends the entire time watching, looking out for her. His eyes follow her across the room, sparkling, with the biggest grin on his face. A smile that says he'll never believe how lucky he is that she said yes, that he's here with her. That, somehow, he gets to be her husband for the rest of his life.

"You know, I was planning on saving this as fodder for my toast"—Emmett smiled at me now, his dimples directly pulled at my soul—"so don't tell anyone you got an early draft. But after Jo and Dave met? I had fifty WhatsApp messages from Dave. Fifty! About a beautiful, intelligent woman he'd met. God, he wouldn't tell me her name, lest he jinx the whole thing. But he told me that he could never go back to a world without her in it. He couldn't stop thinking about her, and he never wanted to. Dave would do—he *will* do—anything for your daughter, Grace. He'll never let Jo slip away. Intimidating parents be damned. I promise."

My mom sniffled as she wiped a tear away from under her sunglasses. "Thank you," she choked out, squeezing Emmett's hand. In that moment, I felt something shift inside me, a fissure line cracking open right through my heart. Was it just the emotions of the week? The excitement of a wedding getting to my head? Because something about Emmett's words made me desperately wish that every sentence was a secret love letter about me.

About us.

"Now isn't that a beauty." Riley whistled as we approached

our final destination. Our little group huddled together, re-positioned in a line. Emmett had subtly, somehow, ended up by my side. Staring up at the lighthouse, an undeniable current vibrated through the air along with its bright, beckoning beam.

Standing with Emmett on my left, my mom on my right, I'd never felt more at home.

CHAPTER

13

THE SCENT OF EMMETT LINGERED LONG AFTER HE left, wrapping itself around me as I sat on the upstairs deck with a glass of rosé. After the lighthouse tour, Emmett walked my mom and me back toward Summer Wind, regaling us with stories of his career with each step. Turns out, his writing had taken him to four continents and countless cities, performing readings at crowded bookstores and luxurious living rooms alike. He was a worldwide literary star, but right now, his hand was so close that I could almost grab it.

As a young artist, my mom had undergone a similar meteoric journey. She spent months in Asia painting monasteries and even a year in Egypt capturing a flourishing street art scene. She and Emmett swapped stories of accomplishments, travel, and the occasional international mischief like schoolmates sharing gum.

Part of me was elated by how easily Emmett and my mom were getting along. The other part of me couldn't help but feel left out. The worldliest endeavors on which Ben and I embarked these days were from our very own kitchen table. We spun a globe and picked a continent, a country to inspire the evening's cocktail selection. Friday nights in Westchester morphed into international destinations by way of fancy ingredients and plastic glassware. We drank caipirinhas and Negronis from the comfort of our worn and peeling barstool chairs. We pretended.

All the while, Emmett was actually out there in the world, his feet walking actual foreign streets, lips tasting actual foreign cuisine. Embarking on actual adventure. Like my mom had. Like Jo would do next. With each story Emmett told now, I pictured myself by his side. Paris, Tokyo, Lisbon. In the front row of his readings, the first to lead a standing ovation after each ending word. Seated next to him in first class, my passport book overflowing with stamps and memories. With love?

As I volleyed my head between the two, nodding along or laughing when appropriate, I tried to make my eyes sparkle with fascination to mask the deep-down feeling that I had missed out on something huge with Emmett that day we said goodbye. Instead, regret started to bubble toward the surface. When I was growing up, my planned path seemed so perfect. Ivy League and the corporate ladder. I checked each box with pride. But lately, it hadn't felt so perfect. The more I saw Emmett now, grown up and a gigantic success, the more I felt like I had missed my train, or rather, that I had hopped off a stop too soon. Was my plan all wrong? Had the universe handed me an out, an opening, an exciting whirlwind alternative, and I had walked right by with blinders on? Why?

Suddenly, I couldn't remember what had stopped me from choosing Emmett in the first place.

Suddenly, I couldn't remember why I had ever forgiven myself for letting him go.

Sipping the driest rosé I could find, I dared my fingers to open back up that Moleskine. Rereading my journals always felt like a violation of privacy against my younger self. I hadn't written these thoughts hoping to be revisited by an older, wiser, wistful version of Amy. The words were for the impetuous and anxious college student holding the pencil. Hoping not to fail the class in the first place. I whispered an apology to that younger Amy and turned the page.

October 21

Dear Writing Seminar Journal,

The first thing you should know is that Ben and I are officially on a break. I'm not sure if that makes him my ex-boyfriend technically, or if we now live in the mystery land of "It's Complicated," but that's where we are: Break City.

That's probably why I haven't written many diary entries recently. I know we are supposed to aim for one entry a week, but it's just . . . my feelings are so strange these days. Not exactly journal-worthy. I'm nervous to even write them down. It's a lot of loneliness. And what lonely person wants to spend their little free time between classes writing down just how lonely they are?

I've tried meditating, like we've been learning in class. At first, there's a sense of calm that fills my entire being. But then my mind wanders, and I find myself thinking about Ben. I wonder how he's doing, if I should ask him to get breakfast at Commons or meet for Pinkberry after class, instead of simply hoping I'll run into him on Locust Walk. (We haven't yet. I hate whoever decided to build the Engineering Quad on the farthest part of campus from Huntsman Hall.) Or maybe I should just wait until he's ready? Play it cool, and let him reach out first? And then I'm reminded of exactly how strange and lonely I'm feeling all over again. Cue: vicious cycle.

While we're on the subject . . . it was Ben's idea to "take a break" in the first place. There were a few fights. He said it wasn't even about seeing other people, per se—he just wants to be able to immerse himself into his engineering coursework, into making new friends and starting a robotics club, without worrying about a loser loner girlfriend waiting for him, sad and lonely in her dorm. Well, he didn't exactly say those last words, but I felt like they were implied.

Ben has been my best friend my entire life. My boyfriend for three and a half years. I thought we'd graduate college together. I assumed we'd get married. But if this is how just our freshman year is going, what's to stop my entire life plan from falling apart?

I want to fix it. If Ben needs space, I'll give it to him. The fact that he suggested we not tell our families about the trial separation, at least not yet, gives me hope that this break won't last for too long. We both know our parents would cry if they found out. Jo would drive herself from Bard to Philly and stay until we reconciled. Dramatics and door slams and professions of destiny would surely ensue. Neither Ben nor I can handle that though, so the B word is strictly off-limits with the family, for now. Fine by me.

But I am craving Jo's opinion on something, even though I don't know how to broach it . . . Emmett. From class. Eek. We've started to hang out more and more. He suggested a weekly study session with our seminar classmates, but so far, I'm the only one who ever shows. Strangely, I don't mind. I sort of love the one-on-one? We sit in the library and talk for hours. His upbringing is wild—born on the East Coast, but then his parents' work moved the family all over. Delhi, London, Milan, even a stint in Madrid. His accent is a blend of the globe. When his parents got divorced last year, Emmett went with his mom to Seattle to finish high school. I can't believe that after traversing the entire planet, he ended up right here at Penn, in West Philly, with me.

My own past seems so small in comparison. Not
that Emmett ever implies that. He says it's cute that
I'm a twin, that my best friends are my family. (Cliché,
ugh, I know!) But he does make fun of me for my
notebook filled with to-do lists, my strict schedule
(sorry not sorry that I eat lunch at 12:30 P.M. every
day), my jam-packed agenda with daily, weekly, and
monthly plans.

The five-year, ten-year dreams I couldn't believe I
actually confessed to him. Graduation summa cum
laude. Marriage by twenty-five. CFO at a PE firm by
forty. House in the suburbs. Corner office. Three kids.
Everything in color-coordinated control.

Emmett couldn't help but laugh when I told him
about it all. Growing up, he barely knew what city he'd
be living in any given year. He stopped planning and
never looked back. He says I should try doing the same.
Normally, I'd roll my eyes and ignore the advice. But
there's just something, well, unusual about him. Yes,
he's late often and his backpack is always a mess.
(What is so hard about using a zipper?!) But he's
creative. Brilliant, really. Ben is brilliant, too, don't get
me wrong. But it's different. Emmett's less strict, more
freeing. Always living in the now. And his sentences
make my heart sing. Jo would probably ask to marry
him on the spot if she read his homework assignments
alone. And I would probably die from jealousy. Ha.

Our study sessions are innocent enough so far, but
yesterday when he looked at me, I found myself almost

wishing for something more. I can practically hear Jo's voice in my head, telling me to get a grip, to focus on winning Ben back. To stick to my to-do list. But there was something about the way Emmett's eyes sparkled that made all my skin cells flutter.

If I'm being honest, Emmett's the reason for this entry in the first place. He just texted me, asking to get dinner next week after class. I tried to call Jo as a distraction, but she sent my three calls right to voicemail. I guess her schedule is a bit more fun than mine is. Although, even if she did answer, I'm not sure what I'd say. I can't talk about the Break. Plus, there's something nice about keeping Emmett to myself.

I haven't answered his text yet, but I think I'm going to say—

"Amy?"

I snapped the notebook closed as fast as a match burned out, hiding it under my hip and out of eyesight. How long had Jo been standing there, staring at me with that empty expression on her face?

"Sorry, I didn't hear you come up."

"We just got back," Jo said. "Wait, are you crying? What's wrong?"

I wiped my eyes and was surprised to pull back fingertips lightly coated in tears. "Allergies," I whispered the lie with a laugh.

Jo's mouth curved into a frown as she sat down in the empty chair next to me. "Everything okay out here?"

I pivoted. "Are you kidding? My sister is getting married in four days. Everything is *amazing*." It felt like I was trying on a cheerful voice in the Lord & Taylor fitting room. I didn't recognize the words even as I spoke them. My heart was still living in the past.

"I'm not some annoying college friend asking you to glue on a smile and wear an ugly dress all week, Amy. I can take it. Honestly, I'd love to talk about something, anything, other than my wedding."

I gulped half of my glass down in one gesture. "I'm fine."

"How was the walk?"

"Beautiful. Perfect weather for it. I think Valerie and Lila had a nice time, too," I lied.

"'Nice time' isn't even a phrase in their vocabulary." Jo's eyes rolled until they landed on what was left of the rosé in my glass. The hovering light pink of a final few sips. "May I?"

"Anything for the bride." I passed the glass her way. "How was the fishing trip?"

Jo licked her lips, finishing the drink off with one gulp. "That's actually why I came up here. I talked to Ben, Ames. He said things have been . . . He's worried." She looked at me with her famed guilt-tripping eyes. "I'm worried."

I tried to keep my voice steady. "You know I hate when you guys talk behind my back." The downside of marrying a family friend, of having a sister and a husband who acted like siblings themselves: worry spread quickly. Even if I begged Ben to zip his lips, to leave Jo out of this or that or whatever situation was distressing me, he still sought her counsel in times of deepest despair. Their secret conversations would result in coincidental check-ins from Jo, inspirational text messages before a high-stakes presentation or supportive phone calls to guide me through a panic attack. Words to wipe away all anxiety.

Especially back when we were kids, there were moments like these when only Jo could get through to me. Like she had the one secret road map through whatever fortress I had inadvertently built around myself, a shield to which only her efforts were penetrable. There were moments when it seemed like only Jo could save me.

It broke my heart, but this was not one of those moments.

Instead, a warm fury started to spread toward them both. Jo knew better than to meddle in our marriage like this, and Ben knew I didn't want to worry my sister with what we'd been going through, not here. Not now, during her wedding week. Not yet. I had tried to warn them. Why wouldn't they listen?

"It's just Ben being Ben. Ignore him," I snapped, exhausted from trying to protect them.

"He's seriously upset."

"It's *seriously* nothing."

"Doesn't look like nothing."

"There's just a lot right now. Work, the house—"

"That's why you haven't been returning my calls? Wallpaper samples and spreadsheets?"

"Responsibilities, Jo. Things every adult besides you seems to have."

"Don't patronize me."

"You wouldn't understand—"

"Explain it to me then!"

"Just drop it, Jo—"

"No, please, if I'm so naive and immature, spell it out and tell me what's going on—"

"You can't help me! You can't fix this! Stop trying!" I shouted. "Just stay out of my marriage." The fury in my voice ripped out and laid before us.

Regretting the escalation immediately, I tried to soften myself, to reach out and squeeze her hand. "You're getting married. Can't we just enjoy that?"

"Sure." She swallowed. But I knew I had stepped too far. Her eyes welled.

How much exactly had Ben told my sister?

Jo looked at me with a piercing sadness, like I was a stranger and not her best friend since the womb. "Enjoy your *reading*." The porch door slammed shut before I could try to stop her. Even if I'd had the chance, I wouldn't have told her to stay a second more.

Of course, she was right: everything was wrong. But I couldn't tell her any of that. Bridezilla or not, no one wanted their wedding week overshadowed by a sister's heartache. It was better this way, I told myself. She'd appreciate the secrets, all of them, in the long run.

My phone vibrated on the chair's white armrest. The name on the screen only made my stomach sicker. Ben. My husband had morphed from a source of joy to a reminder of everything I wanted to avoid. Of everything I needed to expel from my head.

Sending Ben's call to voicemail, I wished I had brought a second bottle of wine. I knew it was escapist, but I craved the buzz of my past with Emmett. The forbidden memories were intoxicating.

A thunderclap filled my ears. I looked up, startled to see that the sky had darkened and heavy clouds gathered on high. The rain started to fall down, first as gentle drops but quickly morphing into a steady stream. My hair grew damp, my jeans covered in puddled stains that looked like polka dots. My cheeks were wet, but the moisture that slipped into my mouth was none other than my own salty tears. My eyes had complemented the atmosphere.

Lightning struck in the distance, and the sky glowed purple. I counted down from fifteen, a lesson learned from a lifetime of summer storms. We'd poke our heads outside with umbrellas or stare with our faces glued to windowpanes, bracing ourselves for the crash to follow. Rain at the beach was rare enough that it became a specialty. Board games and hot chocolate and s'mores made in the microwave. As a kid, I itched for stormy nights, drowning in my dad's spare, over-size Boston University sweatpants, his alma mater. Falling asleep with marshmallow debris still sticky on my palms. What I would give to turn back the clock and retreat into an innocent storm once more.

Nine . . . eight . . . seven . . .

As an adult, rain meant canceled plans or seasonal depression. It meant the sky mirroring the twisting spiral of sadness that lay dormant in your soul. The clouds wept, so you wept right with them. Cathartic for a moment, to look out into the world and for the briefest of moments, to find your reflection staring back.

Three . . . two . . . one . . .

I tried to scream, to match the thunder's cry, but no sound came out of my throat.

My voice was muted. The words were as lost, as trapped, as I was.

A single lightning bolt struck in the distance.

It may have looked electric, but I knew it was just like me. Empty and alone.

WEDNESDAY

CHAPTER

14

B EN AND I SLEPT WITH OUR BACKS INTENTION-
ally facing each other, like strangers sharing a queen
bed on a bachelorette weekend or a school field trip. I had
retired to our room as the rain picked up, feigning a headache and declining the *Casablanca* movie night that had
assembled on the couch. A movie about a rekindled old romance was the very last thing I needed.

Jo wouldn't meet my eyes, still mad after our fight, but I
envied her nonetheless. Swaddled in chunky-knit blankets,
cuddled into the crook of Dave's shoulder where his neck
and collarbone joined. Ben, Mary, Bobby, my parents, and,
surprisingly, Conrad had stretched out on the couch, a dozen
pairs of bare feet propped on the coffee table. A dozen sets of
fingers clutched to personal bowls of popcorn mixed with
Hershey kisses. A Sharp snack tradition, but I still declined.

I envied Ben in that moment, too. Ben and Jo and their

frustrating ability to slip into fiction, into movies and literature and podcasts and poems, to let stories soothe their souls.
I used to love how they bonded without me. Now it just
made me annoyed. They both had this instinct to face the
sun. To stay happy and kind. When had they learned to do
that, if we all grew up right by one another's sides? Was the
fact that my reality was reeling not enough to keep their attention?

Did they have to be having so much fun without me?

Ben must have sensed my sadness because he followed
me as I left the room, echoes of his footsteps ricocheting up
the stairs. "Ames, wait up!" he called out. "You sure we can't
convince you to watch with us?"

"Humphrey Bogart's never really been my thing."

"I'll stay up here then. We can watch the Mets, or play
cards, or just hang out?"

I desperately wanted to say yes, to welcome him back in
our bed and rest my head on his chest and forget everything
that had happened. But I was also desperately afraid of the
topic I knew he would bring up the second we were alone. A
conversation I still wasn't ready for.

Silence was better than a fight, right? It was easier to just
be alone.

"It's fine, I'm tired," I said. "Just want to fall asleep early."

Disappointment spread across Ben's face.

"Maybe tomorrow?" I offered.

"Sure," Ben said, but we both knew it was an empty
promise.

I fell asleep to the patter on the windowsill, but the rain

had passed by morning. When I woke up, I saw a handful of Hershey kisses on the nightstand. A note next to the chocolates in Ben's handwriting read: *Didn't want to wake you to kiss you goodnight. Accept these instead? :) Love you, B. PS— Maybe we can talk later? Just us?*

Why couldn't I just let myself love him back? What was wrong with me?

Slipping out of bed, careful not to shift the mattress, I grabbed a chocolate kiss and tiptoed downstairs to the kitchen. The sun was still hazy, dawn only just melting away. There was nothing more perfect than an early morning in Kismet. Birds sang, but did so quietly, somehow aware of the human hangovers around every corner—emotional and alcoholic alike.

The coffee machine hummed as I matched my shallow breaths to the sound of the water trickling into the pot. Beans brewed, I curled myself up in the windowsill cushion with the biggest mug I could find clasped between my hands. One sip, one breath. The bay window overlooked the pool deck and faced straight out to the beach. I watched faraway seagulls chirp among themselves, imagining a strategy session for their day's agenda: how to best steal Lay's potato chips from the tourists on the sand. How simple it seemed to live and sleep on the beach.

My morning solace would stem from a manmade offering: work. Opening my Outlook app as I dialed my office line, I let the work emails roll in. My shoulders melted down my back as I read through the items I'd missed. Unlike the emotions of this week, these were things I could fix.

"Stop calling! You're on vacation!" Margaret chastised by way of a greeting when she answered my call. I couldn't help but smile as I imagined the venti iced matcha latte next to her keyboard, dripping with condensation onto her desk.

"Good morning to you, too," I said with a laugh. "Any updates? Anything I can help with?"

"You're an addict, Amy," she teased, before updating me on the pipeline.

Accounting took all the things I loved and rolled them into a career. Numbers. Tangibility. Control. The sense of balance when the debits equaled the credits. The fact that there was always a rule to follow meant there was always a right answer to find. A way to make order out of chaos. A happy ending amid the madness.

If only my real life could operate the same.

But when my dad appeared in the doorway, I knew my quiet morning was over. "Wedding duties are calling," I said to Margaret.

"Throw your phone away! I'm not answering if you call again!"

I laughed. "I'll talk to you in a bit."

"I'm serious!"

"Thanks for holding down—"

"Hanging up! Have fun!" she blurted out, as her voice was replaced by a click.

"The fort." My words were matched by silence on the other end of the line.

"Work?" my dad asked, as he poured himself a cup of coffee.

"Never ends."

"It's both a relief and a frustration when you realize that nobody can get anything done without you."

"That's for sure. I'll probably have to spend a good amount of today on my laptop." The lie came easily. Almost shockingly so. Work didn't need me for now, Margaret had made that much clear. In fact, they'd always been respectful of time off, a total rarity in firms like mine. Yet here I was, ready to throw them under the proverbial bus, blame them for taking up my precious vacation hours. Did I need a break from my family so badly that I'd invent a work emergency just for some time to myself?

"Feels like just yesterday I was the one working early in the kitchen, whispering so I wouldn't wake you girls up." Even though my dad had been retired for years, it still felt strange to see him unchained from his old Dell computer. "It's all worth it when you get to the other side."

"It feels endless sometimes," I said. "I'm not sure I'll ever get to where you finished."

"Are you kidding? You and Ben are leaps ahead of where I was at your age. I wish I had your work ethic." His words were meant as a comfort, but they still went in one ear and out the other. Platitudes and paternal praises, nothing more. Yes, our hours were tiring and maybe our titles were impressive. CFO had been my singular goal ever since I started at Eagle Cliff, and hitting that milestone felt like finishing the New York City Marathon: muscles sore from nights at my desk, though admittedly far less sweaty.

In reality, even the high from the promotion faded after

a month. The rush of success evaporated, just as it had after any other accomplishment. My mind fixated immediately on the next test, the next hurdle, the next plan. When would it feel like enough? When my name was on the door of an office building, like my dad's? When my triumphs hung on mantels in museums, like my mom's? Or would it be when Ben's dream came true, and we had a house with kids running around, a hot dinner waiting on a candlelit table? Would our children's lives just become my next series of checklists? I shuddered realizing that days away from turning thirty, I still didn't know any of these answers. Age hadn't brought more clarity, only more concerns.

"You're doing great, Ames." My dad had whipped up plates of egg-in-a-hole breakfast toasts, the yellow yolk soaking its tendrils into fresh country white bread. This was my go-to breakfast growing up, my lucky meal before the SATs, and even the final brunch before my own wedding day began. My father had read my mind in the way only the best fathers did.

"No, *this* is what's great." I raised the plate up as a literal toast. "Thanks, Dad."

"The bride's request. Jo!" he called out. "Breakfast's ready!" The record scratched before I could even pick up my fork and knife. This wasn't really for me. It was for Jo.

Jo and Dave bounded into the kitchen a second later. "I've been dreaming about this since we went to sleep. I still can't believe you've never had this before!" Jo gave my dad a grateful kiss on the cheek before firmly placing a plate in

Dave's outstretched hands. All the while, she refused to meet my eyes. Could she still be mad from yesterday's fight? Our arguments never lasted past the sunrise, a magic rule of sisterhood. Was our charm wearing off like the midnight expiration of a spell?

Dave's eyes grew ten sizes as he took in the plate. "To think, I was almost married before I egged a hole."

"It's true, you can't be a Sharp until you've hole egged," my dad agreed.

Dave treated the room to an exaggerated show of taking his first bite. Dad and Jo cheered, but I kept my eyes fixed down on my own untouched plate. My appetite had vanished.

"Fantastic, really," Dave declared. "Thank you, Sam."

"My treat." My dad smiled. "So, what's on the agenda, today?"

"Dave and I are going to write our vows down at the bay."

"How romantic!" My mom had walked in, sliding her arm around my dad's waist. "If my back wasn't killing me, I'd just have to join you," she teased.

"What happened to your back?" I asked.

"Oh, it's nothing. I must have slept on it funny."

"Shoot, I'm sorry, Mom," Jo said. "Are you still up for meeting the freight ferry in Saltaire?"

"Of course—"

"Jo, if Mom's back hurts she shouldn't be lugging crates of alcohol," I suddenly snapped.

"It's not *just* alcohol," Jo whined.

"I'll go to the ferry," my dad volunteered. "Dave's parents will need to wait twenty-four more hours to pop their egg-in-the-hole cherries. Not too long, just one more day after a lifetime."

"It's fine," I said, sensing the task was going to fall on my shoulders anyway. There was no reason to hurry my dad out of the kitchen or augment my mom's pain. Plus, Summer Wind's walls were making me feel suffocated anyway. "I can do it."

"Thanks, sweetheart," my mom said, rubbing her hand through my hair as if I was a little girl again, offering to take Rocky on a walk. "Want to see if Ben can come with you?"

"He's working." Another lie that came out faster than I should have felt comfortable with. I had no idea if Ben was still sleeping or up working or on the next ferry to escape from his depressed wife and her wedding-crazed family. "I'll go by myself, it's fine."

Just then, Dave's phone pinged. "Perfect timing. El just texted if there was anything he could help with this morning?"

"Great! He can go with Amy," my dad said. Dave's fingers flew across his keyboard.

"Time for him to earn those best man stripes," Jo said. "Perfect."

No, not perfect. "I'm more than capable of a solo freight ferry run," I said, bristling back.

"Sorry, too late, I think," Dave said. "He just texted that he'll meet you outside."

Internally, I moaned. A moment's escape now turned into exactly what I needed to avoid.

Emmett.

★

He was grinning next to the bike stand by the time I found him.

"Four minutes later than Dave said you'd be. Could Mercury be in retrograde?"

I couldn't help but smile as my brain tried to comb through a clever response. Emmett's quips could still leave me tongue-tied. "Funny" was all I could manage, much to Emmett's delight, as I started unlocking the bicycles with the largest wagons attached to the backs.

"You know, I don't think I've ever seen a freight ferry," he said, his index finger tracing one of the handlebars.

"A freight virgin? Prepare for your mind to be blown," I joked, pushing one of the bikes his way. "But the better question is: do you even know how to ride this thing?"

"Please, how else do you think I make my way around Florence?"

I checked my watch. "Not even noon and you're already acting like a pompous jerk. Impressive."

"I can't apologize for living the dream." He laughed, his face fighting off a sheepish grin.

"All right, Armstrong." I hopped up on my bike in one swift motion, calling over my shoulder as I veered sharply out of the driveway. "Try to keep up."

"Cheater!" he shouted back. After a few pedals, I slowed my pace so that Emmett and I could ride side by side, to which, after a single playful attempt to poke me off-balance, he consented. Emmett's emotions had always been capricious. He could be so quiet, so locked inside himself, if he was nearing a deadline or felt consumed with words to write down. But the next day, he was like a movie star. Charming, larger-than-life. Biking with him now, sun on our shoulders and hair blowing off my face, it sure felt like we were in a major motion picture.

Saltaire was the very next town over, but suddenly I found myself wishing it was all the way at the other end of the island. That we'd have to bike for hours to get there, and then turn around and do it all again to return home. An entire day, an entire week, wouldn't have felt long enough to bask in his warmth.

As we pedaled down to Saltaire's town square, we passed quintessential beach houses decorated with quintessential families smiling in front yards. Kids laughing, dogs playing, breakfast on wraparound decks. Summer morning bliss.

"You plan on buying a place out here?" Emmett asked. "There's some seriously stunning real estate."

"One day, I hope. What about you? Beach house in your future?"

Emmett sucked his teeth. "Honestly, the entire concept of home ownership sort of freaks me out."

"This not good enough for you?" I teased. These houses were basically shiny billboards for the Fire Island lifestyle. Sirens singing vacation-themed songs. Americana at its best.

He smiled. "Don't get me wrong. I'd love a big house right here on the ocean. But I'd also love a flat in London and a duplex in Barcelona. It's hard to know where I'll be any given month, with book tours and conferences coming up. Hotels are more my speed these days."

"Well then, you'll simply have to buy a place in all of them." My mind danced back to my passport daydream, how many stamps I would collect by Emmett's side.

"Ha. I just don't want to stop traveling. I love it. I'd live in a new city every year if I could."

"Very nomadic of you," I said, but his words again struck something deep. That wistful urge to pack up and run. My entire schedule felt anchored to a one-hour radius—my parents, Ben's parents, and Jo all within a dozen stops on the Metro-North's Hudson Line. We bought our house in Irvington for that very reason. Yet while my roots crawled down to the deepest depths of soil, Emmett seemed up high in the clouds. Debates over cabinetry styles seemed dreadful; Emmett seemed free.

Free from a permanent address also meant free from rooms that felt bare, lonely. Those empty nests. Haunted, even. "No kids then?" I ventured. The words felt like dares on my tongue.

With a simple shrug of his shoulders, I knew exactly what Emmett meant. Not now, no rush. He took a deep breath in. "I'd never say never, but . . . never. Does that make me an awful person?"

"Just an honest one," I said, hoping my tone sounded light and supportive. Was that envy I was trying to disguise from myself? Just then, our conversation was interrupted by the piercing cry of a toddler. A tantrum forming its thunder as we parked our bikes at Saltaire's dock.

"I mean. Case in point," Emmett said, and I couldn't help but burst out laughing. "Home ownership and whatever that noise is? My top two fears." I was shocked to discover I had no argument.

We had made it to Saltaire right as the freight ferry pulled in, its long platform overflowing with boxes and crates and appliances too hefty for the passenger route. The freight's arrival felt like our carriage turning back into a pumpkin. A reminder that what had started to feel like maybe a date was just an errand in disguise. Yet even when our wagons were brimming with cardboard boxes, filled high with wine and wedding supplies, neither Emmett nor I made any moves back toward Kismet.

"You know, Saltaire Market is not just your average beach town store. They sell the best frozen ices in the tri-state," I said, my voice almost quivering with anticipation. The way the sun shone on his cheeks made my feet turn into dumbbells. I couldn't leave. Not yet. I wanted more make-believe, even though I knew it wouldn't last.

"All the tri-state?"

"Well, at least Long Island."

"I think I have to try it then. Out of respect for Long Island."

"It would really be rude not to." I grabbed his hand to lead him into the Saltaire Market. It started as a gesture just to make sure he followed, but once his fingers were inter-locked with my own, neither of us let go.

My heart raced. This wasn't cheating, I told myself. Just skin and bones and fingernails held against my own. An old friend. Platonic. And yet, even when he lightly squeezed my palm and I felt all my blood rush to my toes, I still held on.

We walked up to the counter, and I asked the clerk for one lemon and one chocolate ice. "What will you have then?" Emmett joked. His giddiness—our giddiness?—was palpable. You could almost reach out and grab it.

"We'll share," I said, swallowing. Sweat was growing under my arms, and I could feel my face turning red. If this was what holding his hand did to me, what would it feel like to kiss again? To try for something more?

My mind flashed to the first time, the only time, that Emmett and I kissed. It was sweet and quick and quiet outside the Septa station. We were tipsy on Franzia and feeling brave. I held his scarf as he held my face, his palm warm against my cheek. He walked me home right after and then we parted ways. One step at a time, we'd said with shy laughs. I could still feel his touch on my skin.

I never told anyone, and then everything changed. Emmett left, and I knew I could never tell anyone now that he was gone.

Was this a second chance or just another secret?

I inhaled, unsure of what I wanted, afraid for the words to even form in my brain, until a nearby voice stole my breath straight out from my throat.

"Amy Sharp?"

I immediately pulled my hand out of Emmett's grasp, snapping back my fingers as if they'd been burned. Reality crashed. Who was that? Had someone seen us? What would they say?

Spinning around, I found the face to match that familiar voice. Staring at me with her eyebrows raised was the worst possible person to have crossed paths with at this moment: Paige. She was a few years younger than Jo and me but a fixture of Fire Island. Her father was the president of the fire department, and her political lineage combined with a dazzling smile and year-round tan made Paige a de facto princess on these shores.

She was also a known gossip queen. I tried not to panic about what she had or had not seen, tried to keep my face a normal color and my breathing even and my body's moisture at bay. Even still, I could feel my stomach starting to twist and turn, nervous sweat coating my lower back.

"Paige! Look at you, all grown up." My voice sounded foreign to my own ears, high-pitched and on guard.

"Amy Sharp! It *is* you. Happy almost Fourth!" she replied with a kiss on each cheek. "Who's your handsome friend?"

"Emmett, nice to meet you." He stretched out his hand, which Paige accepted with a bemused smile on her face. Her manicure was a perfect shade of white-gray. As their fingers touched, I felt something akin to jealousy course through my veins. What was happening? I wanted to push her over, take his hand back in mine. Instead, I just stood there smiling, forcing my emotions to retreat, to recalibrate. To reel it in.

"You look familiar." Paige's brows knit together as she looked him up and down.

Emmett's cheeks turned red. "Just that kind of face, I think."

"He's the best man in Jo's wedding," I managed.

"Of course! I can't believe the weekend's already here. Jo Sharp getting married. It's the talk of the town."

"Honored to be a part of it," he said with a polite smile.

"A part of something, that's for sure. Where's Ben these days?" Was I losing it, or could I see the actual wheels turning in Paige's head? "Don't tell me you're divorced already— my heart would just break."

"Of course not," I quickly said. "He's back at the house, working. We're just running a quick errand for Jo."

"That Jo. What an easy bride. Afternoon ices are *such* a fun errand." She grinned, as if she had solved a mystery, fact-checking my words. "You guys seem like a bridal party I'd party with. If you want to grab a drink before the wedding, you know where to find me." Paige winked in what felt like predominantly (and unnervingly) Emmett's direction before sliding her sunglasses from their resting place on the top of her head down to the bridge of her nose. I never understood how someone could be so cool yet so scary. "See you soon," she sang out, turning to leave as quickly as she'd arrived.

"She seems nice," Emmett offered, once the coast was clear. Even with Paige gone, the energy had shifted. The enchantment broken. I wanted to kick myself for being so careless, for forgetting that we were on a literal island with friends and family members around every turn. Friends who took mental notes about everything they saw and swapped secrets as readily as ice cubes for glasses of wine on the beach. I didn't know what Paige saw, but I wasn't naive. I knew she suspected something.

The frozen ices were ready, but I'd lost my appetite. Emmett happily dove into both, oblivious to my dejection. I glanced at my phone to check the time and was shocked to see three missed calls and four unread text messages from Ben. The latest read:

Ben: Need to talk. Meet me at the beach. ASAP.

CHAPTER

15

A MILLION PANICKED THOUGHTS RACED THROUGH my head as I pedaled back to Summer Wind. A chill had settled in the space between Emmett and me, and not just from the frozen treats. I knew Emmett wanted to stay in Saltaire longer, live in the dream instead of assuming our roles as fake strangers back with the wedding party. And he could not have been thrilled that the impetus for our quick return was none other than my husband.

What did Ben need to talk about? Could whatever Paige saw have somehow spread that quickly, fluttering through the streets from Saltaire to Kismet to Summer Wind's front steps? There were dozens of legitimate reasons why Ben could and should be upset with me. For ignoring him since we arrived, for sniping every chance I could. For shying away at his touch and spending the morning biking and giggling and swooning over another man.

I just had no idea which it might be.

Imagine my shock when I climbed up to the top of the beach's entry steps and saw not an angry husband with his arms crossed or a suitcase packed for a dramatic escape but, rather, a picnic.

I had spent the afternoon with another man while my husband prepared a picnic.

I had fantasized about kissing another man while my husband secretly shopped at the Kismet Market, snuck groceries to the beach. While he arranged this thoughtful surprise.

I swallowed my growing guilt and shoved memories of Emmett to the side.

"What is all this?" I marveled as I neared the spread. It was something straight out of a magazine, or at the very least, a sponsored Instagram advertisement. On top of a checkered blanket sat cheese and meats, bundles of grapes and fig jam galore. There was a basket of crostini breads and cheesy garlic sticks. A white wine chilled in a marble cooler, and my heart swelled when I realized it was a Beaujolais vintage, from a vineyard we visited on our honeymoon in France. Two plump pillows sat facing the ocean, and a simple baby-blue balloon floated along, affixed to a pastel tasseled umbrella. Ben stood with two glasses of wine pre-poured and a sheepish smile on his face.

"Happy birthday, babe."

I ran up to Ben and kissed him so hard, he nearly spilled both glasses of wine. After he paused momentarily to secure them safely on a tiny beach table, already topped with straw baskets of serving ware and cutlery and a single, perfect cupcake, Ben wrapped his arms around my body and pulled in tight. My husband was six inches taller than I was, which I always thought was the perfect height difference—I could easily tuck my head right under his chin without even having to stretch my neck.

As he kept his lips pressed tight against my forehead, I wished he'd never let go.

"I just wanted to do something special for you, before the wedding events kick into even higher gear," he whispered. "I know things have been—"

"Shhh," I cut him off, reaching up to kiss his scruffy cheek. "It's perfect."

His eyes shone so blue I could have forgotten my own name. In that instance, nothing else mattered. We sat with our ankles hooked against each other's, taste-testing the Brie and the Gouda, debating a favorite from the cheese board. Aside from a particularly nosey seagull, we somehow had a quiet corner of the beach to ourselves. A miraculous serenity before the holiday weekend's crescendo. By the time we reached the bottom of the bottle, the sky had turned a pale pink and the waves sang a lullaby with their gentle crashes. Our own slice of heaven.

"I missed sitting like this. We should have come out here sooner," Ben said.

I knew what he meant. There was something about the stillness of the beach that begged us to look inward, to inspect our every pore. A panacea we had been craving. My head on Ben's shoulder, my mind started to play all the times we'd seeped our souls in sand-covered conversation.

"Remember when we flipped a seashell to decide which house to buy?" Ben smiled. Of course he was thinking the same thing I was, reading my own brain.

"And then right again, to decide which color to paint the walls?" I laughed back.

"I'm still glad I lost that one. You were totally right about Pigeon Gray."

"When am I not right?" I teased, the way we used to. Pretending I believed my words.

"We've spent so many days like this," Ben said. "Remember before we moved to Penn? We sat here for three full hours after everyone went back to the house. Your parents thought we drowned."

A laugh. "Instead, we were just driving ourselves up a wall guessing all the ways college could change us." I shook my head. "I wanted to think of every solution in advance, every plan to stop any and all change right in its tracks."

It was ironic. As if any of my prepping had ever successfully prevented anything.

"Well, I still think I made the best plan Fire Island has ever seen." Ben pressed his arm around me tighter.

"Call me biased, but I agree." I knew the exact plan, the exact beach conversation he was referring to. The exact June weekend six years ago, when I hadn't even wanted to come out to Fire Island in the first place.

After a week preoccupied with a deal closure at work, all I craved that Friday night was bed and a Shake Shack burger. I hadn't even had time to wash my hair, let alone maintain a manicure, so rushing from the LIRR to the 7:30 P.M. ferry couldn't have ranked farther toward the bottom of my to-do list. Yet Ben insisted. "Sunshine is the only logical solution to a week trapped under the fluorescents of your office cubicle," he'd said. I only relented when he offered to pack my bag himself. But I warned him: no partying, no late nights. That weekend, I just wanted to catch up on sleep.

Friday night had been a strange blessing. Instead of the usual revolving door of family friends stopping for drinks or dragging us out dancing, Summer Wind was shockingly quiet. Even my parents seemed tongue-tied, suggesting just a movie before an early bedtime.

But when the house still echoed with silence come morning, I began to think something was wrong. There was no Dad in the kitchen toasting bagels, no Mom or sister sketching by the pool. No boyfriend even, snoring gently atop the next pillow over. Until my phone pinged:

Ben: Meet me at the beach?

I threw on a cover-up and headed toward the sand. "Walk?" Ben suggested once I had arrived, taking my hand and leading me eastward along the shoreline, toward the lighthouse. We let our feet get wet, skin coated in that sticky brown sand that wedged between the toes. Silence for a moment, the kind of trusted quiet when the pressure to fill the void with endless noise evaporated. Ben and I had always been that way; after a lifetime together, we had no need for words just for words' sake.

The next words he said were studied ones, ones he'd later claim to have practiced in the shower for weeks, whispered under the auditory cover of the steady water's stream. Internal rehearsals hadn't prepared him for the real deal, heart racing and words freezing up, and while he swore he repeated full sentences a few times over, I couldn't remember a thing. His voice was muted as I just watched his teeth taking different shapes. The only thing running through my mind was "Amy Sharp, you are so damn lucky in love."

When Ben got down on one knee, and I finally realized what was happening, I had to ask him to please, please start again—I hadn't been listening hard enough. We both cracked up, but he obliged, repeating the entire ritual from the top. He knocked my heart out, again.

After my gleeful "Yes, yes, yes!" Ben took my hand, cushion-cut diamond secured and sparkling, and led me closer to the lighthouse. There, holding glasses of champagne with beaming grins were Jo and both sets of our parents, along with best friends and relatives. When our loved ones clinked their glasses, Ben picked me up and kissed me. I could feel his entire body shaking, his palms clammy, his arm hair standing straight like a pin. It only made me love him more; his body revealing just how nervous he had been all the while.

Could he have ever thought I would say no?

This had been our lifelong plan. Engagement had actually been a beach discussion the summer prior. After Ben gently probed if—hypothetically—he presented me with a ring, would I—hypothetically—accept (answer: a resounding yes), he didn't bring up any of the other details again. I was anxious at first, knowing a life change was coming and I couldn't surround it with checklists, itineraries, and budgetary columns. My trust in Ben, for our future, carried me blindly. In the end, it had been perfect. The secrecy all paid off.

Now I worried if Ben could trust me. If he even should.

"Make a wish," Ben sang, shaking me back to the current sandy scene. I stared at the cupcake, candle aglow, but my mind went blank. Where to start with wishes when I needed so many? With the mocking flame extinguished, we did what we did best. We walked.

"Thirty," I said to Ben, to the sky, to anyone who would listen. "It feels hard to believe."

"At any age, you'll be the most beautiful person in the world. Even eighty. Even a hundred!"

"Eighty? Slow your roll, sir. Lots of life before we get there." Eighty felt impossible sometimes. A lifetime away. Recently, if I tried to picture myself even three years older, it felt like someone had spilled boiling water all over the keyboard of my brain. An error message: CANNOT COMPUTE.

Now the same old elephant exploded in the space between us. Any inkling, any thought about the future was always accompanied by the inevitable question of kids.

As teenagers in love, Ben and I daydreamed about parenthood. Twin boys named Daniel and Hudson, a big house near an apple orchard, soccer games on Sunday and cider donuts after a big win. But as we'd gotten older, and as that vision crawled within reach, I found myself repelling it. It was suddenly too real, too soon, too possible. I avoided it all the more.

Benchmarks turned into excuses—not until we're married, not until I'm promoted, not until we buy a house. First things first, I thought. In reality, it was just "baby things last."

It was never that I didn't want kids. From the moment I held my first doll, I wanted kids. I'd naively make a mental list of ways I would and would not raise them—I'd never yell, I'd always bring hot chocolate in bed if they were sad. I would be a mom to rival all moms . . . when the time came. One day, instead of showcasing the morning's hour, I just assumed my alarm clock would announce: *You're ready!* A moment of clarity would beam through my being, and our lives would seamlessly and miraculously transition into that of parents.

Real adulthood would begin.

Instead, the alarm rang, but then the clock broke and vanished. Now I wasn't sure how we would ever go back. How we could ever try again.

"Amy," Ben began now. I tried to caution him with my eyes, but it seemed he was sick of signals, fed up with warnings. "I know you don't want to talk about it—"

"You think?"

"Please, Amy."

"Don't ruin it, Bear. Can't we just have one nice, normal day?"

"None of this is normal! *We* don't feel normal anymore—"

"So let's just pretend. Just one more week. Until after the wedding." I went to grab his hand, but Ben had moved away.

"Pretending that we're fine won't fix anything," he choked.

"Neither will telling everyone and ruining what's supposed to be a nice week."

"I'm not saying we have to tell everyone! We don't even have to tell Jo! I just want to talk to you."

"So why did you talk to Jo then? On the fishing trip? I really wish you wouldn't always run to her when things got hard. Now she hates me, too."

"No one hates you, Amy. I just thought Jo could get through to you in a way that I clearly can't. You barely say three words at a time to me anymore!"

"Because you're always looking at me like I'm some fragile thing about to break!"

"I'm not going to apologize for being worried—"

"I just need space, okay?"

"Space? Come on, Ames. All I've given you is space!"

"I don't want to talk about it."

"You never do! I just want us to get better—"

"Maybe I'm not ready to be better," I snapped. "Why are you? Why is it so easy for you to just be happy? To forget everything so soon?"

"Are you kidding? You think I'm happy? Are you crazy?"

"Now I'm 'crazy'?"

"You know what I mean." Ben sighed. "Amy, I get that you aren't ready to try again. I will wait until you're ready, no question, no problem. But I'm scared. This isn't us. All this silence, this 'space'?" Ben threw up his hands. "How much more space can you take until you're gone? Up on the moon and never coming back down?"

"Ben, come on—"

"I don't know what you're thinking anymore, if you think it's just your fault—"

"My *fault*?"

"And I don't know why you think this is something only you are dealing with. Some burden only assigned to you. Because I'm here, too, Amy. I am hurting. So much. It's awful. But if I pushed you away, who would be left?"

"There's nothing left anyway," I said, anger slipping out.

"Is that what you want?" he went on. "For me to be gone?"

Of course not, I thought. But it was like his words were daggers, slicing right through my vocal cords. I couldn't respond.

"Jesus, Amy. I want to help, but if you won't let me . . . I'm just not sure how much longer we can keep doing this."

My cheeks were wet with tears. "Just leave then. Please."

Ben looked over at my face, winced when he saw that I was crying. "Amy, don't cry."

"Just go." I needed him gone, to let his words, his threats, marinate in my body.

"At least come back to the house with me."

"Please, Ben. That's what I want for my birthday, okay? For you to leave me alone." The words spilled out of me like vitriol. But I needed to say them, if only to twist the knife deeper into my own heart. To punish myself for everything I'd done, to push Ben further, to give him more ammo to not come back. I didn't deserve his goodness anymore.

I needed to feel every inch of my own hurt. To watch every piece of my own heart shatter. Because of course Ben was right. Pushing him away didn't make anything feel better. It didn't bring back what we had lost.

It didn't ensure it would never happen again.

It only made it easier to fill myself up with sadness.

It only made it easier to hate myself for it even more.

"Fine," Ben said. He looked as if he wanted to say something else, but instead he just shook his head. He didn't need to verbalize what I knew he was thinking. *There Amy goes, ruining it all.* He turned around without so much as a goodbye.

It was unfair, but a quiet piece of me still hoped that he'd look back and glance my way. Grab me by the arms, absorb me into a hug, and carry me home. That he'd see through my selfish smoke show of anger, see the real pain. The fear that I was broken, that I would always be broken, and that he wouldn't love me because of it. That no one would.

The fear that life would never be the same.

The fear that one day, I could do something so horrible that even Ben, my Ben, wouldn't stay.

Just like that, he walked away.

CHAPTER

16

I T HAD BEEN TEN WEEKS OF SECRECY. OF CODED
smiles and mischievous grins, living in an entire world
that only Ben and I knew existed. We dreamed up the heart-
consuming ways we'd share the news, invite others into our
growing new world. A sweater embroidered with "grandma,"
a sonogram left just so, out on the kitchen table and waiting
to be discovered.

Superstitions had always haunted me. I skipped cracked
pavement, avoided thirteenth floors, knocked on the nearest
wood I could find whenever anyone made a wish. I don't
even dare to imagine the Mets actually winning when we're
at Citi Field, and the word "traffic" is as bad as "Beetlejuice"
when making record time in the car.

When a month passed without my period, I stayed calm.
I tried not to dwell on that March date night with Ben, after
which we'd come home and carelessly shrugged off the idea

of protection as fast as we tugged off each other's clothes. We had been in those early-day stages, the thinking-about-starting-to-talk-about-trying phase. Ben was practically born ready for fatherhood, but his pleading glances always were paired with patience, too. That night his eyes had shone. His smile so convincing.

One night, I thought. Sure. That couldn't possibly be all it would take. It felt too easy, too predictable. Okay, okay. Let's give it just one try.

Of course, my ovaries didn't care about the fact that I wasn't ready. That the items on my pre-baby checklist—make partner, go on a cross-country road trip, remodel the bathroom—continued to multiply overnight. That I worried about the reality of giving up weekends and sleep and my disposable income all to a new human being.

That I feared the type of mother I might actually be.

When those two parallel lines appeared, Ben knew better than to question my jinx avoidance: we didn't say a word. Instead, we silently stared, Ben's hands on his head. Could it be? I called in late to work and drove straight to the doctor's office, waiting the longest two hours of my life for a break in the schedule to have my blood drawn. Fueled by the need for conclusive proof.

Even when that call from the doctor confirmed my results, a part of me refused to believe it. A tumult of thoughts and concerns and celebrations took up residency in my brain all at once. It wasn't until I had to stay home sick from work because of the nausea that I let myself breathe, just a little. Show the semblance of a smile.

Nausea was a good sign.

It was actually happening.

Anxiety flooded (the hormones weren't magic), but so did excitement. I had nine months to plan, to throw myself into research and checklists and a calendar of appointments. Butterflies seemed to fly out of my fingertips with each parenting book I read, each crib I researched.

Suddenly it felt so natural. I had been scaring myself for so long with parenthood fears that even a monster under my bed couldn't have lived up to the horrifying expectations. The anticipation of ever being pregnant had paralyzed me into never wanting to proceed. An impulsive decision was my unexpected antidote. I could do this.

We could do this.

We counted down to the end of the first trimester, to the nuchal scan. All the while, Ben begged that we tell our parents sooner, tell Jo. I considered it, even scheduled a lunch with my family just to finally announce the news. Personalized presents. A big reveal. But when our entrées were cleared and the check arrived, my throat tasted like sandpaper. I wasn't ready. I couldn't share the truth. Flowy sweaters, leggings, and lunch sodas would suffice until I was completely sure. Until the baby was completely safe.

In hindsight, when I lay awake and stared up at the ceiling, I wondered if I had jinxed this right then and there. If the baby sensed my years of aversion and didn't feel welcome in my home. Didn't feel like part of my plan. Did my superstition, my stress, my fears, pave way for the fall?

Did the baby know I hadn't thought I was ready?

Did this mean I had never really been ready at all?

My doctor assured me that was impossible, but medical explanations didn't soothe the aching feeling in my gut. It didn't mask the invasive smell of the hospital walls or placate the time-stopping memory of the awful spotting, the pain and fears that had brought us to its fluorescent wings in the first place. It didn't speed up the empty heart rate on the scan. The beat we had naively drummed our fingers to just weeks earlier now vanished.

Disappeared.

The baby was gone before anyone even knew that one had arrived.

Ben and I said our singular goodbyes, but the absence prevailed. It was in every corner, every conversation. The pain the only reminder of what had been. "I'm fine" didn't cut it, but how else to answer my mom's phone calls checking in? How to smile through Jo's wedding countdown when my insides were empty? We had four weeks until Jo's ceremony. Three weeks until we needed to pack our bags and head to Kismet.

How were we to explain the aftershock from an earthquake no one else knew had struck our house and left our hearts in pieces?

Days in bed turned into weeks of silence. My body had healed but nothing was normal. Ben and I didn't know how to fit back into our roles. Our plan, our great foolish plan. What was the point of pretending? Life had pivoted and left us directionless. Ben wanted to talk, to process, to try again as soon as the doctor said we could. But any suggestion of another pregnancy caused my soul to unravel. How could we ever open ourselves back up? Why plan to try again when a consequence could leave us with this much heartbreak? Ben begged me to talk, but I felt frozen. I couldn't seem to verbalize this fear that had moved into my bones. The pessimistic possibilities that I didn't want him hearing.

What if all this pain just happened again?

What if Ben stopped loving me because of it?

Sentences started but never formed. We were together, but I'd never felt more alone. Doors slammed as even innocent questions erupted into arguments, saying all the words but the ones we needed. I raised my voice, we both did, desperate to feel something scratch inside. When I licked my chapped lips, my raw vocal cords felt like the only reminder of the pain I craved. A piece of me was gone; another piece of me was terrified. I couldn't just carry on without a hurting sensation in my core, an ever-present tap on the shoulder, a reminder of what had been and what could be.

All of it was easier to just ignore. Quiet was the only thing I could stomach.

I slipped away, so Ben begged me again to call Jo, to call my mom, my dad, to call anyone. To finally talk and to tell. We settled instead on a therapist. A woman named Nina became a new life vest. Amber hair and glasses and a gentle voice that lulled me back to life. Sessions whenever I needed them. She didn't push or prod, but rather, she legitimized my reaction. She made room for all my fears.

All we had were our bodies, she said. We had to listen when they cried.

Our secret world was to be forever covered in ashes, a civilization left behind. Maybe one day a tourist would walk through, take a photo, wonder how it all went sour.

CHAPTER

17

"BULLSHIT," TYLER ROARED. CONSIDERING HOW many secrets I held, I was a surprisingly terrible liar when it came to cards.

Dinner at Summer Wind had been tense. Ben and Jo sat lost in their phones, and my mom kept starting to tell some story or another, only to be cut off by a warning glance from my dad. Meanwhile, Dave's parents had taken him and Lila to the Inn for dinner, a final Beaumont-only family meal before more guests trickled in tomorrow. Jo and I hadn't spoken all day, so I didn't know if she was offended by being excluded by Valerie and Conrad. If it confirmed her fears that they never liked her in the first place. If she had wanted me to plan a rival outing for her and our family instead. I couldn't imagine Ben's parents taking only him out for a family dinner so close to our own wedding—the whole point of the ceremony was an *addition* to one's nuclear unit. Did it feel like a slap in Jo's face for Dave's family to be preserving what would soon cease to be?

Whether Jo was hurt or worried or not, I found myself missing the Beaumonts' presence at our kitchen table. I would have given my left arm to nod along to some tirade from Valerie or stare at Lila's permanent frown. Anything to distract me from the painfully quiet echoes of my family's slurp and chew.

It was hard to believe we were here for a celebration.

A text from Mary changed everything.

Mary: Party at Party of Five. Now.

The text was followed by a string of beach-, alcohol-, and fire-related emojis.

Ben and Jo both uncharacteristically claimed fatigue, preferring to stay home instead, but I knew that the Party of Five house was exactly the after-dinner change of scenery that I needed.

I could hear their music blasting before I even made it to the front steps. I vowed in that moment to never take being "just a wedding guest" for granted. If I didn't wear the mantle of bridesmaid—or worse, maid of honor—for the rest of my life, a complaint would never once leave my lips.

"Welcome to the fun house!" Mary greeted me now, gesturing toward their display as if she were Kismet's very own Vanna White. The cousins had ordered pizza, and a buffalo chicken dip was cooking in the oven. A bong rested on the table, scattered between joints and empty beer cans. My mind flashed to weeknights at Ben's college frat house, smoking weed and watching reruns of *It's Always Sunny in Philadelphia* for hours on end.

I quickly pushed the memory away. I'd had enough Ben for the day.

Instead, simultaneous relief and disappointment washed over me when I saw Bobby and Tyler on the couch, a Mets game on in the background. No sign of Emmett. I had deliberated texting him before I came over, sending a warning that I was stopping by. But then I kept remembering the utter lack of warning he had given me by even showing up this week. A taste of his own medicine didn't seem so out of line. Even still, I wondered if he could hear my voice echoing through the hallways when I called out: "Tequila, anyone?"

Rounds of shots followed, but they couldn't distract me for long. As Mary and Tyler inched closer, as if drawn by an unspoken magnet, my own heart swelled with desire. Flirting was fun. Flirting was easy. The first steps were the simple ones, daring kisses and fingers grazing, testing out a hold. What no one told you was that it only got harder from there. Trust and relationships and not getting sick of someone else's loud laugh and morning breath ten years later.

Dating was easy; living was harder.

I hated that I couldn't feel settled, just knowing Emmett might be right upstairs. It was like goose bumps had been tattooed on my forearms, and the anticipation of whether I'd see him had made my entire bloodstream cold. Anticipation, yes, but also anger. At Ben and at myself. It was like a portal had opened and there was no turning back. The tequila didn't help either. After months of expectant sobriety, my body was still getting used to the quick buzz.

"Amy! Game time! Come play," Tyler said, beckoning me to where he and Mary had settled on the couch, a deck of cards prepped on the table. A few rounds of the bluffing card game BS followed, before Tyler suggested switching to President.

"We need a fourth player, though," Tyler said. "Bob-man? You want in?"

"Ugh, not that game," Bobby complained from across the room, his eyes still glued to the baseball broadcast. "I'm out."

"Come on, it'll be fun," Mary pled, but Bobby put his hand up to silence his sister.

"You only think it's fun because I always lose."

"We do need a fourth player," I said.

"Go ask El," Bobby huffed.

"He's 'writing,'" Tyler said.

"Ames, you ask him," Mary said with an impossible-to-deny smile. "Please? He can't say no to the maid of honor. That's a wedding week faux pas."

I hesitated.

"Pleeeeeeease," my cousin begged.

"Fine. I'll try." I groaned, fighting a grin from growing on my face, too. It was just a simple question. An innocent invite. What could go wrong? "No promises."

"Thank you, Amy!" Mary and Tyler sang.

They were charming as a couple, whether I liked it or not. So, I blamed their charm when I found myself knocking on Emmett's bedroom door, drawn again right back to his orbit.

His cologne greeted me before I even had a chance to bring my hand back down to my side. "What's up?" he asked, his head cocked to the side as his door swung open.

"We need a fourth for a card game. Want to join the party?" I coughed out.

Emmett looked back inside his room. I followed his gaze to an unmade bed covered in notebooks, a laptop still open, the keys worn and torn, practically falling off. A suitcase stuffed with still-packed flannels, despite the air's warmth. It was so colorful, so chaotic, compared to my and Ben's tedious display.

The mess was sexy.

"I guess a break can't hurt," he decided. "But can we go outside first? I don't think I can handle more games yet. Card games, I mean." He smiled, and my heart sped up.

"A little fresh air can't hurt," I said, following Emmett almost trancelike until our feet found Party of Five's wraparound deck. Sitting outside was innocent, right? Mary and Tyler would just have to wait.

We settled on the outdoor swing, facing out into the darkening street.

"How's the book going?" I asked, after a few moments of charged silence.

He smiled. "Great, actually. I feel strangely inspired here."

"That's great." I felt my face flush.

"It's like there are muses everywhere I turn." A flutter.

"You should come here more often then." A dare.

"How about Labor Day?" He grinned. I could barely find the words with which to respond before he added, "I'm actually headed to Marseille in August. I'll be there most of the fall. Usually write best when there's as little English as possible."

"Well, I do speak French." I hadn't actually spoken French since college, considering the little travel Ben and I found ourselves embarking on of late. That didn't stop my mind from imagining a future Rosetta Stone course, refreshing for a writers' retreat, a season abroad.

"Good to know." Emmett kicked and we were swinging, the bench moving with the air. Our friends' muffled voices seemed light-years away. The party inside belonged in another world. Only the crickets within our reach.

It almost felt like he might lean in and maybe even try to kiss me (would I let him?), until a cough from the street made my hair stand up straight. Another cough. My heart dropped. Was someone watching us? Spying on us again?

"Just do it," someone whispered. A spiral of nervous giggles exploded out from hiding.

"Ugh, fine," a second voice relented before the click-clack of heels made their way out from the darkened street, up the stairs and under Party of Five's porch lighting.

It was a woman. About my age. A tourist, I surmised, since I didn't recognize her, in town for the holiday. That still didn't explain why she was standing at our doorstep.

"Can we help you?" I called out, trying to mask my apprehension.

"Sorry," she blurted, "this must look super weird. My friends dared me." She laughed. "Are you E. L. Murphy?"

Even in the dark, I could sense Emmett blushing. "Guilty."

"I told you!" a voice that must have belonged to her friend called from the dark.

"There's a rumor on Instagram that you're here. I can't believe it's true!" I had no idea if Paige was a regular on literary message boards, but I still had a nagging feeling that she was the source behind this rumor's spread. "We're sorry to bother you," the girl said, but the excitement in her voice indicated otherwise.

"It's not a bother at all," Emmett replied.

"It's just, and no worries if not, totally no worries, but do you think if we came by tomorrow, we could maybe possibly please get your autograph?"

It took everything in me not to burst out laughing. His autograph? It wasn't like Emmett was a movie star, his face blown up across millions of big screens, chasing cars or fighting bad guys. And yet, this stranger, this fan, looked at Emmett like he had singled her out in a crowd and left his handprint on her heart.

"Of course. Come by any time." Emmett had stood up by now to shake the fan's hand.

"Ah! Really?! You're amazing. Thank you so much. This is amazing! I can't believe we met E. L. Murphy. And his girlfriend!" she squealed, dancing off to her friends before I could correct her assumption. Submerged by the darkness as quickly as she'd appeared.

By the time Emmett turned back to me, his face was crimson. "Don't even say it."

"Oh my God." I laughed. "You have a fan club?! Can I join?"

"Not one more word." His face flashed a toothy grin. He couldn't believe it either. How surreal, to have strangers stop you on the street. To sing your praises for nothing in return. To have your words mean so much that someone would cease fear of all social decorum and come knock on your literal doorstep.

To have created something that made you worth knowing.

He sat back down on the bench, chuckling into his own hands. "Was that terrible?"

"It was cute," I admitted, daring to knock my knee against his. Skin to skin. How could something so wrong feel so natural? My mind once again played that film reel, like a projector against the back of my skull. Life with Emmett. Autographs with fans. It didn't seem so bad.

A crash inside Party of Five jolted us back to reality. "My fault!" Tyler called out from the windows. Instead of cards, they'd built a de facto pong table, which must have just fallen over. Beer was flowing onto the floor. I took it as my cue to leave. A wake-up call, whether restful or not. Mary and Tyler would need a rain check. I couldn't stay, knowing all that still waited for me back at Summer Wind.

Emmett offered to escort me home, but I knew these streets like I knew my own hand. I didn't need a chaperone. Especially not a dangerously handsome one, in the dark, with so much tequila in my bloodstream.

"Goodnight then," Emmett said. But as I walked away, he followed me down into the street. He was now just a few inches away, our bodies nearly touching. An electricity jolt exploded between us as I leaned forward and rested my arms around his neck. I don't know if it was the alcohol or the way the beach's breeze wound down Lighthouse Walk and whispered goose bumps on my skin, but I turned my head and kissed Emmett's cheek. It was soft, a small kiss, but when his beard scratched my chin, I wanted to buy real estate next to his neck.

"Goodnight," I said, turning to leave before I did something I'd definitely regret. I didn't have to look over my shoulder to know he was still staring after me. His attention a ray of heat, a fire. My back was covered in smoke. I was relieved and disappointed in equal measure that I didn't hear him running after me. That he let me walk away.

I hummed to myself as I walked home, until I heard a drunken hiccup coming from our pool deck. There, sprawled on a lounge chair with a drink in one hand and her phone in the other, lay my sister, Jo. From the looks of the white, foamy beverage, I could tell she had opened our Rocket Fuel mix without me.

"The queen has returned," Jo called out. Judging by the sound of her voice, she'd drank even more than I had.

"Looks like you've had quite the evening." I sat down at the edge of her pool chair, my fingers fidgeting with the plastic rubber bands.

"Could say the same about yourself."

"Thanks for waiting on the Rocket Fuel, by the way. How much of that did you drink?"

Jo simply shrugged in response, but I could see the near-empty package next to her chair.

Too much.

"Where's Dave?"

"Where's Ben?"

Touché.

"You should see them over there, it's like summer camp," I said.

"Glad someone's having fun." Jo sighed, another hiccup escaping from her chest.

Jo's cloudy face caught me off guard. It wasn't like her to feel so sullen, so weighed down. I felt out of step with my sister, like we were operating on distant planes. For once, I was the one flying, impetuous in the breeze. Jo looked like she was crashing on the pavement.

"You should've come, Jo. Everyone's in Kismet because they want to spend time with the bride—"

"Stop saying that word." Her eyelids stayed squeezing together. "I just want to go home."

My heart broke. Weddings were stressful, and it hit me like a knife to the side: I had abandoned my sister. I had thought I had been protecting her, but instead I was just pushing her away. She was out of her element, so unused to being tied down. And in the thick of wedding preparation, she'd capsized and I hadn't been there to right the ship. What kind of maid of honor, what kind of sister, was I?

I took a deep breath in. I needed to apologize for not being more of a support system. For not being a better twin. To confess the truth about Emmett. And maybe even finally share the worst heartbreak of them all.

The one about the niece or nephew who almost was but now wasn't.

Yet before I could say anything, her phone pinged from an incoming text. The screen glowed with a name I hadn't seen in years. A name that only meant trouble. A name we had no room for this week.

Zach Webb.

"Really, Jo?" Her eyes flung open as she grabbed for her phone, positioning the screen away from my eyeline, but it was too late. "What could Zach possibly have to say to you right now?" I heard the anger rise in my voice like an avalanche, but I didn't feel like stopping it.

"I—I can explain," Jo stuttered, but my idea of a drunken confession had already transformed from reconciliation to disappointed rage. The fight with Ben, the frustration with Emmett. It all flew out of me and into Jo's face.

"What do you even have to say to a loser like him?"

Jo rolled her eyes. "You wouldn't get it."

"He cheated on you, Jo!"

"Thanks, I remember—"

"He put empty beer cans in our mailbox!"

"Can I talk for one second? Jesus, Amy. You've always had Ben, you don't know what it's like—"

"Yeah, you're right. I don't get it. Not at all. You get everything you want, all the time. Always. And yet for some incomprehensible reason you're out here drunk texting your high school ex-boyfriend. Like some washed-up prom queen."

Jo's eyes bored through me as I choked down the irony

like vomit in my throat. This was different, I told myself. Jo's behavior was nothing like my own.

She was the one getting married in three days.

She was the reason we were all out here in Fire Island in the first place.

It was time for Jo to grow up. To enter the adult world.

To stop choosing romance over realism.

Zach was bad news. He always had been. What was she thinking?

"When I said seventeen, I didn't mean literally," I scoffed, my limbs practically pulsating with pent-up anger.

Jo just glared at me. "Fuck you."

She stormed inside and slammed the door behind her.

THURSDAY

WHEN WE WERE PLANNING JO'S FIRE ISLAND week, my mom considered it a stroke of genius to transform the kitchen one morning into a manicure and massage parlor for the Beaumont and Sharp women. Familial bonding by way of relaxation and a healthy dose of essential oils. She had curated a playlist of calming melodies, scattered bud vases with frangipani flowers throughout the room. Candles were lit in every cranny, and she had even had custom plush bathrobes hand-embroidered with each of our names right over our hearts. *Amy, Jo, Grace, Valerie,* and *Lila.*

But my mom never could have predicted the hangovers and the white-hot heartache that would be haunting Summer Wind when the morning finally arrived.

As the manicurist cut my cuticles, I had to keep extracting my hand from her clutches to rub my forehead, willing away the pain that had moved into both temples, courtesy of five tequila shots and two heated arguments from the day before. If Jo and I had been on thin ice earlier, we were drowning in frozen water by now. When Jo stumbled into the room, her hair in a messy bun and bags under her eyes, she slumped down in the chair as far away from me as possible. She didn't even meet my gaze.

My dad passed out coffee and croissants, apron donned, but no one had much of an appetite for breakfast treats or bridal fun. My mom was quiet, off in her own head, whereas Valerie kept stepping into the hallway to make hushed phone calls, her nails still wrapped in tinfoil sheets. Meanwhile, Lila's eye rolls could have lifted her straight up to the moon. I wished she could take me with her, to a galaxy far, far away.

After a first pour of coffee, Jo must have felt pressure to fill the air. She began polling the room for advice on nail color. I was surprised to hear that her throat was hoarse. From last night's tears? I shuddered thinking she could have any left to spare on Zach.

When my mom suggested a red—something bold and chic yet very Jo—Valerie groaned. "Good God, please not red."

My mom's face blushed instantly.

"Jo could pull off red, if she wanted," I said. I wasn't interested in complimenting Jo or stroking her ego, but I couldn't leave my mom raftless at sea against such a moody mother-in-law.

"A light pink should be the only color on a bride when she's getting married. Nude lips, nude nails, white gown. It's tradition," insisted Valerie. I selected a light pink manicure for my own wedding, so I could hardly fight Valerie there.

"Maybe a white nail, then?" Lila offered. It was a surprising olive branch from someone I wasn't entirely convinced had even been listening to the conversation.

"That's actually a great—" Jo started, before Lila cut her off, quickly adding with her signature sass, "Not that it matters anyway. It's just a wedding." The reconciliatory twig tossed back on the floor. An awkward silence resumed.

Looking down at my fresh manicure, I resisted the urge to peel off the nude polish. To chip away the paint and skin alike. Instead, I excused myself from the kitchen entirely. My maid of honor record was already horrific, but I had no energy left to play pretend. I didn't want a massage, or a manicure, or a morning filled with small talk. And I definitely didn't want anyone touching my body, smoothing away at skin that felt like it was teeming with nerves. Working my hands, my neck, my back.

Except, a small part of me wondered, maybe Emmett?

I bailed on our wedding itinerary and found Emmett at the pool. In the same second that I walked outside, he was climbing up the pool's ladder, body dripping, shaking out his wet hair. I inhaled sharply. Talk about timing. I needed to look somewhere else, to control my roller coaster of feelings. My cousins' voices offered just the distraction. On the side of the pool deck, tucked off in the shade, I found Bobby, Mary, Tyler, and Ben seated in a semicircle around a wagon, paint cans stacked up next to a cardboard poster board.

The Fourth of July float. The decorating station my parents had prepared. How had I forgotten? Every summer, the Kismet Fire Department hosted a Fourth of July parade. Families transformed wagons into painted parade "floats," wore matching costumes, and marched through the streets. It was something Jo and I always did together. While some kids dressed as Disney stars or Olympic athletes, we eschewed patriotism for birthday flare. We painted the wagon like a Funfetti cake and stood tall inside like two twin-flame candles. I hated the attention, but Jo always held one hand tight, forcing me to wave with the other, making me feel brave as our parents tugged our float along.

Eventually we aged out of the parade, preferring to spend the morning nursing our birthday-eve hangovers, but for Jo's wedding week, we wanted to share our nostalgia with the guests. Anyone interested could paint a spare wagon and even walk in Saturday's parade before Jo and Dave's ceremony began. Never ones to say no to a good time, it shouldn't have come as a surprise that Bobby and Mary were Team Parade. So here they were, and it looked like they'd enlisted Tyler and Ben, too.

"Nice paint job on that thing," I called out to Ben as I walked over to their group. "But I think you have to get ready with Dave on the wedding morning. Brother-in-law duties override parade participation, I'm afraid."

"I know, all good, just wanted to help for now." Ben smiled, hopping up to kiss my cheek. It felt so natural, which only made me feel numb. "Nails look nice, by the way. Hey, shouldn't you be getting a facial or something?"

"Massage, actually, but I canceled. Too hungover."

"Oh yeah? Didn't realize last night got so rowdy." Ben's eyebrows rose in concern. I felt my blood warm, and I knew it wasn't from the sun's heat. I simply shrugged in response, praying Ben didn't notice how Emmett kept glancing my way from across the backyard, toweling his body dry.

"You feeling okay? Do you want anything—" Ben started to ask, but Mary's gleeful voice interrupted him as she waved a paintbrush in my direction. "Yay! Amy's come to help us out!"

"What's the vision here?" I asked, hoping I sounded happy and normal, not anxious and aloof. "American flags? Stars and stripes? Maybe Lady Liberty?"

"Do we look that basic to you?" Bobby said in mock horror. "Try Mount Rushmore. You're looking at the best Abraham Lincoln Kismet has seen since, well, Abraham Lincoln."

He held up the large cardboard poster, which, upon closer inspection, had already been covered with impressive sketches of Theodore Roosevelt, George Washington, and Thomas Jefferson. There was a gaping hole where Abraham Lincoln's head should have been. "My face will go there, and Mary and Tyler will pull the wagon. We're just working on securing my beard."

I couldn't help but laugh, glad that someone was leaning into the Kismet vacation. "My dad might have an old beard in the storage closet. Sometimes they do Halloween out here."

"I can check," Ben offered. "I'll bring some lemonade out, too."

"Can you add some gin to that, Benny-boy?" Bobby asked.

"Naturally." Ben laughed back.

"You rock, man. Thanks," Tyler said, as Ben excused himself into the house.

My legs felt shaky, the hangover really kicking in. I needed to lie down. "You guys have fun. I need some last-minute work on my tan," I said, and headed to a lounge chair. Surprisingly, Emmett was gone. I hadn't seen him leave, but I was grateful to have the pool, have the moment, to myself.

From across the deck, I watched Bobby, Mary, and Tyler flick paint at one another, decorating their monument-inspired scene. Their happiness felt out of reach. I longed to doze off, but my mind was restless. Instead, I reached into my beach bag. Hidden away with my ear pods and SPF 30 was the Moleskine. Not the standard summer read, but I hoped it would provide answers. Guidance. The very least: a much-needed escape. When the coast was clear and I knew no one was looking, I opened the page.

November 11

Dear Writing Seminar Journal,

I cut class today. (I'm sorry, Kate!) I can't quite believe it: Amy Sharp skipped school.

It wasn't my idea. In fact, I was so nervous about being late after the statistics review session went waaay long that I ran straight from Huntsman to Fisher 303. Emmett was by the door waiting for me, like he'd started doing every Tuesday and Thursday. He took one look at my sweaty forehead before checking his watch. "Welp, class started three minutes ago. What do you say? Try again next time?"

I couldn't find the words to protest. He took my hand and practically danced me down the stairs until our feet found College Green. The leaves had just started turning yellow and brown. We sat on the grass, coats zippered up to our chins, and listened to the sun.

It was perfect.

This semester has been overwhelming, to say the least. Classes, deadlines, group projects—I'm having trouble keeping up. It's wild to think one thing is keeping me going, but it's true. Emmett is the bright spot of every day. Ben is still MIA, and Jo is answering one call in three. They both have thrown themselves full force into the "undergrad lifestyle." Jo is already on the board for the Young Poets' Society, and my mom said that Ben's mom said that Ben just won his first robotics competition. (It's the worst grapevine ever, by the way—I had to pretend that I knew all about it.) Meanwhile, I found out that all my floormates have a group chat without me.

On the plus side, I have gotten really good at eating meals alone.

Thankfully, there's Emmett.

We've started hanging out almost every day. Getting coffee at Saxbys or meeting at Van Pelt Library to study in the stacks. He always brings chocolate or little goodies with him to our meets. Last week, he brought a daisy he'd picked from the quad's garden. Now my heart skips when I see him coming, wondering what treat he might have hidden away.

Something has definitely been building between us, but we've both avoided discussing it directly. We smile longer, brush shoulders when we walk. He even showed me a draft of a new short story he's working on, and I don't know if my heart was just willing it to be true, but I think it's based on me. A twin in a new city who falls in love when she least expects it. I could barely focus on his actual sentences; my heart was beating so fast as I read his words.

Even still, we never say anything more specific about our relationship. The idea of Us. At least, we never said anything specific until approximately thirty minutes ago.

Thirty minutes ago, Emmett asked me out. On a DATE. Not just dinner after class, but a real, proper, get-dressed-up-and-pick-you-up-at-seven DATE.

Dinner, this Friday night. Downtown, in Center City. The restaurant is near a local poetry reading. He thought we could stop there first, if I didn't mind? We'd take the Septa and maybe even hold hands? I said yes immediately.

Now I've spent the last half hour trying to calm my brain. The meditations didn't work, so I picked up this pen. I am excited. So excited. But I'm also scared. I've never been on a date with anyone other than Ben. I've never even kissed anyone other than Ben.

I know what you're thinking. I should stop worrying about Ben. It was his idea to take a break. Until yesterday, I hadn't even heard from Ben in weeks. But then, my phone buzzed, and his name appeared. Ben texted to corroborate our stories before we head home for Thanksgiving. Solidify our lies. We still haven't told our parents about us. I hate lying to my family, but I'd hate the look on their faces when they heard the truth even more.

I'm not quite sure why Ben won't just put me out of my misery, call the whole thing off. Not that I have any interest in ending our relationship either. I should really just wait. Stick to the plan. I'm a patient person. I can handle this.

But if I'm supposed to be waiting . . . does going on a date with Emmett count as a betrayal? The lack of boundaries, the ambiguous rules—it's all starting to bog me down.

Emmett thinks I should stop waiting. He hates that Ben is trying to keep me on the sidelines. Emmett's parents went through a rocky divorce after years of trying to make something work when in reality, it was like rotten milk: plain old expired. Their waiting, their delaying of the inevitable . . . it crushed him, he said. That's really why he doesn't believe in planning. "Nothing is guaranteed, even your parents' marriage."

Awful. It's been hard for him to trust since then, but he said I make it easy. Being together . . . I know what he means.

I think it might just be time that I start listening to Emmett.

"Lemonade!" Ben called out, interrupting my read, but my mind was still in the notebook. Dreaming in the past. That first date, penne vodka and poems. That first kiss afterward. The taste of Emmett's promise. My mind was a mess. I needed to get out of there.

Instead, I felt the weight of a cold liquid hit my legs. I looked down at the wet red paint, streaked against my calf. Whipping my head around, I saw Bobby and Mary holding up the soaked brushes, their faces shining with guilty grins.

"Library hour is over," Bobby shouted. "Come have fun."

I groaned, but I had to laugh. "Let me just rinse this cute new tattoo off." It was impossible to stay mad at my cousins, even when my romantic life was making my heart cramp.

The outdoor shower would do just the trick.

Hidden off behind the house, the wooden walls blended into the backyard's trees. It was a respite, a secret annex, like a portal to an enchanted world where you could be inside and outside at the same time. The shower was split in half, the first chamber serving as a dressing room of sorts. Hooks for towels and bikinis alike, a space to shake off sand before stepping into the larger shower portion. I stripped down. Overhead, the sun beamed straight down, its reflection flickering off the showerhead. It was silly, but the excitement of staring up at the sky while your body soaked in suds never waned with time. The childlike wonder remained.

The shower smelled like Rainbath soap. A giant container of our favorite bodywash had rested on the shower ledge for almost thirty years. I closed my eyes and let the water fall over me. Not just my legs, but my entire body. Peace.

Until, against the steady pulse of the water pressure, I heard voices rise from within the house. Conrad and Valerie.

Eavesdropping is rude, I told myself. *Don't even think about it, Amy.*

When I heard the word "Jo," I turned the shower right off. It didn't matter that Jo and I were on rough terms—my sisterly duty kicked into gear as I pressed my head against the wall and willed my eardrums wider. Braced to listen. Dave's parents' whispers trickled through the nearby guest bedroom window, which they must have left propped open to let the fresh afternoon air in. Now their hushed secrets were flying out.

"It won't last," Valerie snapped. I could hear her jaw popping even from here, her teeth surely flared like a dog protecting its bone.

"It has to. Vows are vows," Conrad fought back.

"Vows are superficial promises that sound pretty. This is real life, Conrad. We need a real-life solution."

"I wish you'd have some hope. Some optimism."

"We're past optimism. Way past. It's a mismatch. Broken—"

"So, let's fix it!" Conrad was shouting, his voice alight.

"It's beyond repair. What do you do with a broken toy?" Valerie's tone was thick with condescension. "You throw it out. This is the only way."

A quiet.

"You're right."

"I know."

"It doesn't make it any easier."

"This is hard for me, too."

"It's what has to be done."

"Think of our family, Conrad. Our future. The kids," Valerie said sadly.

"I know. We'll end it. For them."

A door closed, and I heard the sound of faint footsteps walking back up the stairs.

My body started shaking.

I needed to warn Jo. She had been right all along—Valerie and Conrad were against her from the start. They were going to try to break up their marriage, call off the wedding. I had to tell Jo what I had heard.

Wrapping myself up quickly in a spare beach towel, I grabbed my things and ran inside the house, leaping up the stairs to Jo's bedroom. Knuckles rapped repeatedly on the door, but neither Jo nor Dave called back from inside.

I hated snooping on my sister. There had always been an unwritten promise for privacy, and trespassing in bedrooms was implicitly forbidden. But those rules were made when we were children, when the only secrets were the ones between us and the rest of the world.

With bated breath, I turned the knob and opened her door. I would just take a peek, make sure everything seemed okay, that Dave's parents hadn't already poisoned Jo and left her to die in her beach house's bedroom. This was a favor to Jo, I told myself. I nearly even believed it.

To my relief, there were no bodies, no one suffocating in the bed. Just sheets half made, a bikini hooked and drying from the post. Orderly, even for Jo. I let my mind catch its breath as I pulled out my phone, resolving to send Jo a quick text instead. I typed out a message:

@Jo—Find me when you're back? Need to talk.

Instantaneously, a ping echoed from nearby Jo's bed. Tiptoeing closer, I saw that her phone was poking out from under her pillow, a long white charging wire connecting it to the extension cord on the floor. Jo leaving her phone behind wasn't unusual.

But then my stomach sank even further.

Because staring at the phone, I glimpsed the messages that hovered, unread and ready for receival, in Jo's newly lit-up lock screen.

Amy: Find me when you're back? Need to talk.

Dave: Meet me at the dock? It's important.

Jack B (Goldman): Can I get my sweater back then? Pretty sure it was cashmere . . .

Brendan Hinge: Hey stranger. Long time no talk.

Zach Webb: Sorry I missed your call. Try again tonight?

I rushed to the window in my bedroom, where I had a straight view out onto the pool deck. No Jo or Dave in sight. They were gone, and I was too late.

I sank down onto Jo's bed, my towel falling to the side, my skin now dry and itchy. My body felt three sizes too small. I bit at a cuticle until I felt blood in my tongue, new manicure ruined.

All these messages.

Missed calls from Zach.

I gulped.

What had Jo gotten herself into?

I NEEDED TO WARN JO ABOUT VALERIE AND CON-
rad's secret plan, but it soon become clear that Jo had no
interest in heeding my warnings. In fact, it felt more and
more like she had no interest in even talking to me at all.

By the time Jo and Dave finally crossed back through
Summer Wind's threshold, my sister sped upstairs like a
bandit. I only caught a quick glimpse of her face, but it was
enough to see that her cheeks were puffy, her eyes red. Traces
of leftover tears.

Cornering Dave in the kitchen, I tried for answers.
"What's wrong? What's going on?"

"Nothing's wrong!"

"Was Jo crying?"

His face wrinkled. "Er, yes, but—"

"I should go talk to her," I said.

"It's fine! Wedding prep. As they say, emotions run high,"
Dave said with a forced laugh.

"I'll just go check on her, make sure she's okay—"

"Amy?" Dave cut me off, putting his hand on my shoulder to stop me from running up the stairs after my sister. He lowered his voice to a furtive whisper. "I got this. Promise."

I swallowed. Had Jo told Dave about our fight? Was he under instructions to keep me far from Jo's radius? Or did I just need to finally get used to a new hero swooping in to save my sister? Dave certainly looked at her with love. When they were together, it seemed like they were floating. But Valerie's glare could have even Don Quixote shaking in his boots. Would Dave be able to stand up to his parents? Throw in texts from an ex-boyfriend (or three?) and the entire novel felt like its pages were doomed to split from the seams.

It went against my every nature to pause my sisterly protection, but before I could argue, a door slammed downstairs. Dave's face darkened at the echoing sound. His parents' guest room. "I'll handle that. Just let Jo be for a bit." He grimaced before adding "please" and disappearing. Meanwhile, Jo's bedroom door stayed firmly shut the rest of the afternoon. I followed Dave's advice and let it stay that way.

By the time I saw my sister and her fiancé again, we were at the beach. Jo's approaching face, starlit against the glow of scattered tiki torches and string lights, made me feel like I was hallucinating. Here and now, she looked perfect. Sleek high ponytail, light pink maxi dress. Warm eyes and not a worry on her face. A goddess approaching mere mortals.

Had I been the only one dreaming up her danger?

I kept my eyes trained on Jo as she made her way toward

the shoreline, toward the clam bake crowd. Traditionally on
the Sunday of Labor Day weekend, we invited the entire
town to join us at sunset for a Sharp beachside ritual. Resi-
dents donned white linens and fluttering dresses in a final
hurrah before autumn lulled us back to city jobs and winter
houses. The summer chapter concluded with lobsters and sau-
vignon blanc and fire pits for s'mores. Kids played hide-and-
seek or told ghost stories at the ocean's edge while parents
promised playdates and tailgates, insisting we'd all see one
another again very soon. It mimicked the buzz of a last day
at camp, but instead of yearbook signings, there were endless
rounds of farewell toasts and shots and sundaes until the ca-
terers sang their last call. Our closest friends always wound
up following us back to Summer Wind and watching the
sunrise from our deck. It was like Christmas; no one wanted
to retire to sleep because that meant the night was over. Summer's magic had ended, and a slew of ordinary days lay ahead.

This year, Jo's nuptials warranted shifting the clam bake
to an earlier date in the summer schedule. By now, dozens
more of Jo and Dave's wedding guests had arrived, both local Kismet neighbors and distant relatives alike. I found Jo
greeting these adoring newcomers and decided I needed to
pull her aside at last.

"Jo, is everything okay?"

Her smile didn't fade. "Why wouldn't it be?"

"Well, last night, for starters—"

"I can't get into that right now," she quickly whispered
behind her teeth, frozen still in a forced grin.

"And earlier today, I overheard Valerie and Conrad. About you. It sounded bad, Jo."

Her facade faltered for a moment. One drop, one break.

"I can say something to them, if you want me to?" I offered. "Fix it all, Amy-style?"

"Just leave it alone!" she snapped like a bone breaking.

"Sorry, I was just trying to help," I said, wincing.

Suddenly, Jo's winning smile was back as quickly as it had gone. Her face like a mask, a hostess's beam for the record books. "It's fine. Everything is fine. Enjoy the party!" she instructed, as if I were a random cousin here for the booze and not her twin. Her maid of honor. I blinked and Jo was gone, waving to an uncle by the bar, resuming her place by Dave's side. Hand in hand with her new other half, her new secret keeper. At least she had someone by her side. For now.

At the same time, Mary greeted me with a much-needed vodka soda. "Ben's deep in some sports conversation with Tyler and Mr. Watts. Thought you could use one of these."

"You're a savior, thank you," I said, trying to shake Jo's strange mood off my shoulders. If she wasn't worried, then I shouldn't be either. Right? Nina said we could only help people who wanted to be helped. Did that count for sisters, too? I willed my breath to slow down, to settle.

"You're the one saving me," Mary said, laughing. "I couldn't even tell you what sport they were talking about. Hockey? Baseball? Professional? College? I had to get out of there."

"That's Mr. Watts for you," I said. "He'll keep them going for another solid hour or so."

"Guess you're my date then." She looked over at Tyler with doe eyes. The yearn of a crush looked unusual but radiant across her face.

"Come on, I'll introduce you to some of our more interesting friends." Mary and I made the rounds, cocktail chatter with family friend Julian, whose collegiate lacrosse team won the championship this past spring, or our second cousin Brittany, who had designed a new makeup collection set to launch this fall. We nodded along to Mrs. Henry's updates about her daughter Regan's summer SAT prep—"You can't start too early!"—and gave best wishes to Mr. Post, whose doctor just scheduled him for hip surgery that winter.

Life was happening all around us. Gatherings like these proved it so. Anecdotal check-ins were reminders that the world was always turning, seasons bringing hardship and joys, moments of hope and heartache—even if you hastily tried to hit pause. We all were on the same collision course. No wonder life felt like spinning—technically, we always were.

I blamed it on gravity when I nearly toppled over at the sight of Paige chatting with Emmett by the shellfish tower. My nerves kicked in as Mary and I inched our way into their conversation, until I saw Emmett notice me and his eyes wash over with relief. I silently prayed that neither had given away any incriminating information about my past. Paige couldn't keep a secret to save her life.

When the conversation steered toward Paige and Mary's overlapping friends—the two happened to run in similar Manhattan circles—I excused myself for another drink. Emmett recognized the out and took it like a desperately welcomed life preserver, following me to the bar. I wanted to inquire after every detail that Paige had told him, to make sure our secret was intact, but my head was whirling, at a loss for words. All I could manage was to ask what drink he wanted next.

"Sweet tea vodka," he said with a wink.

"A local now, are you?"

"When in Rome."

Cocktails in hand, we strolled over to one of the fire pits and sat down on a small bench, looking out at the sea. I tried to momentarily let go of my fears for Jo, to forget about Ben and all our past pain. All the pain that the future still promised.

Instead, I watched Emmett's face glow a deep orange in the flame's frame.

After just a few sips, I felt the vodka pulsing straight to my head. I mentally added up the nearly nonexistent calories I'd consumed today, registering that almond-buttered toast could only stretch so far. Part of me knew I should excuse myself, shovel some arancini balls quickly down my throat. But the other part of me couldn't bear the idea of leaving Emmett's side. It was a trance, a spell, a trick of the fire's lighting. I knew it. But that didn't make it any easier to break.

Emmett interrupted the silence first. "I've been debating whether or not to tell you this . . ."

My entire body froze with anticipation.

"I actually missed the first three ferries before coming here on Sunday. That's why I was so late."

I cocked my head, not sure how to measure the import of that reveal. "Busy day?"

"Not at all," he said. "I watched the first come in—the parents and dogs and screaming children all racing to hop on board. I watched families claim their seats on the top floor, readjust their bags, put on their sunglasses and smooth windswept hair. And then, I watched the ferry leave."

"Sounds kind of creepy, if you ask me."

He laughed. "I couldn't bring myself to board. The next ferry came and went, exactly the same. By the third, I'd had the good sense to watch from that clam bar next door—"

"Nicky's?"

"That's the one. I ordered a corn chowder." He shook his head at the memory. "Ate it like a coward."

"You were scared?"

"Terrified," Emmett whispered.

"It's just a wedding; it can't bite," I said, trying to soften the air. He smiled, his glass once again to his lips.

"By the time the fourth ferry came in, I knew it was now or never."

"Just imagine—poor Dave, stood up at the dock."

"It wasn't Dave I was worried about," Emmett said. "But now that I'm here, that we're here, I'm so glad I boarded that ferry, Amy." While his eyes didn't drift from the firewood, it felt like he was looking right into my soul.

I swallowed, my throat suddenly dry. "Me too," I admitted to Emmett as much as to myself.

"Here," Emmett said, reaching into his shirt's front pocket. "This is for you." A small flower twirled between his fingertips. A dandelion, plucked from a bush along the sandy Lighthouse Walk. When we were in college, his gifts would send a warmth through my bones. A decade later, my body's response hadn't changed a bit. I accepted the flower while trying to hide what I knew the gesture meant.

He was feeling as reminiscent as I was.

We both finished our glasses with quickening gulps. Afraid and excited over what the other might say next. Emmett excused himself first, making me promise I wouldn't dare move as he doubled back to the bar to replenish our drinks. He was gone mere minutes, but long enough to have charmed the bartender into giving him an entire bottle of Firefly vodka.

We alternated sips and stories, each pass of the bottle back an excuse for a lingering touch, a scoot of an inch closer on the bench. We pretended not to notice while not changing a thing. I ignored the knowledge that my parents were here somewhere, that Jo might need my help. I knew dozens of our closest friends and family members were behind us and possibly watching. Ben, too. Eyebrows were likely raised, questions being asked, but this time, I didn't care. I was sick of being in charge, of playing a part, of always being the one who had to follow every rule. What was the point of planning? All planning ever did was set me up for heartbreak.

It was like Emmett had always said.

It was time to live in the now.

It could have been thirty minutes or three hours. The party had melted away along with my worries, my stress. Together, we were on fire.

Ben was our extinguisher.

Reality resumed when I heard Ben's voice call out from behind our shoulders. "Amy? I brought you some food."

There wasn't enough time to re-create the distance that should have separated myself from Emmett, so I stood up, hoping to erase the clue altogether.

"Thank you," I managed, tucking a hair behind my ear.

"Thought you might be hungry." Ben stumbled over his words, his tipsy brain visibly trying to compute the tension he'd interrupted. "Everything okay here?"

"Couldn't be better. A drink?" Emmett cut in.

"I'm good, thanks," Ben said. "Actually, Emmett, could you give us a moment?"

Emmett's face dropped, but he quickly recovered. "Cheers," he said, grabbing the bottle and giving me one last smile before heading back in the direction of the party.

"What's the deal with that guy? Every time I look for you, you're either standing with him or staring at him." Ben was drunk, but he wasn't wrong.

I was mortified. Caught and careless, carried away. But

I still couldn't bring myself to confess. "He's Dave's best friend. You know that."

"Are you sure that's all?"

"Ben, I only just met the guy this week. I don't know his life story."

"Well, you two looked pretty comfortable to me."

"He's no one."

"I just feel like ever since we've gotten here, you've been keeping something from me. Is it him? Are you into him or something?"

"Just calm down—"

"Don't tell me to calm down! I know what I'm seeing, Amy. Things between us aren't perfect right now, but is *this* what you want? Some sad writer?"

"He's not sad, Ben, he's brilliant. He's exciting and different, and you couldn't be like him if you tried." My voice exploded before I could control it. Drunken declarations leached from my throat.

Ben's face went white. "Wait. Do you really have some crush on him? Are you serious right now? After all we've been through?" Ben's voice was loud and laced with anger.

"It's not what you think."

"You're such a bad liar." Ben went to walk away but couldn't let it go. "Fine. Do what you want. Just don't blame me when you wake up and realize everything's still broken."

"*Broken?*" I could feel my body trembling now. It was everything I had been thinking, the reality I had been fearing. "Me, you mean. I'm the broken one."

Ben didn't respond. He just lifted his arms in surrender. His eyes tired, spent. No fight left in them.

Ben was done.

My breath cut; my vision blurred. It felt like my blood was leaving my body. "I have to go," I said, brushing the falling tears off my face as I shoved past my husband. Walking as fast as I could back to the house without alerting unwanted attention from the crowd.

Broken. Hearing it from Ben's mouth finally made it true.

My body, my heart, my mind. Our future. All of it was broken.

I was broken.

Summer Wind called like a beacon, but I wouldn't let myself step inside. I wasn't ready. I wasn't deserving to return home yet, to hide in my bedroom under the harbor of my covers until Ben came calling with his apologetic look. With his determination to finish our conversation sober and sullen in the morning.

I wasn't ready to face the reality that this time, maybe Ben wouldn't come calling at all.

I kept walking. Down the street, to the go-to hiding place of my youth. Tucked behind the tennis courts, a small alley with a raised barrier just high enough to double as a bench. I let my limbs rest, folded over with my head in my hands. I cried.

Losing Ben had always been the scariest possibility. We had grown together, so an uncoupling was unimaginable.

When we were younger, Ben would jest that if we ever broke up, he'd send me a bill. It was a joke, but more than that, it was a testament to just how serious about the other we had always been. We were seventeen and operating as if we had shared bank accounts. After that one freshman semester apart, marriage was never a question, never a doubt. Ben was my future; I knew it in my bones.

I just assumed he would always choose me, too.

His words tonight were vicious but deserved. More than deserved. I had doled out only cruelty, and it was natural that he'd reach his limit. After all we had been through, why couldn't I see that? Why did I do this to him? To us? I couldn't stomach the answer. The terrifying sensation that maybe we just weren't meant to be after all.

Was this a happily ever after at its end?

"Amy?" a voice suddenly called out from the darkness.

"Ben?" I asked, hopeful and afraid.

The figure stepped out of the shadows, his face revealed under the lamppost.

It was Emmett.

Part of me blamed him. If Emmett hadn't shown up, none of this would be happening. He was the distraction taking over my brain, making me act like a teenager and forget my bearings. My responsibilities and my routine, the life I'd spent decades building. Perfecting. Protecting.

But the other part of me swooned that he was here. That he had come after me this time. Could this be the universe giving me a sign? Like the maxims my mom raised us saying, printed on bath towels and bedroom signs alike. Let it be. Destiny. Karma. When one door closes, and so on. Emmett had nothing to do with my miscarriage. He hadn't built a rift between me and my sister. That was all me.

So, when I stood and ran to Emmett, when I jumped in his arms and kissed him with all the passion and sadness and anger and hopefulness that had laid dormant for a decade, I knew I only had myself to blame.

FRIDAY

CHAPTER

20

I KISSED EMMETT LAST NIGHT. THE WORDS DIDN'T FIT right in my brain. I kissed Emmett, I leapt into his arms like a damsel in distress, but it didn't feel like a romance film. It didn't feel like a happy ending. It felt awkward and wrong, like jamming together two puzzle pieces from polar parts of the pattern. From different puzzles altogether. The decade's worth of pent-up emotions rolled up into a not-so-fairy-tale display.

"Hi," he had said, putting me down. My feet were on the ground, but I had felt anything but stable.

"Hi" was all I could manage back. What was happening? He had moved to kiss me again, his hands tight around my waist, but I had pulled away. "People might see."

"Let them," he had dared, tugging my fingers. His hand was warm in mine, despite a chill in the summer night's air. I rubbed my thumb up and down the bones of his index finger, taking in the bump near his knuckle, a blistering cuticle by his nail. How strange—to hold something again after years, so familiar yet so new.

"Not here." I croaked out the words, my throat still frozen.

"Come with me then." Emmett took my arm and led me back to the Party of Five house. My feet must have followed on autopilot because my mind was racing on some other plane. In denial and terrified yet curious all at the same time. So many parts of me wanted to give Emmett exactly what he wanted. What I had led him to believe *I* wanted. Not just the polite Amy, the people pleaser eager for approval, but also the girl with the Moleskine notebook. That freshman who met Emmett, who kissed Emmett once and had for an instant imagined a different life for herself.

It was a daydream I'd revisit. If Ben canceled a date night, bailed on a plan. Silly disappointments, and I'd trick myself into an exit strategy. A fantasy. My mind would wander and wonder, *What would Emmett do?* The self-loathing that accompanied those thoughts would keep me up for nights on end. I knew it was selfish and pointless and cruel. But pity didn't stop the fantasy from sneaking back in every once in a while.

Of course, that same fantasy was never supposed to come back into my reality. It was never supposed to actualize itself in the form of a six-foot-three, handsome, acclaimed writer no more than four inches from my eyes. I was never supposed to be following him into a guest bedroom, to see his comforter unfolded, his books on the floor. To feel the fabric of his favorite flannel warm against my skin.

He was never supposed to pull me closer, one hand on my hip, the other clenched in my hair. He was never supposed to kiss my neck, my ear, my cheek. My lips. He was never supposed to breathe me in like smoke, like candy. But here he was.

"I can't believe this is happening," he said, pausing just to rest his forehead against my own. "I never stopped thinking about you. Wanting this. Wanting you. God, you know you're even more gorgeous than you were in college?"

I couldn't respond; the words wouldn't form. It was happening and my senses were overwhelmed. Because from the moment it started, I knew it needed to end. Being with Emmett felt off now. His lips too small, his tongue too big. His nose threatened to slam right in my eye. His face too high up that it strained my neck. Instead, each kiss felt like I was breaking. Sinking. Walking down a path I paved but needed to demolish.

It felt wrong.

It was wrong.

I was kissing Emmett, but it was Ben's nose I missed. Ben's hands, Ben's tongue, Ben's smell. The way Ben's face felt against mine like a jigsaw designed by the gods.

I was kissing Emmett, but it didn't feel like a fantasy at all.

I pulled my body away, my arms falling to my sides like weights.

Ben. I needed to get back to Ben.

"I'm sorry," I whispered.

"What's wrong?"

"I can't do this." I needed to get out of there, fast.

"Yes, you can. Just be here. Me and you. *This* moment. Us. No more plans, remember?" His eyes were big and yearning.

"Emmett—" I started.

"Amy. I was lost when we met, but then you gave me hope. It didn't matter that my parents weren't talking. That I wasn't 'high school cool,' that I hadn't gone to prom." He laughed at the memory. "You saw all that and sat next to me still. You kissed me still. You felt this, too, I know it. I loved you from the moment I saw you, Amy." He kissed my cheek, venturing into me again, but I didn't relent.

I couldn't.

This wasn't what I wanted. What had I been thinking? Who had I become?

"We'll talk tomorrow, promise," I said quickly, whirling around before he could stop me. Before I could make any of this even worse.

"Wait!" he called after me. "Stop!" The thump of my heartbeat drowned out his pining words as I ran down the stairs. I couldn't turn around. "Amy, come back! Don't do this again!" I heard his shout, his voice crack, but I couldn't listen.

I couldn't let in the memory.

I didn't dare look back until I had made it to Summer Wind's driveway.

Ben had slept on the couch. Early in the morning, it must have been around dawn, I heard the door creak open, followed by the sounds of Ben grabbing a change of clothes. Even with my eyes tightly closed, I felt the pressure of his gaze. Was he thinking of crawling into bed? Of kissing my forehead to wake me up? Or was he contemplating how many more days until he never had to share my space again? Spineless, I kept my eyes held closed tight. Ben sighed, and the door closed behind him without so much as a word.

Now I grabbed his vacant pillow and smothered it on top of my face. Rolling over, I checked my Outlook inbox, the most recent item being an email from Margaret saying that the office was closing for the long weekend and a reminder to get off my phone. Great.

Maybe I should just go back to sleep, I thought. Wake up when the wedding was over. My eyes closed, desperate for darkness and sleep and anything other than having to face Ben and Emmett and my complicated heart, but I was soon awoken by new voices drifting down the hollow hall.

Jo and Dave approached, and it sounded like they were fighting.

"What the hell are we supposed to do about it, Jo?" Dave's whisper cut through my bones as if he'd shouted, causing my whole body to wince. I had never seen Dave angry, or even demonstrate signs of a temper. When his voice morphed back down to lower decibels, I strained to make out what they were saying. Whatever it was, it didn't sound pretty.

Had Dave glimpsed her secret texts? Had his parents' furtive agenda been unveiled? I ushered away my nagging fear that maybe Jo was just as broken as I was. Doomed for unhappiness. Two sides of the same rusted coin, both of us slinking back to washed-up romances instead of nourishing the worthy ones standing front and center. Could Jo fix what I clearly couldn't? Or would we sail home on a ferry as an almost-bride and a divorcée, with canceled plans, tattered veils, and broken promises?

The echo of Jo's sob and a slammed door crawled under my doorway. In that moment, I prayed that our genetic similarities only expanded so far. Twins but not identical.

It was a day before the wedding, and everything seemed to be falling apart.

Needing coffee, I finally dragged myself out of bed and tiptoed downstairs to the kitchen, thinking the coast might be clear. I couldn't handle any human interaction just yet. When I heard Conrad, Valerie, and Lila bickering downstairs, I hid my body against the wall, held my breath. The specifics of their mutterings were hard to decipher, but I swore I heard something about contracts and cancellation policies. Moving boxes and refunds. Were they planning to move Jo out of Dave's apartment after they canceled the wedding? To pack her up and ship her out of their family? For sale, but not for us?

My phone buzzed, announcing a new text on my phone.

My screen displayed a stream of messages that had already poured in from Emmett that morning. Unread and unanswered. Reminders that last night was neither a dream nor a nightmare but a real-life mistake.

> **Emmett:** Hi. Can we talk about last night? Please?

> **Emmett:** Yoga on the beach? I'll bring the coffee.

> **Emmett:** Fine, fine, no yoga necessary. Just want to see your face again.

He would not be ignored. I would have to deal with the consequences.

Gazing out the hallway window, I caught a glimpse of Ben and my dad arranging flower garlands on an army of golf carts assembled in our driveway. Our rented transportation fleet to the rehearsal dinner at Le Dock in Fair Harbor tonight, just a few towns over. Too far to walk, and since there are no cars permitted on Fire Island, golf carts had become the next best solution.

Now I felt something like motion sickness just thinking about sitting in a small vehicle by Ben's side.

Would he smell the betrayal on my skin, cheap and strong?

From the next window over, I saw Mary, Bobby, and Tyler relaxing on floats in the pool, frozen cocktails in hand despite the early hour, sunglasses on their faces. Oh right, I remembered. We were on a beach vacation. A celebration. At least someone was having fun at Jo's wedding, even if the bridal party was bound in misery. Carefree music played from our Bose speaker system (Bobby must have connected his phone), and it traveled up to the windowpane. Knocking on it almost, mocking me. "Girls just wanna have fun," it sang.

I had to lie down.

I slunk back to my room, silently clicking the door shut behind me. I turned off my phone and urged my mind to do the same. My thoughts were racing with drafts of sentences, rehearsing all the explanations and excuses and apologies that I owed. As I tallied up my debt, I realized just how deep I was in. I needed silence, peace, to figure this out.

Instead, a knock on the door. "Amy?" My mom's gentle voice floated through the wood. "You awake?" My throat was so heavy, I knew I'd start crying if I even attempted a response. I didn't want to be pitied when I knew I was the one causing all the pain.

"I'm here if you want to talk," she said to the silence. A moment longer, and I heard her footsteps patter away. Tears stained my cheeks, and like a coward, I willed myself back to sleep.

CHAPTER
21

"SHOOT! SLOW DOWN JUST A LITTLE, BEN?"

"Give it a rest, Mary," Bobby groaned. "I feel like I'm on a soap opera. Just calm down."

"I don't want the wind to mess up my hair too much!"

"You just want to look perfect so Tyler will make out with you on the beach tonight!"

"Shut up!"

"You know I'm right!"

"He's cute," Mary said, pouting. "Sue me!"

My cousins were bickering in the back seat of the golf cart, but ever since we pulled out of Summer Wind's driveway, a numbness had consumed my core. The colors and noises passed in a blur, every sense out of sync. As Ben drove to the rehearsal dinner, he and I pretended like everything was fine. Like last night hadn't been an explosion. Like we still had so much left to say to each other. Polite laughter at Bobby's jokes, polite encouragement of Mary's smitten yearning from the back seat as Ben kept his eyes on the road. All while my head felt detached from my body.

I knew I was unprepared. The afternoon had passed in a fog until I woke up from an uncharacteristic nap soaked with sweat, subdued in a panic. My speech. Rolling over in bed and glancing at the alarm clock, I felt my stomach drop.

It was already five o'clock, and I had completely forgotten to practice my speech.

The maid of honor and best man had been instructed to give their toasts at Friday's rehearsal dinner, allegedly to save more time during the reception for dancing. Jo promised my widely known fear of public speaking hadn't played a role in this decision, but I knew deep down that she was solely doing this to save me. I could handle reciting one short toast at the rehearsal dinner, in front of a small group of friends and family, we both agreed. Definitely.

That was, I could handle reciting one short toast in front of a small group of friends and family if, of course, I had managed to learn my lines. Months ago, I had googled "maid of honor speeches" and hand-copied the generic results onto a stack of three-by-five index cards, never to be reviewed again. Now, I pulled those forsaken note cards from my wedding planning binder and grimaced at what I had prepared. An Oxford dictionary opening about the definition of "soulmates" followed by mundane clichés and platitudes. No one expected groundbreaking literature from me, the sister without a creative-writing bone in her body, but the words still felt like one more reminder of all the ways I'd disappoint my sister, my family, myself. I wanted to tear the cards up into a thousand pieces, but instead I just tucked them into my purse. Even with practice, they'd be far from perfect. Just like everything else this week.

A half hour later, Ben knocked on our door. "Amy? How's the speech prep going?" he called out as he turned the knob, poking his head into the room like a stranger, polite and perfunctory.

I was still in my pajamas. No makeup on my face. Hair under a baseball cap. Ben noticed my ensemble and shot me a look of concern.

"Sorry, been dealing with a work emergency," I lied. "Lost track of time."

"Ah, sorry. I made you a good-luck latte," he said, stepping fully into the room and handing me a large ceramic mug. The words "Kismet Is for Lovers" were printed on the front, above a beachy photo of my parents. A favor from their anniversary party ten years ago. Was Ben using it as a sign? "Thought maybe if you weren't still practicing, we could talk."

His voice was so quiet, so sad. It made my heart ache.

"Thank you." I accepted our favorite warm drink (cinnamon for good luck, rum for good measure) and tried to hide how much my hands were shaking. I took a slow sip so that I wouldn't have to speak. So that I wouldn't have to make eye contact with my husband because I was so ashamed, so terrified of what he might say next.

Ben inhaled, ready to begin, to break up with me probably, to demand the answers and apologies I knew I needed to give him. That I wanted to give him. If only I could find the words.

But then my phone rang on the nightstand.

Hiding the device from Ben's sight, I mumbled a quick, gutless lie. "More work, probably. Let me just finish this up. Then I'll come down? We can talk before we head out?" I spoke quickly, so that my voice wouldn't crack into pieces.

"Amy, come on—"

"I'll be right down," I whispered. "Promise."

Ben looked at me with his knowing blue eyes. He nodded. He closed the door to our bedroom, but he might as well have been closing the door on me. On us. On everything I ruined.

My phone screen didn't help.

2 MISSED CALLS FROM EMMETT.

Emmett: Can we at least talk about what happened?

Emmett: Amy??

I flung my phone across the room like it was a grenade. The screen shattered, but I didn't even flinch. I wanted to cry but knew the entire house would hear the echoes if I did. They would hear for themselves how everything was collapsing around me.

It was way too late now to meet with Emmett in person, to smooth over the mistakes from last night before seeing each other again, face-to-face in front of my entire family.

Hiding a flirt or a beam of chemistry was one thing. Hiding hurt was like hiding a mountain. Emmett was now added to the ever-growing list of wedding guests who would prefer if I boarded the first ferry home.

Luckily, the rehearsal dinner's seating arrangement at Le Dock was assigned in advance, so I wasn't going to be subjected to cafeteria nightmares of eating at a table all alone. Still, it felt like walking into a powder keg; I held my breath as we opened the restaurant's door.

The room was arranged with one long dais-style table down the center. Families alternately woven along each side, intentionally designed to mix up the Sharps and the Beaumonts. Mingling galore. As a result, Ben and I were seated face-to-face with Dave's parents. Great. It took everything in me not to confront them about what I'd overhead, but I bit my tongue. That would only make matters with my sister worse. If Jo didn't want my help, I wouldn't give it. Instead, I offered a strained hello while cursing the seating chart I had made weeks ago. I would have traded anything to be placed at the table's end, where I could hang my head and avoid all conversation for the duration of the evening. Unsurprisingly, Conrad and Valerie looked as if they felt the exact same way. Both parents had deep bags under their eyes, hollowed-out cheekbones, lips glued together. So much for small talk.

Jo and Dave were seated in the middle. Even in exhaustion, Jo was the actress of our family, and tonight she looked determined to play the part despite whatever earlier hallway arguments had erupted. Blond hair fell in loose waves around her face. She wore a white crop top with matching white culottes, paired with three-inch strappy white heels. It was a rehearsal dinner outfit of bridal dreams.

So why did I feel like even Jo was bracing for a catastrophe?

A clink against a champagne glass stopped my spiral.

"Plato once said, 'At the touch of love, everyone becomes a poet,'" Dave's voice sang through the space. "I think we can all agree that Plato would have been permanently speaking in verse, limericks even, if he ever met Joanna Sharp. His brain would have been filled only with rhymes. With melodies.

"It feels like just yesterday Jo walked into my life and turned my days into poems," Dave went on. "I can't quite believe that come tomorrow, she'll be my wife. They say marriage is forever. And with Jo, I want the longest forever a lifetime can hold. I promise that I will look forward to every single day. Every poem. I already am. Here's to our tomorrow, and the many, many, many tomorrows to come." Dave kissed Jo's cheek as the room applauded.

I clapped my hands along with the guests, but my fingers barely felt like my own.

"Lovely speech," I said to Conrad and Valerie, just to fill the air as we picked up our cutlery and began the first course. My appetite had waned, so I relegated myself to cutting the tuna tartare into a thousand pieces.

"He must have learned that from you both," Ben added. I knew he was trying to be kind, the courteous in-law working to keep conversation flowing. Yet when Conrad abruptly dropped his flatware back on the tablecloth, the color drained from Ben's face.

"Excuse me," Conrad muttered, before bolting up and rushing to the bathroom.

"Stomach pains," Valerie explained away with a tight-lipped frown, after an awkward pause had swallowed us into silence.

"Poor guy," Ben said.

"Better tonight than at the wedding, I guess," I said. Why was it always easier to say the meaningless words than the deserving ones?

Valerie huffed, and the reticence resumed. As she chewed, I noticed her gaze repeatedly track down from her plate to up and over where Jo and Dave were seated.

Maybe Dave's romanticism had stirred something in me, but in the conversational lull, I knew it was time. To meet Ben's eyes, to take us out of this silence, this stress, before we were broken for good. I was dying to pull him away so I could properly confess about last night, to at last apologize for everything. To finally start to process, to talk about all that we had endured, all that we had lost, together. I tried to summon the courage, but just as I turned my body toward Ben's and went to grab his hand, he stood up.

"I'll see if there's an aux cord or a speaker that I can plug my phone into," Ben said, his feet already moving toward the waitstaff, his phone already open to his Spotify app. I hadn't even realized that there was no background music, so deafening were the voices in my own head. This was just another quintessential Ben-ism, ever attuned to what might need fixing. We used to be a dream duo that way: I planned big picture, and Ben executed the details. Our own version of Chip and Jo Gaines. Now it seemed like we weren't even playing in the same stadium, let alone for the same team.

Yet when Ray LaMontagne's "You Are the Best Thing" started to spill out from the speakers, goose bumps took over an entire layer of my skin.

This was our wedding song. It played during our first dance, as we grinned through each note. I had been nervous about the attention, all the eyes glued on our untrained steps. One hand on my waist, the other holding my own, Ben had whispered in that moment: "Don't worry so much, just look at me. We are all that matters." The guests, the fears, the entire world, had instantly melted away. Ben's arms were the most reassuring place to be. How could I ever have wanted to be anywhere other than surrounded by his warmth?

As Ben walked back to the table now, he gave me a smile from across the room. A secret signal, that song. We would be okay, it said. We were all that mattered. We, too, could forgive and recover and heal. We could move on, maybe even dream again.

We could survive everything, together.

Yet our peaceful coda was interrupted by the clink-clink of a knife against a champagne glass once again. From the far end of the table, Emmett stood up and cleared his throat. He smiled, but his cheeks were red, his forehead glistening. When the guests at last hushed down into a quiet, he made the exaggerated motion of checking his watch. "Dave said I should give my toast when the appetizer course was finished, and I'd hate to mess up his schedule. You might not guess it, but Dave is rather beholden to a calendar." The room laughed, but I braced for a crash. Emmett's grin was still plastered across his face, but the tone of his voice confirmed my suspicion.

Emmett was drunk.

Too drunk.

"When Dave first asked me to be his best man, I actually said no." The crowd chuckled, but my grip only tightened on the rim of my chair. "What could I offer by way of matrimonial support? I told Dave no, and yet, he brought me here anyway. I'm sorry Dave, but I feel that it's my duty to now share what I've spent the past decade discovering: love does not exist."

My heart stopped, but Emmett continued. "It's not even just that I don't believe in it! I'll say it again, for those in the back of the room." Emmett's eyes now scanned the room and landed right on my own. "Love does not exist.

"It's a social construct." Emmett's voice sped up. "A capitalistic creation. Fabricated for feudal partnerships and family legacies alone. You think love makes you happy? No, it's a way for overpriced industries and bridal companies to trick you into wanting a wedding, to take your money. It's a way for unhappy parents to show off to their friends, unhappy lovers to hide behind rings and dances and expensive venues. Island getaways, if you will.

"Love, marriage, they don't make people happy. They make people *boring*. They take away your freedom, trap you in the mundane. Marriage isn't paradise—it's ordering from the same sushi restaurant even though their delivery is always late, their spicy tuna always soggier than you remembered. Marriage is having the same conversation over and over on repeat as you sit on a lumpy couch and wonder why you'll never live up to what you see in the movies. The lies you knowingly buy.

"Love doesn't make you happy, it only makes you cruel. Dave, buddy, friend. I'm sorry to say that your future with Jo will probably not be happy. I hope I'm wrong, but"— Emmett simply shrugged his shoulders—"I'm not wrong often. Ask Jo's sister for my empirical evidence if you're so inclined. If your bride is anything like her sister, well, good luck."

Goodwill darkened into gasps and shudders. Jo caught my glance and mouthed, "What the hell?" but I could only shake my head. Only shrug. I tried not to let my own eyes fill with tears as I felt everyone around the room fix their gaze directly on me.

"Congratulations, Dave and Jo, on your eternal heartbreak." Emmett chugged what remained of his champagne and stormed outside. The door slammed behind him.

CHAPTER

22

BEN RUSHED BACK TOWARD OUR TABLE, HIS FACE filled with all the questions I knew he was desperate to ask, but I couldn't tackle my husband's guilt right now. I needed to solve one crisis at a time. Pushing up from my chair and grabbing my still-full glass of champagne for courage, for something to occupy my shaking hands, I followed Emmett out into the courtyard.

The sun had only just begun setting, but a chill was in the air. Emmett sat at a patio table, his head hanging low, a lit cigarette in his hands. When he heard me approach, he stared at me with a frozen glare.

"Now you want to talk?"

"Emmett, I can explain—"

"You know what, Amy? I don't even care. I don't want your explanations or your excuses or to see your dumb, pouty, infuriatingly perfect face ever again." His voice careering.

"Look, I'm sorry," I begged. "I shouldn't have gone back with you. That's my fault, but it's no reason to ruin my sister's rehearsal dinner. Hate me all you want, but leave Jo out of it."

"She'll survive. Honestly, Dave should be thanking me. Get away from the Sharp twins before it's too late." Anger mixed with alcohol, his words slurred more than I'd ever seen.

"You're past drunk, Emmett. Go home, sober up—"

"That's your apology? 'Go home and sober up'?"

"I'm sorry, Emmett. I am. After last night . . . I should have called. Texted you back. That's my fault. Ben and I— we're working through something right now. I'm not myself. It wasn't fair of me, I know, but you, this . . . was just bad timing. A distraction. A mistake. Nothing more." I hadn't planned these words but as they fell out, I knew they were the honest ones.

"Ben isn't right for you. He's never been right for you, and you know it."

"That's not true—"

"I'm in love with you, Amy! I always have been." He rose now, stepping toward me. "Come with me to France this fall. Forget about all this, let me show you how happy you could be. With me."

My head was spinning. In one universe, these were the exact words a girl would swoon to hear. A confession of love, a promise for adventure. For passion. On paper, perfection. Yet in reality? With my two feet on this very ground?

My mind played out that version of a life with Emmett, but this time, the notes were flat, the sounds garbled. I could see it clearly. His career would always come before mine. We'd always be traveling but never settling down. I pictured our hotel rooms, always messy, suitcases half unpacked. What had seemed so exciting now made my chest tight, my hopes feel small. How could I pick up and just follow wherever his writing whims sent him? Would I just quit the career I loved, the profession I'd devoted a decade to earning? Title transformed, CFO to fan club president, always in the audience but never onstage.

What about my family? Our family? A future without kids. No backyards, no swings, no soccer games. No tiny limbs learning to crawl. A forever empty nest. A lifetime of peace and quiet I now knew deep down I'd regret, no matter the risk required in trying again.

Ben.

My heart panged. It had been a whirlwind excitement, a hypnotizing hypothetical. I thought being with Emmett would have made my life feel bigger, but instead, facing the potential of it, everything seemed stunted. Wrong. Ben was the life I wanted. Ben was who made me feel known, even in our worst pain.

Emmett was just a fantasy outgrown, expired.

"I can't," I choked out. "I won't. I'm sorry."

Emmett's eyes drew toward the ground, his brown leather shoes shining in the dusk. A moment of quiet, before the escape of a hate-filled laugh. "Christ. I can't believe I fell for your act. Trusted you all over again." Those shoes now inched in my direction. He was getting closer, an arm waving with a cigarette still accusatorily outstretched. "At least in college it was cute."

"*College?*"

I spun around and saw my biggest fear come to fruition. Ben and Jo had followed us outside. Their faces were white, their jaws hanging open.

The champagne flute I had been instinctively clutching fell from my fingers, crashing with a deafening roar. The pieces were flung awry, scattering across the ground.

There was no putting this back together again.

"Did he just say *college*?" Jo asked again.

"Guys, I can explain—" I started.

"You know what?" Emmett interrupted, his voice on fire. "I should be thanking you. If I'd stayed at Penn with you, *for* you, I would have ended up in some soul-sucking corporate job, with some cookie-cutter house in the suburbs, changing diapers and regretting the day I'd ever learned your name." Emmett accentuated each syllable with a wave of his cigarette. Each word crept dangerously closer to my face, until Ben jumped in between us like a human shield, just as the ash nearly brushed my cheek.

"Get away from my wife, asshole."

"You can have her. I'll keep the book sales." Emmett smoldered as he flicked his cigarette and stormed off into the darkened night.

"Thank you," I whispered to my husband, who was still

holding on to my arm protectively. Triggered by my words though, Ben dropped his hands at once. His face winced, like I was painful to the touch, a hot stove or sharpened edge.

"What the hell, Amy?" Ben shouted like he had been shot.

"You *know* him?" Jo snapped.

"From college. Freshman year."

"I've never seen him before," Ben said.

"He transferred by the spring."

"After our break?" Ben asked, his voice small.

"We stayed in touch. Until we didn't," I said, watching as Jo's eyes widened, her mind piecing together what that meant. Who this man must be. The Brainy Guy I had called her about. A chapter I swore was over.

Light bulb.

"You've known Emmett all week, but you lied to our faces?" Jo's voice climbed in tenor, matching the height of her eyebrows. "Are you serious? Does Dave know?"

I shook my head.

"That speech, Amy. That outburst? What's happening?" Ben asked.

"Ben, you really didn't know about this?" Jo's shriek continued. His silence was answer enough. "What's going on, Amy?!"

"It's not what it looks like." My tongue suddenly felt numb and fuzzy. Sentences trapped behind my teeth.

"It looks like you hooked up with my fiancé's best man, hours before my wedding."

I had to laugh. That was how she wanted to frame it? "At least I'm not calling my asshole ex-boyfriend days before getting married!"

"Lying to your entire family's better? What, were you guys sleeping around behind our backs? Meeting up in the night and giggling about how clueless we all were?"

"It's not even like that! We only kissed, I swear!" I was losing control.

Ben's hands flew to his forehead. "I can't handle this right now. I'm going back to the house—"

"Ben, I'm so sorry. It was just once, and it meant nothing. I only love you, Ben, only you, I promise."

Ben just shook his head. "How?"

"Bear?"

"How could you?" Ben's voice cracked and broke my heart in two.

"Wait, listen—"

But Ben held up his hand, ignoring my eyes, my presence entirely. "Jo, I can drive you back if you want," he said instead.

Jo, now seated on the bench's edge, tears in her eyes, waved him off. "I can't leave yet."

"I'll come with you," I begged. "I'll explain everything."

"I can't talk to you right now, Amy."

"Please, I can explain."

"I need space—"

"Let me explain, apologize—"

"*Space*, Amy." Ben shook his head. "Space. You of all people should get that."

"Wait!" I tried to grab his arm, but Ben shrugged me off.

"Don't. Touch me." Ben's throat was cold, holding back a storm of hurt and anger and everything I had fed him blindly for a week.

"I'm sorry," I whispered.

Ben slid into a golf cart. Its ignition rattled on, roared to match the anguish in our veins. With a screech, Ben was gone.

"Jo, I swear I can explain," I started.

"It's never your fault, is it?"

"You don't understand. Things have been really hard—"

"Ben is my family, Amy. I can't believe you'd do this to him."

"I know." I swallowed.

"I don't think you do know. You strut around like you're in some picture-perfect relationship, with this perfect, fairy-tale life," Jo muttered, her eyes pooling. "But it's all a lie, isn't it?"

The restaurant's back door swung open before I could defend myself. "Everyone okay out here?" Dave surveyed the scene, rushed to Jo as soon as he saw her. "Hey, hey, why are you crying?"

Jo welcomed his embrace, her tears staining his shirt. "I'll tell you everything tomorrow," her muffled voice sniffled into his chest. "We should get back to the party."

Dave looked over to me for answers I couldn't give him. But then his eyes kept tracking up and over my shoulder, narrowing in on a figure hovering in the shadows near the dock.

"Who's out there?" he asked, and I whipped my head around to match his sight.

Zach Webb walked out from the shadows.

"Uh, hey," Zach called out.

"What are you doing here?" I asked, imploring. My head whipped back toward Jo, but she wouldn't meet my eyes.

"Jo said she wanted to talk. I saw on social that you guys were in Fire Island, thought I'd come and hang."

"I just . . . I just meant a phone call," Jo stammered.

"Jo? Who is this?" Dave cut in, his voice steady but nervous.

"You left out the part that you were here for your wedding." Zach indicated the party inside with his hand. The sign visible that read "Congrats, Joanna & Dave!" The crying bride decked in white. "I mean, I'm not *not* into it. But it's a little weird."

"Wait, why are you here?" Dave asked again.

"Jo invited me."

"I didn't *invite* you to anything," Jo cut in, but Dave's face was growing pale.

"Zach, you should really leave," I said.

"Wait, you know him, too?" Dave looked to me. Again, I watched the pieces fall around. A life-size Jenga, the secrets toppled one by one. "*Zach* Zach?" Dave's eyebrows soared to the heavens. "High school Zach?"

"I just wanted to talk," Jo insisted again.

"I thought you were saying goodbye to your exes. Not inviting them to our wedding—"

"This is just a misunderstanding, Dave, I can explain—" Jo started.

"I don't have time for this. Our guests are waiting," Dave said before retreating back inside. Back to where our parents and cousins alike were staring out, wondering if and when it might become appropriate to start in on dinner without the bride in her seat. Forks and knives held anxiously in awaiting hands.

"Hey, Jo. Wow, you look amazing—"

"Get out of here, Zach. You shouldn't be here," I snapped.

"I think Jo can answer for herself."

"And this is Jo's answer," I said. "Tomorrow my sister is marrying an NYU professor who lives in a brownstone off Washington Square Park. He is successful and distinguished, but he's so much more than that. He is kind and generous and thoughtful. He's caring. And he looks at my sister like she is his whole world. Like she's his greatest ending, not just some resting place to pass on by. He is quite literally magic, and all you've ever been is mean. So you can leave now, Zach. Forever. Jo doesn't want you here."

With his arms raised in surrender and his voice a huff, Zach finally turned and headed back toward the dock, where a group of his friends had gathered outside the yacht club. When he was safely at a distance, I turned back to console Jo. She was wiping tears off her face.

"Thanks for that, but it's really not what you think." Her voice was bitter.

"I get it, Jo."

"No, you don't, Amy. I wasn't crawling back to Zach like some 'washed-up prom queen.'" I flinched as she threw my cruel words back at me. "I've been reaching out to *all* my exes. For *closure*. To write an ending for each story." She shrugged. "It was Mom's idea."

"What? Really? Why?"

"I knew you wouldn't understand. You don't even have an ex-boyfriend. You don't know what it's like." She shook her head. "I thought it would help me feel ready. Less afraid. I had left Zach off my list because I know how much darkness he stirs in me. But being back here, seeing those Rocket Fuels and remembering all those nights . . . it bolstered me to dial his number, despite how horrible he was. It was supposed to just be a phone call, but he clearly got the wrong idea. And obviously, so did you."

My stomach flipped. Had I really just imagined it all? Projected my unhappiness onto her face like a slideshow?

I was all wrong. Jo wasn't drowning; she hadn't sunken like my ship. It was solely me and my own misery that lay broken at the bottom of the sea.

"Jo, I'm sorry," I choked out.

"My whole life I wanted to be more like you," Jo scoffed. "You made everything look so easy. A dream husband given to you at birth while the rest of us had to flounder. You think I liked being the single sister? The untethered Sharp? Floating away because no one would catch me?" Jo's voice cracked in her throat. "Now I've found someone. It's scary every day. But I love him. And you've gone and ruined it all. I don't even know who you are anymore."

"Jo, please, I'm so sorry. You know me. I'll make this right. I can make it right." I stepped closer, needing to reach out and hug my sister, bridge the monstrous space between us, but she held up her hands.

"Just stop, Amy." Her voice cracked. "Just stop."

Jo turned and vanished back into Le Dock, returning to the festivities inside. Through the windows, I saw her whisper in Dave's ear. An apology, or at the very least, a promise of an ample answer in the morning. Her reasonings, her reassurance. He squeezed her shoulder, and Jo beamed with sorry eyes toward the remaining family members. The main course streamed in, escorted by the waitstaff, as entrée plates filled the table. Candles danced, and the room sparkled again.

Nobody seemed to miss me, and I couldn't blame them. I walked home alone.

SATURDAY

CHAPTER

23

E MMETT'S VOICE ON REPLAY HAUNTED MY SLEEP.
"Ben isn't right for you." I sounded out his words over
and over in my mouth. In the bright light of the morning,
early sunshine seeping in, I realized why they stuck with me.
They were familiar: the exact five words he had said to me a
decade earlier. I didn't need my freshman-year diary to tell
me that. The memories flooded back on their own.

It was a cold night outside my dorm room. Twinkle lights
danced throughout the decorated streets; a mid-December
snow had transformed the campus into a Christmas fairy
tale. The stressors of first-time finals and end-of-semester
projects disguised anxiety with holiday merriment, and the
anticipation of a three-week-long break beckoned within
reach.

Emmett and I had turned in our final writing seminar
projects together. An essay on meditation gurus through the

ages, along with the presentation of our completed journals. Kate scanned through our ink-stained pages with an approving grin, but I held my breath the entire time. Emmett stood behind my shoulder as I prayed he didn't glimpse the shape of his own name repeated throughout my homework's lines.

We walked back to the dorms as the sun made its descent. We stopped for mochas and made small talk about upcoming holiday plans, but Emmett wasn't his usually loquacious self. I couldn't have guessed what thoughts consumed his mind, but I knew exactly which words I felt like I was bending over backward to avoid: Ben and I had gotten back together. Two weeks earlier, Ben had shown up outside my dorm room with a bouquet of flowers and tears on his face. He was never much of a crier, so I immediately assumed the worst: that he was mid-route to a funeral or a hospital or another nightmarish tragedy. An apology was the last thing I expected.

Ben filled the room with sorries, explanations, and lists of mistakes. The stress of university, a fear of failure, a fear of change in general. The misguided belief that any of this transition would be easier without me right by his side. Although I appreciated the window into his behavior, I knew I didn't need any of it. It was a relief to hear, an overdue comfort, but I had never, and would never, stop loving Ben. He was my future, my everything, my favorite thing. The person I wanted to be with when the rest of the world was stripped away. His laugh, his smile, his brain, his quiet kindness. As much a part of me as any cell in my body. We were built for each other; we had built each other together. I had my boyfriend and best friend back. In that moment, that was all I cared about. Ben wrapped me up in a hug and it felt like coming home.

Only now, Emmett was banging on the doors, demanding I kick Ben out and change the locks.

A light snow fell as we reached the quad's arched gates. When I let slip that Ben's parents would be coming to pick us both up, to drive us home for our first collegiate winter break the very next day, Emmett suddenly reached out and grabbed my hand. His fingers felt like icicles, but I didn't let go.

"Amy," he started, his eyes moving from the soles of his worn sneakers up to my own gaze. "Hi."

I laughed because I didn't know what else to do. "Hi."

"I don't really know how to say this, but I know that I need to. I think I love you, Amy. I think I'm in love with you." He leaned in to kiss me, but no grand orchestras played. Instead, I dodged out of the way.

My heart raced with guilt. It felt like a plane had taken off, a train zoomed out of Thirtieth Street Station. My mind sped through a montage of memories from the past month. My head resting on his shoulder on our late-night Septa ride. His scarf, my cheek. Grazing fingers under the table at the library and neither of us letting go. A secret hope, a secret option, if I was ready. *When* I was ready, he'd said. Emmett knew all about Ben. Of course he knew about Ben.

I just was never quite ready to let Ben go. I would never want to let Ben go.

Now, with Emmett standing right in front of me, I knew exactly where the train was headed. I had laid down those initial rails, but somewhere in transit, my map had rerouted its desired course. Our destinations diverged.

"I'm so sorry," I said, pulling my hand away.

Emmett's face refused to break. "We have a connection. This is special, I know it."

"It is special. And you really mean so much to me. I'm so grateful for our friendship—"

"Friendship?"

"I'm sorry, Emmett." My voice was small. "Maybe there's a universe where this can be something more, but for now, in this life, it just can't be."

"It's him, isn't it?"

I was silent.

"You just took him back?"

"It's not like that—"

"Back to your 'plan'? Christ, you and your sacred plans."

"I won't apologize for knowing what I want—"

"I trusted you."

"You can still trust me. We can still be friends—"

"He's not right for you, Amy." Emmett's voice rang out. "You need someone more. Someone who challenges you, who pushes you—"

"He does, Emmett," I said. "He is right for me. He's everything and more. I love him. I'm so sorry."

"Whatever." The air was cold, but Emmett's face turned hot with anger. A quickening emotion spreading like rapid fire through his pores. "God, I always knew love was just for fools. You, my parents. What a waste of time. Thank you for proving my point. Saving me the future heartache."

"Come on, you know that's not true," I started.

"Goodbye, Amy." As Emmett turned and walked away, a piece of my heart went with him. A first new crush, the second person I'd ever kissed. A frightening but compelling glimpse of a future without Ben.

But a glimpse was all he would ever be.

A few weeks later, Emmett apologized for his harsh words and alerted me to his transfer status. I'd never know if I was the reason he left, or just a part of it, but he was gone by January. Over the years, we half-heartedly tried to keep in touch, but calls and video chats always ended the same. He wanted something I would never be able to give him. A friendship could never have been enough. We decided silence was the best course forward. To seal the door firmly closed. Eventually, he was all the way gone, and all I had left was the memory of the snow falling down, dusting my writing seminar journal with a soft white powder as I stood outside waiting until the power of Emmett's words had finally faded away.

That night, I wrote the journal's final chapter and vowed to never read it again.

If only I had read those last pages of that Moleskine days earlier, I might have saved us all the heartache.

I had made countless mistakes. It seemed my regret list

had grown exponentially this week. But Ben had never been a regret. Choosing this life with him, this destiny, was not something I would ever again consider undoing. I just needed to make him see that.

My mom yawned from across the room, her body and mind beginning to rise. My dad had snuck out a half hour or so ago, pecking me quickly on the forehead before he left. It felt like I was six years old again, waking up sandwiched between my parents after a night of terrors, consumed by the fear of monsters under my bed. Woken by a goodbye kiss from Dad before he left for the train station. The second the door closed, I would sprawl over onto his side of the bed. Sneakily giggling as I stretched, my head taking over the center of his pillow, still warm. Breathing in his fading scent like family stardust.

While I may not have refused squeezing onto my parents' mattress, even at thirty, I owed a debt of gratitude last night to the sleeper chaise in their master suite. After ducking out early from the rehearsal dinner, I hung my head and walked all the way back to Summer Wind. My toes crunched and my heels ached with each step, but my body craved the retribution. The pain.

My remorse only magnified when I returned home and tiptoed up the stairs, heels at last in hand, only to realize that Ben had locked our bedroom door. I didn't blame him. Pattering down the hall, I twisted my parents' door handle in defeat. The chaise shrouded me like a long-lost lover as I let my head rest and drifted to sleep.

"Happy birthday," my mom now called out from across the room. The sun shone so brightly, my mom's smile so pure, I almost momentarily forgot what had led me to this morning's mother-daughter sleepover in the first place. She opened her arms wide, an invitation.

"Happy Fourth," I said as I crawled into her bed. Jo and I had spent many birthday mornings doing just this, usually with more laughter and singing and jumping up and down until the bedframe threatened to give way. Her absence now was a noticeable ache. It felt wrong to have Jo missing from the mattress.

"So, last night . . ." my mom broached. I groaned, throwing my dad's pillow over my face. Faux suffocating, but still a small smile. My mom had a way of diving right into conflict resolution, even before a morning coffee.

"I don't want to talk about it," I muffled from behind the pillow. A loose feather floated up and landed on my fingernail.

"You don't have to talk," my mom said, as she plucked the feather off my hand and twirled it between her own fingers. "Just listen?"

"Fine," I gave in, turning onto my side, my head propped in my hands.

"Marriage is a tricky feat. It's sort of like a wild animal. It needs to be fed, to be nurtured. But sometimes it needs to be left alone, to explore unobserved and find its footing. To attack and growl, need be."

"Am I the beast? Sorry, I'm not tracking."

My mom slowly sucked in a deep breath. "I, too, nearly dipped my toes in the tempting pool of infidelity."

I bolted upright. "Wait, what? First of all, I haven't 'dipped' in anything—"

"I've seen the way you looked at him this week. I may be getting older, but I'm not blind. And that speech . . ."

I felt my cheeks redden. "I can explain—"

My mom stopped me with a halt sign. "I know you can. But you don't have to."

"Wait . . . You cheated on Dad?" I couldn't believe it. "Why have you never told us? When did it even happen?"

"I didn't cheat on your father. But I came very close, abhorrently close."

"What?" I shook my head. "Really? When?"

"Your senior year of college. Your father was preparing to retire, but that meant months of endless nights at the office. Polishing his legacy to perfection. I was in a lonely place. Restless but terrified. I didn't know what life would look like when you two graduated. All my loved ones seemed to be nearing these huge changes, these huge accomplishments. My own work felt uninspired. I hadn't even picked up a brush in years. These were all excuses, of course. Deep down, I was scared, so I was selfish. And then, an old friend came to town. A painter I'd crossed paths with in Italy. He was romantic, always had been, tan and gentle with a certain touch—"

"Don't need those details, Mom."

"Right." She smiled as she tucked a fallen strand of gray hair behind her ears. "The point is it was wrong. The temptation alone had wrecked me. I moved out for nearly a month, lived in the city. I needed time with my thoughts. See, it wasn't just the potential betrayal of your father. It was my own betrayal with myself. That I had let myself be wound so tight in fear from change that I ushered right in my own fallibility. So afraid of the future that I risked ruining something that had been perfect all along," she said.

"And Dad? He was okay?"

"We got there, in due time. It was a wake-up call for both of us. A reminder. 'Happily ever after' sounds simple in love songs, but the truth? It's work. Hard work, every day. Choosing time and time again to come back to the person you made that very first promise with. *That's* the real destiny. Something you choose."

"You make it look so easy."

"Oh Amy." My mom sighed. "I see so much of myself in you."

I had to laugh. "Because we both broke promises?"

"Because we're both human. Mistakes are in our nature. And apologies are, too."

"What if Ben hates me forever? What if he ends—" My heart cut off my voice, wavering and weighed down with the threat of tears.

"You can run yourself in circles with 'what ifs' and 'why nots.' The truth is the only way forward. And forgiveness," she said, "also means forgiving *yourself* in due time, too."

I wiped my eyes. "I've never felt so lost."

My mom took my hand and squeezed it tight, just like

she used to when I was a little girl, worried about test scores or tryouts or birthday parties for which I hadn't received an invitation.

"There can be strength in the wander, sweet girl. You just have to let it guide you in the now." She was right. Of course, she was right. I had spent so long craving perfection, convincing myself that nothing I did would ever be good enough, that I built myself my very own runway to falter. No more excuses, I vowed. I would fix everything. Even if it was messy.

Looking over at my mom, my heart hurt knowing she had been holding on to such a secret. "Thank you" was all I could manage, my emotions still choked in my throat.

"I've been meaning to tell you girls about it for a long, long time. A warning," she said, wrapping her arms around me in a hug. "I suppose I granted myself the passivity, claiming I needed the timing to be 'just right.' It's overdue, and I'm sorry."

"It's okay, Mom." I squeezed hard. "Who knew you could keep a secret for so long?"

She laughed. "There's a lot you don't know," she joked back, her eyebrows raised in intrigue. "Just wait until you're thirty-one."

"This year feels different already." I tossed my pillow over at her. Growing up, I hadn't always been welcoming of these types of moments with my mom. Teenagers didn't want to hear about patience and acceptance during their first fights with boyfriends or betrayals with best friends. Now, I felt grateful. My mom had dealt in similar heartache, and somehow still persevered to the other end intact. Maybe I could get through this, too. Even my parents weren't perfect. Maybe no one was. Maybe I didn't have to be perfect.

I just had to try to get back to the good.

The apology list was long, but I knew who was first in line.

W HEN I KNOCKED ON HER DOOR, I WASN'T SURE she would answer.

After exiting my parents' bedroom (more realistically, being kicked out so my mom could meditate and perform her morning sun salutations before taking a shower), I tiptoed first to my bedroom. Ear pressed tightly against the wooden door, I didn't hear any sound of Ben awake, any rustle of his morning movement. A rotation of the knob confirmed Ben's absence, and my hopes sank at the empty room. Even though I was worried about what I'd next say to him, a bigger part of me missed him desperately. But I guessed reconciliation with Ben would have to wait.

Instead, I opened my closet door and slid out a thick envelope from the front pocket of my suitcase. In black Sharpie, I had drawn a big "30" surrounded by confetti and birthday hats all over the light pink envelope. Now, the childish markings made me wince. I wanted to grab a pen, cross out the doodles, and write "I'M SORRY" in bright block letters instead.

Cards were my and Jo's specialty. Their secret messages had a way of jumping off the page and holding your hand, grabbing you tight. Jo's words gave the world warmth. They elevated Christmas stockings, celebratory gift baskets, even maid of honor "proposals" to new heights, and they were the only thing we had ever exchanged on July 4. Twinhood was a gift, and a card our persistent reminder to give both thanks and celebrations.

Now, I hoped my card could embody every apology I owed her, too.

Jo opened her door and froze when she saw the card in my hand. A small smile forced its spread, despite her furrowed eyebrows. In the other hand, I held out a coffee, still steaming from the pot my dad had been mid-brewing. Sensing that I had no time to explain, my dad had just wished me luck with his eyes.

Now, hesitantly, Jo accepted both the card and the coffee and granted me entry into her room. It smelled like a garden: flowers covered every surface. "Wedding day surprise. Dave's not a big planner, but apparently, he's a romantic. Who knew?" she said, gesturing toward the bouquets. "Anyway, he went for an early-morning beach trip with his parents, so I'm all yours." She looked out the window, toward the waves crashing in the distance.

I had forgotten that her bedroom had such a direct view of the beach. When we first moved into Summer Wind, Jo and I had rock-paper-scissored to decide who could claim their new bedroom first. I had, being me, suggested deciding by birth order, but that rarely worked when you only held a two-hundred-second seniority; I thought three minutes mattered, Jo begged to differ. I had been disappointed when Jo's rock broke my scissors and she picked the room where you could easily look out at the ocean.

Now, we could just make out Dave and his dad swimming in the ocean, Valerie and Lila sitting on a towel by the edge. I watched Dave dive into the waves, relieved each time his head resurfaced. A new brotherly protection surged within me, transformed from strangers to siblings.

Then my face reddened when I remembered that if Jo had been looking out that very same window earlier this week, she could have seen my and Emmett's morning yoga session. My and Ben's picnic fight. How much did she already know, already piece together on her own, before I'd even had the chance to confess?

"I guess now's the time." Jo pulled an envelope out from her purse, hanging off her nearby reading chair. "Happy birthday," she said, handing the card to me. "You can read it later, or throw it out, or whatever." Her shoulders were puffed up, her face a scowl.

Before I knew what was happening, an uncontrollable laughter seized my body. I couldn't stop it. The anxiety, the lies, the pretending. It all broke and bubbled out.

Jo looked at me like I had four heads growing out of my neck. "What's wrong with you?"

I wanted to answer but a wheezing laugh was the only response I could muster. Explanations were futile.

Jo shook her head, letting out a few exasperated chuckles of her own. "You are so strange, honestly."

"*This* is so strange!" I croaked, trying to settle my breath between hiccups. "I've had a stomachache for days. I hate fighting with you. More than anything." Never before in our lifetime had our sister squabbles lasted this long. It was uncharted territory, and I was struggling to navigate my way out of the mess I'd created.

"Then why did you do it?"

I sat on Jo's bed, hoping she'd join me, but instead my sister shifted her body back again toward the window, in the direction of her very-soon-to-be husband. "I just want this day to be over," she said, her voice tiny and timid.

"It's going to be perfect, Jo. He's amazing. I'm so happy for you. I know it's a corny thing to say, but I really am. The way you look at each other, even when the world is falling apart around you? It's beautiful. Really. I'm so sorry that I ever suggested otherwise, that you'd do something to jeopardize it all."

"It's okay. I know from the outside this all probably seems red-flag-level fast. Especially compared to you and Benny." She smiled sadly. "We all know I've woken up and changed my mind before. But when I'm with Dave, everything feels different. Right. Worth the rush." She sighed. "Still, it's been overwhelming, the idea of commitment . . ."

"The Exes Project?" I asked, my eyebrows raised. "All go okay with Dave after last night?"

"I told him I was reaching out to them. He knew how scared I was, even though I was pretending not to be. We just didn't think anyone would, you know . . . show up." She shuddered with a laugh.

"The ghosts of boyfriends past," I teased.

"It helped, though. The closure of it. Or, I guess, the relativity. None of those guys hold a candle to how I feel with Dave."

"Mom's advice never fails," I said. A quiet surrounded us. "Jo . . ." I started.

"Why did you do it?" my sister asked again, but her voice was free from anger this time. It was layered with curiosity instead.

I took a deep breath in. It was time. "We were pregnant. Ben and I."

Jo stood frozen by the window.

"That's not an excuse, I know. I take full responsibility for lying to you, and to Ben. For not telling everyone the truth about Emmett. I just want you to know the whole picture. You should have known already. Ben wanted to tell you as soon as we took the test. And then he begged me to tell you as soon as it was gone, but I . . ." My gaze hadn't left my hands, clenched into fists, clammy palms leaving damp marks on the envelope from Jo. "I just couldn't."

"Oh Amy." When I heard Jo's voice from across the room, I looked up and saw her white face, her eyes welled. "I'm so sorry."

"I didn't want to bother you. I thought it would make everyone too sad and depressed, that it would ruin your wedding. And now I've gone on to ruin it anyway just by showing up."

"Selfish," Jo sputtered. My body turned to ice. How could I have damaged an apology, too? Would this be the last straw, the last fight between sisters? Was this the end of Amy and Jo?

"Do you really think I could be that selfish?" Jo's voice quivered.

"What? Jo, *I* didn't want to be the selfish one. To make everything about me and my problems when we should only be celebrating you."

"As if we haven't spent our entire lifetime sharing the spotlight?" Jo shook her head. "I could have handled it, Amy. I could have helped. Do Mom and Dad know?"

"Not yet." I winced.

Jo moved toward me then, her arms wrapping me in a hug. "There is always room enough for both of our heart-aches and our joys, Ames. We grow together, that's what we do."

"I'm so sorry, Jo," I said, my voice muffled into her shoulder.

"I'm so sorry that you were holding this alone. I'm always here to share your pain."

Jo sat down on the bed next to me, and I let my head rest on her shoulder.

"Ben must have been heartbroken, too. He's been talking about babies since your wedding night." Jo was right. Of course Ben was reeling. Mourning the same cruel loss that I was. And instead of sharing our unspeakable grief, our brutal pain, I had pushed him miles away, left him adrift.

"I made a mess of it with him. He'll never forgive me."

"I would never dare doubt the extent of that man's kindness. It's like his superpower." Jo smiled. "But it can't hurt to beg and plead a little," she teased.

"I'm ready to grovel, trust me. I owe every ounce of it."

"Can't believe Emmett is Brainy Guy all these years later. Dave's birthday parties are going to be pretty awkward." She laughed. "He came by this morning, you know. Emmett. Iced coffees and bacon, egg, and cheeses from the Market in his hands, profuse apologies to both Dave and me. He said he didn't mean a word of that speech, begged to still be allowed as Dave's best man. We were the first stop on his morning's forgiveness tour, too."

"I'll smooth everything over. I promise."

"What really happened with you two?"

I held my face in my hands. "I don't want to talk about it."

"Amy . . ."

"We kissed—"

"Amy!"

"But it's done. It was nothing. Just an old feeling. I guess I needed to confirm it was a mistake or something. But it was."

"I believe you."

"I wanted to tell you everything."

"No more secrets?" Jo outstretched her pinky for a promise like we used to make as children, swearing not to tell about sneaking out after bedtime or swiping an extra cookie for dessert.

"None." I smiled, hooking my finger around hers. Relief flooded. One relationship salvaged, for now. It was terrifying to think how close I had come to losing it. "I can't believe it's your wedding day."

"I know, right? I sort of thought I'd never get married," Jo said with a laugh.

"Your words, not mine," I teased, but my heart was swelling. It wasn't pride, exactly, but it felt good to see Jo making choices for Jo. Taking charge. Even if the decisions were surprising.

"Okay, sorry, I have another secret," Jo said, prompting me to lightly punch her arm.

"I'm listening," I said, laughing.

She inhaled. "I only picked July Fourth as our wedding date because I knew that would mean you'd come. You'd never miss our birthday."

"But you thought I'd miss your wedding?!"

"I wasn't sure! I know it sounds irrational, but deep down, well . . . we just felt so far apart. I was afraid. You were always so busy, with work and the new house. Now I know what must have also been keeping you away." Jo squeezed my hand, acknowledging the space we had lost, the secret pain that pushed me into hiding. "Sometimes it just feels like you're the one with this real adult mature life, and I'm just running around trying to write about it. I wanted to make it easy for you. Our birthday, Kismet. It seems foolish now, and you probably think I'm the the worst sister ever for getting married today of all days. But I had to be sure you'd show."

Protestations ran through my mind. The ludicrous thought that I'd ever miss Jo's wedding. That I wouldn't clear my schedule for any chance to see her, to be with my family. Our growing families. Not to mention the small kernel of satisfaction that at least she finally admitted the slightly selfish date choice. None of it mattered. My sister had believed that there was a possibility that I would miss one of the most important days of her life. I silently vowed to never let her, or anyone I cared about, feel that same sense of doubt or distance again.

"I love you, Jo." I squeezed her hand. "Now, let's get you married."

CHAPTER

25

I T MIGHT HAVE JUST BEEN MY IMAGINATION, BUT IT
felt like the air at Summer Wind had turned, like the
light freshness after a storm. There was a brightness in the
hallways, the creaks in the staircase sounding like song.

After leaving Jo's bedroom so that she could quickly
shower and shave her legs before the glam team's arrival, I
retreated to my room and hid her birthday card away in my
purse. I wasn't ready to read it yet. My heart panged when I
noticed Ben was still missing, along with his suit and wedding accoutrements. He must have already ventured down
to the first-floor den, where Dave, my dad, and the other
bridal-party men were soon set to gather. Whereas the wom-
en's itinerary detailed hours of hair and makeup prep, the
guys would spend the afternoon drinking beer and watching baseball, only to tussle in some hair gel and throw on
their ties a few moments before the photographer's arrival.

Any other day, I knew Ben would have much preferred to spend the afternoon with me and Jo. I willed away the encroaching fears of how he and Emmett might interact together after last night's revelations. There was no place in Summer Wind where Ben could find a moment's peace today, Dave's best man a stark reminder of his wife's treachery.

I counted down the seconds until I could talk to him. To explain. To apologize. Every passing minute felt like the image in my head was growing sharper, Ben's face the only view I wanted to see.

Jo's voice drifted in tune, down the hallway from our upstairs bathroom. A sound I hadn't heard all week. Only then did I realize how strange its earlier absence had been. I listened closer as the lyrics to "I Want to Hold Your Hand" by the Beatles danced from the shower straight into my room. Our favorite song, ever since we were children. We'd sit on my dad's lap, each assigned one knee, as we'd bounce and shout along with the record player. Its melody became a family anthem. When in doubt, reach out. Communicate, connect. My mom's brand of wisdom trickling in with the Beatles' sound waves when we least expected it. Jo's shower performance this morning was a reminder of just that.

When the water pressure shut off, I opened my door and applauded loudly into the hallway. "Bravo! *Brava!*" I called out in her direction. "Encore!"

"Shut up!" Jo shouted back, but I could practically hear the smile on her cheeks.

"The hair stylist will be here in fifteen minutes," I reminded her, my voice reverberating out and down the hall with excitement.

It felt natural to resume the role of sister-in-chief. It had always been my favorite part to play. My duties for the rest of the day were simple: follow the plan. My Plan. A binder contained three identical printed copies of the day's itinerary, along with a detailed shot list for the photographer and a contact information cheat sheet. The latter was just an extra safeguard, considering I had already inputted every vendor's name, number, and backup number into my phone's address book weeks ago.

Gathered in my parents' suite once more, it seemed that at last, all the ladies were on their best behavior. While Jo's curls were being set, my mom and I danced to a curated playlist of wedding anthems so catchy that even Lila tapped her feet along to the beat. Any nervousness Jo had displayed toward today's decision seemed to have evaporated into thin air. Whereas I could barely form a sentence the morning of my wedding, so anxious about the day's remaining to-dos, the looming "I dos," and starving from months of an absurd bridal diet (no dairy, no gluten, a charcoal juice a day— what had I been thinking?), Jo seemed once again at peace. She washed down a bagel and lox spread with a mimosa and a smile.

When the conversation lulled, Valerie cleared her throat. Standing up, she clinked her champagne glass with the closest knife, still coated in a light swath of cream cheese. A bemusing sight in the hands of a woman who detested mess.

My mom and I met eyes from across the room and held our breath. The next words out of Valerie's mouth were poised on a precipice, teetering on the edge of disaster.

Was she about to pull the plug on the celebration entirely?

"While I've always found public speaking a bit uncouth, there is something I feel rather compelled to say," Valerie said, stopping to clear her throat. My stomach flipped. "When Dave told me that he was engaged to be wed, I was disappointed. My Davey has always been so strong, so sophisticated, always on his own. I feared a secondary presence would change that. Distract him from his studies. Thwart his career. And after this week, and all the drinking and partying and crowds of people . . ." Valerie paused, her face tight in a scowl. "I know I was right."

"Now, listen, Valerie," my mom interrupted, ready to defend her daughter, only to be stopped by Valerie's raised hand. I swallowed, my throat dry.

"I was right about the distractions. The changes. But I was wrong to be disappointed. Jo, you make my son more himself. He has been happier this week than I've seen him in years. And he told me he's been researching Fire Island while we've been here. He might make it his next paper topic. Even his career seems to be in safe hands. After a week in this house, watching and getting to know you all, I'm ready to admit that I perhaps may have been wrong."

"Thank you, Valerie," Jo said, surprised.

"Thank *you*," Valerie said, her champagne glass raised.

"If I liked hugs, I'd give you one. But alas." Valerie just shrugged her shoulders, before sitting back down. I tried not to laugh as I looked at Jo. Whatever I had been expecting from Valerie, it had certainly not been an emotional declaration of any sort.

A knock on the door prompted the room to inhale with that sense of wedding day excitement. A reminder that we were mere passengers on a ship that would launch whether we were ready or not. The door opened and in walked the photographer, Laurie, a charming Texan whom Jo had crossed paths with during a photography class at Bard and vowed to hire for all the major photographic events of her life to come. One of the best things about Jo was that she always kept her promises.

"Jo Sharp, you might be the most stunning bride I've ever seen," Laurie announced.

"I doubt that," Jo said, beaming, "but I might be your most organized. Ames? The list?"

Laurie let out a cackle as she took in the stapled packet of pages I placed in her outstretched hands. "I've seen shot lists worse than this, trust me. Once I even had a client print me out a facial-recognition guide for each family member. Headshots titled 'Grandma' and 'Brother's Ex-Girlfriend—*avoid.*'"

"Amy's thirty-second breakdown has to be a first, though," my mom said, elbowing me in the rib.

"First of all—ow. Second, just wait. You will all thank me tomorrow, I promise."

Laurie referenced the time on her wristwatch. "Well, looks like we're already sixty seconds behind. Let's get started!" The photographer started posing Jo and my mom in "getting ready" stances, snapping photos as we sipped champagne and zipped up her jumpsuit. As Jo's blond hair was given a few final perfect curls, her cheeks a final graze of rouge, her lips a final hint of gloss, butterflies flew throughout my own stomach. This was happening.

My mom appeared by my side, squeezed my arm. "Ready?"

"We're not the ones getting married, Mom."

Still, she smirked. "Ready?" she repeated.

"Yes," I whispered to her. "Time for the first look!" I called out to the room.

Laurie guided Jo to the doorway. "See you guys for family portraits on the beach in—"

"Thirty," I said instinctively. The timeline tattooed on my brain. The old Amy was back.

"Perfect," Laurie said. "Let's go take a look at that groom of yours."

Jo suddenly stopped in her steps. My heart froze. I felt my mom tense up beside me. Jo turned to us, her eyes watery, and I couldn't help but fear the worst.

She coughed a little to clear her throat. "I just want to say—" Her lips were moving, but her voice caught.

"We love you," I said. On behalf of the room, the family, the town, the world.

"Thank you," she managed.

"Now go, dear! Dave's going to think you stood him

up!" Valerie ordered. Lila cracked up as Jo nodded and followed Laurie down the hallway. Once we heard her footsteps on the staircase and the front door closing behind her, my mom and I rushed over to the window overlooking the deck. Peering through the pane, we spied Dave standing alone, a grin up to his ears, waiting for his bride to tap his shoulder. His navy suit complemented the ocean.

"Could my mom and I watch with you guys?" Lila asked, startling me slightly. She had spoken so little this week that I still hadn't grown accustomed to her voice.

"Of course, sweetheart," my mom said, pulling Valerie closer to the window, two mothers with bird's eye views of their children's special day. Past the deck, beyond the hedged fences, I could just make out the heads of my dad and Ben. Even Emmett was seemingly reconciled, huddled with the men and trying to avoid the sun. Before I could even begin to wonder what the three of them could possibly be discussing, I heard Dave shout, "Holy shit!"

Valerie's hand flew to her mouth. "Language, David," she whispered under her breath.

Despite our view from stories high above, Dave and Jo's joy was crystal clear. Jo stunned like a lightning bolt to the heart, and when Dave reclaimed his composure, he picked up my sister and twirled her around. A princess in a storybook. As Laurie positioned the couple throughout the deck for bridal portraits, Jo and Dave beamed like teenagers in love, stealing kisses and clinging hands whenever they could. Connected by a matrimonial magnet, the pull never

ceasing. When Laurie led them down the driveway and
steered them toward the beach, the entire house seemed to
savor the stillness, the leftover sips of their love.

From up above, I fought to keep my eyes trained anywhere other than on Ben's and Emmett's faces. It took every
ounce of willpower to keep my eyes fixed on the pool, the
deck, my hands. Anywhere but on them.

Yet when I did finally lift my chin and gaze out in the
direction where I'd last seen them standing, the only eyes
staring back at mine were Emmett's.

Ben was gone.

A MISSING BROTHER-IN-LAW IS NOT A WEDDING-day stereotype for good reason. Brides with cold feet, a groom on the run, even parental day-of drama is unfortunate but expected. Those are the relationships taking center stage. Those are the ones at risk of failure. A brother-in-law flung into hiding should never earn a square on anyone's wedding day Bingo card.

Yet when I saw the empty space on the sidewalk where Ben's feet had just stood, I knew something was wrong. I raced to my bedroom, praying that maybe Ben had snuck in for a few moments of quiet before the ceremony. Almost mockingly, the room was just as empty as I had left it, pillows fluffed and sheets pressed tightly into hospital corners with no sign of a restful husband-once-been. A dial tone filled my pounding eardrums as I called Ben for the third time. And for the third time, I heard only ringing followed by a voicemail greeting. His digital voice, recorded and far away.

"Dad, have you seen Ben?" I called out, my hands shaking as I walked into the kitchen. Ben was probably just out for a walk, I told myself. This was normal. His absence now didn't mean anything about our future. Right?

"Not since the first look." My dad raised his eyebrows in my direction. "Are you feeling okay, Ames? Your face is, uh, different . . ." he said with a wince.

"Totally. Couldn't be better," I said, suppressing my fear. Maybe I could find a short-term comfort by folding myself back up and into the day's itinerary. "You and Mom should head to the beach for parent portraits. I'll get Ben and we'll meet you down there in a few."

"Aye, aye, Lieutenant," he said, but the family nickname didn't make me feel any more in control. Instead, I grimaced and turned toward the hallway, but my dad caught my arm.

He gave me a small smile that warmed my heart, like when he'd tuck me into bed with an extra blanket. "Relationships . . . they weave," he said now. "What matters is just getting them back on track. It's putting in the work. And no one works harder than you, my girl. You can do this."

I swallowed, eyes brimming. I thought my dad had been blind to my marital woes, my extramarital temptations. Had he been watching all along?

My dad patted my shoulder before taking a sip of the whiskey he'd just poured for himself. When he caught me glancing at his midday cocktail, his lips curled into a smile. "What? I'm a little nervous."

I burst out laughing, which made my dad chuckle, too. A momentary release. "It's going to be great," I promised. "Everything is going to be great. I can fix this."

It had been my constant refrain all week. If only I could make myself believe it.

If only I could just find Ben.

Unfortunately, the path surrounding Summer Wind had already been overtaken with the Kismet Fire Department's Fourth of July parade. The streets were filled with families holding flags, children in red-and-blue bathing suits waving as the floats looped their way up and down the town's streets. Holiday bliss as far as the eye could see, all to the soundtrack of a local marching band playing patriotic tunes. It was usually my favorite part of the weekend, of the entire summer.

Now it was just in my way. I elbowed past kids, jumping over the decorated wagons (despite my high heels), hurrying past the stand selling hot dogs and raffling off the annual "Wagon of Cheer," filled to the brim with every alcohol imaginable. Out of the corners of my eyes, I glimpsed Bobby, Mary, and Tyler heading back to Party of Five, presidential costumes in hand. Their Mount Rushmore float had been in the earlier portion of the parade so that they'd have time to celebrate and still change before the wedding, and from the looks of the grins on their faces, it must have been a success. I quickened my pace toward them—had Ben simply gone to cheer on the cousins as their float went by?—but my stomach dropped when I realized Ben wasn't by their sides.

Ben wasn't anywhere to be found.

As the sky's rays beamed down, a pool of wet humidity grew at the nape of my neck. I cursed my hair, strands frizzing already, but mostly I just cursed myself. A glance at my phone screen filled my stomach with dread. No new messages or missed calls from Ben, and I had one minute to get to the beach in time for family photos. I held my breath and hustled toward the shore, speed walking as fast as I could. A balance in punctuality while preventing my sweat-covered forehead from being memorialized in Jo's wedding album for perpetuity.

When I saw a man in a gray suit standing at the top of the beach's entrance stairs, I felt a flood of relief wash over me. My future restored in an instant, fears conquered.

The peace shattered a few steps later when the man's head turned in my direction.

It was only Emmett.

When Emmett saw me, his mouth dropped, surely stunned and nervous and awkward to be in such close proximity for the first time since last night's drunken tirade. His lips began to form my name, but I had no time for pleasantries or apologies alike.

The beach now in full view at the top of the stairs, I could make out Jo and my parents posing for pictures, Valerie and Conrad admiring from a distance, even Lila not staring at her phone.

No Ben.

"What did you say to him?" I shouted, my jaw clenched tight.

"Wait, what?"

"Ben. What did you say to him?" My mind raced through the dozens of devastating conversations the two men could have had this morning. The exaggerated versions of events, jealous histories. A chemical explosion waiting to set fire. I should never have let it happen.

"I don't know what you're talking about, nothing—"

"He's gone. I can't find him anywhere."

My eyes wandered again to the clear patch of sand in the distance where the wedding would take place. The stage was set for bliss. Ten rows of white chairs lined up facing the waves. Anchored at the shoreline and centered between the aisles stood a simple brass structure draped with satin. Delicate white and pink flowers traced up and down its sides. I shuddered, remembering how Ben and my dad had constructed that arch just days earlier.

Emmett followed my eyeline. When he noticed the absence for himself, his spine straightened. "I'll find him."

"It's fine—"

"You have to get down there. I can do this."

I hesitated. The last thing I needed was Emmett tracking down Ben and pushing, driving him even further away. But what else could I do? Time was running out.

"Please, Amy. Let me do this." His eyes shone with all the apologies he couldn't yet say.

"Fine," I said. Emmett nodded slightly before pounding

down the stairs, off to find Ben where I couldn't. I just prayed he'd have more luck than I did.

I needed him to.

"Amy!" Jo called out, as I reluctantly made my way toward the beach, hesitant to pause my search for Ben. The bridal families had gathered by the ocean, their laughter trailing through the wind like campfire smoke, their happiness so ablaze that you could almost reach out and touch it. Not me. Their joy felt like a direct affront to my still-racing mind.

Laurie looked at me with a grin from behind her camera. "You're late!" she teased.

When I didn't laugh back, Jo immediately pulled me aside. "Where's Ben?" she whispered.

"We're going to have to take photos without him." It was all I could manage to keep my voice from cracking.

I watched as Jo decoded the clues in her mind. Ben was the most reliable, most caring person either of us had ever met. His absence spoke volumes. She squeezed my hand, pity in her pupils. "We have all night for photos."

I locked the aching part of my heart away as Laurie placed us in formations, the Sharps and the Beaumonts photographed in every possible arrangement. Behind us, the waves crashed as the air danced with the smell of salt and eucalyptus. We posed until our cheeks grew tight, my smile plastered so firmly that I nearly lost feeling in my face. Excuses flew out of my mouth to explain Ben's nonattendance. Stomachache. Urgent work call. Double-checking the reception setup was just to Jo's liking. White lies while the truth stayed locked away.

The excuses didn't prevent my mom's constant knowing glances, trying to catch my attention every chance she could get. I did my best to ignore her. There were no words she could say that could comfort me now. If Ben was willing to miss Jo's wedding, it meant the unimaginable had come true. I pushed away the image of Ben speeding off on the first ferry to Bay Shore. Suitcase packed, a divorce lawyer on the phone. Until we knew what Ben was thinking, there was nothing that my mom or Jo or my dad or anyone could do. The blame, the responsibility, fell squarely on me, along with this phase of silent, teeming heartache.

"Now, everyone, point and smile at the happy couple!" Laurie instructed.

I extended my hand but couldn't stop my index finger from shaking. My legs itched to run off the beach, to find Ben and hold his face in my hands. To apologize at last, to explain, to promise to never put him through anything like this for as long as we lived.

"What's next again, Amy?" Jo's question sucked me back to the surface.

"Just about time for you and Dave to head back to Summer Wind. The guests should start trickling in any minute," I said, hiding the sadness soaking my words.

"We'll take photos with Ben after the ceremony," Dave said. He looked at me with a silent understanding, a small smile. My heart tugged with gratitude as he grabbed Jo's hand. "Shall we?"

"Are you sure you don't want us to wait a little longer?" Jo asked, but I shook my head.

"Go on. I think I already see Uncle Neal idling on the steps."

As Jo and Dave and both sets of parents were guided off the beach, back to Summer Wind, where they would wait until it was time for the procession, I walked over to where a violinist and a cellist were setting up by the back row of chairs. A folding table propped up, its tablecloth covered in stacks of paper programs for the ceremony. Passing them out was originally a task for both the maid of honor and best man. I grimaced that Emmett was still nowhere in sight. It couldn't be a good sign that he still hadn't been able to track down Ben.

"Need some help?" Lila's voice once again snuck up behind me. Her face shone, albeit a bit sadly. Nodding wordlessly, I moved over and allowed Lila to grab a stack.

She fingered the edges of the paper as we stood quietly. I knew I must have seemed rude, silent, and standoffish, but my body felt like it would combust if I put it through another round of wedding weekend small talk. Worries were already zipping at the highest echelon throughout my every pore; I was having a hard enough time keeping up a conversation with just myself.

"Marriage sucks," Lila said with a sigh at last, breaking the silence. "It's unnatural to think that one person can be with just one other person for their entire lifetime. Life is long. People get old. How do I know who I'll want to be with when I'm seventy-five?" Lila stared at me with such a genuine conviction that I realized she was hoping for a literal answer.

"Well, even when you get older, you still stay you. I think the baseline stays the same," I said.

She snorted. "Sorry, sorry," she said with a laugh, covering her face. "That's just so wrong. People change five ways before lunch. At least the people I know."

"Then you just have to find someone who changes along with you."

"I hope Dave and Jo make it. No matter what my mom—"

"They will," I said firmly, before she could finish her train of thought. Whatever doubts I had before coming to Fire Island had been dispelled.

It was only my own relationship that I was worried about.

"You guys are cool twins. I always wanted a sister."

"It has its ups and downs," I said, painfully aware of all I'd done to risk our bond this week alone. "But still, I wouldn't trade it for the world."

"Jealous." Lila seemed to smile and frown at the same time, her mouth a curvy line. In that moment, I knew I would never understand the enigma that was Lila Beaumont. But I had glimpsed a part of her, and it was a start, at least.

"Well, now you have two sisters," I said, watching Lila's eyebrow slightly raise. "Jo and I are a package deal. When she gets back from the honeymoon, we should do a girls' brunch. Sisters and sisters-in-law only."

"I don't think that's how in-law-hood works," Lila said, laughing, "but I'm down."

As the sun fell from the sky, guests began to trickle onto the sand. Lila and I handed out programs to each newcomer.

Groom side, bride side. *How was the ferry?* Small talk and big smiles. My cheeks were kissed, hands shaken, shoulders hugged, but my body felt cold. Trapped and waiting. I just hoped the programs weren't stained with damp prints from my clammy palms.

When Emmett finally appeared, I held my breath. He was alone. Emmett pulled me to the side as Lila covered program distribution for the both of us.

"Did you find him?" I begged, the words hardly leaving my mouth before my eyes started to fill with tears. Verbalizing my anxiety only made the emotions worse.

Emmett barely shook his head.

"What's that supposed to mean?" I whispered hoarsely.

"Amy, I am so sorry. For everything," he said instead. "I've repented all day to everyone but you. I was a mess last night, foolish and stupid and drunk. So drunk. It wasn't the real me—"

"Emmett, what about—"

"Please, just let me finish before whatever happens next." He cut me off, his hands raised.

"Okay," I said, my voice small.

"Seeing you again this week brought everything right back. And instead of using this as a chance to finally just be your friend, I got in the way of everything. It was reckless and immature, and I am so sorry."

His words, though poorly timed, struck a chord. We had all been acting like headstrong teenagers, lustful and lamenting and leaning into loose whims. A beach vacation could do that in the best of times, the smell of the ocean a constant temptation to set inhibitions free.

"It was my fault, too. I'm so sorry," I said. There was no point in grudges or anger. The only concern I had was finding Ben. All that energy I'd spent failing to forget Emmett suddenly evaporated, like air releasing from a balloon. Spent, done. "Growing up is harder than we thought, huh?" I said.

Emmett smiled, relieved. "Friends?" He reached out his hand in my direction, just as he had done all those days ago on the cold bathroom floor. But this time, his eyes told me he meant it sincerely.

"Maybe one day," I said. It would have been easy to play along, but I was tired of empty promises. "Let's try to survive this wedding first."

"Fair enough." Emmett dropped his hand. "And, Amy? I really hope you and Ben get through this."

"Me too," I whispered. Scanning the crowd, I choked down the disappointment that Ben's face still wasn't shining out among the guests. Was my sister's wedding going to double as my separation? Dozens of friends and relatives had taken their seats, an excited roar of chatter swelling with anticipation. Lila smiled at me from her chair as I made my way to the arch. Emmett's eyes met mine from across the aisle, where he stood ready to bear witness by Dave's side. Suddenly, Emmett wiped his eyes with the backs of his hands. Was even the cynic feeling sentimental? Emotions were on fire.

A quiet hum as the violinist placed her bow against the

instrument's string. At the beach's entrance, Dave appeared at the top of the stairs, arm in arm with his parents. I inhaled sharply. It was happening.

As the music swelled, I looked into the throng of guests and saw a flood of faces winking at me. Uncles and cousins and best friends. "Your sister is about to get married!" their smiles screamed. "This is one of the best days of your life!" What no one else seemed to notice was the empty chair in the front row.

Reserved for Ben. Vacant.

CHAPTER

27

A S DAVE AND HIS PARENTS APPROACHED THE
aisle, I fought the urge to flee. My hands were sweaty,
my vision blurred. The ceremony was beginning, and my
husband was nowhere to be found. My feet longed to run off
the beach, through the streets of Kismet, calling Ben's name
as if I were in some romantic dating show gone terribly
wrong, but a runaway maid of honor would have only made
the afternoon's agony that much worse.

Dave and his parents walked with careful steps down
the sandy aisle before hugging their son and taking their
seats in the front row. Conrad's face was painted with a
proud expression, his eyes aglow and a toothy grin stretching from ear to ear. Valerie's expressions were naturally more
withdrawn, a closed-lipped smile, a serious stride. Yet, upon
closer inspection, I could tell that her cheeks were red with
adrenaline, and her eyes shone with a watery hue that brewed

just before tears broke through. Dave turned around, his back toward the sea and his gaze landing on the foundation of his every joy and wonder.

The guests heard Jo's laughter before they even saw her face. Whipping their heads in the direction of the source, our relatives stood up with anticipation as Jo made her way down the stairs, my parents on either side. Jo in white, my parents dressed both in shades of blue. A vision. And in classic Jo fashion, her laughter continued as she made her way toward the aisle. She winked at friends, waved to our younger cousins. There was no severity in her ceremony, no stuffiness or pomp. She hated taking herself too seriously, and her wedding would be no exception. At a moment when usually a bride might feel stressed or even pass out, Jo managed to put the entire beach at ease with one look. Her happiness was contagious.

Jo, walking down the aisle with my parents. Her future husband, tears staining his cheeks as he greeted his bride. These were moments that we had dreamed about since we were schoolgirls in the backyard. The wedding was here, but as the officiant began the ceremony and spoke of Jo and Dave's love, the colors turned gray. Cold. It had been Jo and Amy and Ben for decades. Our trio. A celebration, a major life event happening without my husband beside us, felt like riding a broken tricycle. Everything was wrong.

I tried to keep my eyes on Jo, to listen attentively to the officiant's voice. To will myself to forget Ben and focus on all the luckiness, all the beauty, that I had for now in front of me. Yet even as he recounted the story of how Dave and Jo first met, his words sounded more and more like gibberish to my distracted ears.

Until I heard a cough.

I followed the sound. There, alone at the very back of the rows of chairs, almost disguised against the dunes, stood Ben. A light gray suit, a light pink tie. The most handsome human I'd ever seen.

My heart raced as we made eye contact. Yards away and his face still sent goose bumps up my arms. Even though my eyes filled with tears, I could just make out the blurred sight of Ben raising his hand up in greeting and mouthing a quiet "Hi."

"Hi," I whispered back.

He smiled. I melted.

Thanking every god and goddess in the universe, I tried to maintain composure as my stomach did a thousand backflips in reprieve. My thoughts raced, a game plan splayed out in front of me. Ben was still in Kismet. All I needed was one chance, one conversation. He didn't even have to forgive me. He could still board the next ferry, tell me never to come home. I just needed to look into his eyes, hold his hand if he'd allow it, and explain myself.

But first, Jo needed to be finished getting married.

For the duration of the ceremony, I kept a constant tab on Ben. He never did claim his assigned seat, naturally hesitant to cause unwanted attention or interrupt the ceremony by conspicuously sliding into the very front row, but it didn't seem to impact his enjoyment. Every time I looked his way, Ben was either grinning, laughing, or wiping at his eyes.

In fact, the entire audience seemed subscribed to only those emotions as Jo and Dave read their vows. While Dave's vows were more traditional, Jo's promises were disguised as a poem about Dave's hands. She played on the theme of their partnership, committed to striding hand in hand through life, and even hinted at the future, smaller hands he might hold one day in his. Surprisingly, the mention of my future niece or nephew didn't trigger any sadness or pain. Any jealousy or anger. Instead, it filled me with hope. Jo swore to take Dave's hand, whether the skin had grown rough or smooth, bruised or wrinkled, manicured or dirty, and to hold on tight.

I did my best to focus on their words, but my mind seemed hard-pressed to remain in place. When I wasn't stealing glances in Ben's direction, I felt like I was transported back in time. Flashbacks flooded from my own wedding day. Memories of my and Ben's vows filled my inner dialogue. We had stood in front of our loved ones and promised a lifelong commitment to laughter and compassion. To competing for the best pun. To always bringing each other a glass of water before bed or giving a back scratch after a long day. To making space for quiet and for cheers as needed, happy or sad or a little bit of both.

To trusting, to listening, to loving at every turn.

To traveling alongside the other, no matter the curves in the road. Growing just as we had always done. As we promised to always do.

Now, those promises rang in my ears. How had I let myself forget, fall so far from the partner I promised I'd be?

I closed my eyes and saw Ben's face during our ceremony. I remembered his eyes. They shone with hope. They filled with tears, something so rare for Ben, usually strait-laced, emotions close to his chest. Our entire wedding day, Ben had a constant watering at his eyeline, so much so that his mother followed him around with travel-size packs of tissues. "This is just so perfect" was all he could manage by way of explanation for his unexpected tears. It only made me want to marry him even more.

It was perfect. He was perfect.

We could still be perfect, too. We would find a way to heal us, to continue growing and laughing together.

I would do whatever it took to fix us, to protect us.

I had to.

The sound of the crowd bursting into applause snapped me out of my trance. I heard my voice cheering out, felt my hands turn red from clapping as Jo and Dave were pronounced husband and wife. The violin cued Jo and Dave's recession off the beach. A few steps in, and they raised their interlocked hands above their heads, triumphant.

They did it. We were witnesses to magic.

My mom and dad followed after the happy couple, trailed by Valerie and Conrad. All four parents' faces were flushed with emotion. As the music crescendoed, I knew that Emmett and I were supposed to walk out next, the only members of the two-person bridal party to follow the bride and groom in exaltation. But before hooking my hand around

Emmett's outstretched elbow, I peeked out once more toward
the dunes from where Ben had watched the ceremony. Self-
conscious and anxious about touching Emmett again, even
in a purely platonic way, I craved a secret smile with Ben, a
telegraphic code that this elbow holding meant nothing, that
this would soon be behind us.

Yet all that remained in the patch by the dunes were
scarcely visible sandy footprints. He was already gone. Vanished like the wind.

Emmett led me down the path, past tearstained faces
and waving relatives. This time, however, Ben's absence emboldened me. He'd shown up once. That was enough for
now. Waving back with my free hand, I dared let a smile
occupy my face.

I would find him again.

CHAPTER

28

THE GROOM ADMIRING HIS BRIDE AS SHE WALKED
down the aisle. A father telling a family tale, tears in
his eyes as he toasted a new beginning. A bouquet flying in
the air, caught in eager hands as a signal for all the future
love still to come.

Everyone had their favorite parts of a wedding, but my
favorite was always the dancing. After the photographer's
checklist was blotted with crossed-out lines, after the rings
were safely exchanged on shaking fingers, after the parents'
toasts were completed and the risk of embarrassing stories safely avoided (or, at the very least, survived), I relished
watching a bride's face as the band upped the tempo and the
real party began. An exhale for the ages as a moment of relaxation finally settled in. It didn't matter anymore if her
father-in-law hated the codfish or her aunt was squirreling
away the spare Q-tips from the bathroom in her purse. The

music set all that free, paved the final way toward celebration at last.

Now, though, the crowded dance floor felt like my biggest adversary. An invading army, against which my only defense was an empty champagne flute and the steadfast determination to find my husband.

Immediately after the ceremony, Emmett and I had led the five-block charge from the ocean to the Out. The restaurant had been transformed into a dreamscape. String lights glowed over the patio. Round tables arranged in a semicircle to create a dance floor in front of the stage where the Rich Mahogany Band played as guests mingled toward their seats. Flowers seemed to grow from every surface, sprouting from every corner, as waiters passed trays of champagne and tequila shots right along with hors d'oeuvres. I popped a bacon-wrapped scallop between my lips as I scanned the crowd, trying but failing to catch a glimpse of Ben's black hair among the bobbing heads and chatting faces. Finding my seat, I tempered my disappointment when I confirmed that Ben's place setting remained untouched.

Where had my husband gone? And when would it be an appropriate time to ditch the wedding proceedings and search for him again?

"Still no Ben?" Bobby asked, startling me slightly even though he had read my mind. I looked up and saw Bobby folding his suit jacket over the back of his chair, just down the table from my own, and rolling up the sleeves of his button-down shirt. Exposed forearms were always the first indicator of the transition to the reception phase of a party.

My frown sufficed as answer enough to his question.

Mary popped up by his side with puppy-dog eyes. "Can we at least get you a drink?"

"I'm set," I said, lifting my champagne glass. "You?"

"I'm still hungover from last night." Mary shrugged. "No drinking for me tonight." Maybe we all could have used more sobriety this week.

The uplighting behind the band dimmed to a purple glow. I trained my eyes away from my cousins' pitying gazes and over to the stage, where an emcee stood. As the spotlight focused, I recognized the man holding the microphone as Riley. In classic small-town fashion, he'd transitioned from Kismet tour guide to wedding host with a snap of stage lighting and a trusty tuxedo rental.

"Hello, ladies and gentlemen!" Riley's bubbling voice boomed out from the loudspeakers. "It is with great honor that I welcome, for the first time ever, the newest Mr. and Mrs. Beaumont!" The guests cheered and the band erupted into song as Jo and Dave danced their way into the space. Sparklers were lit to toast their entrance, casting the patio in a luminous blaze. I winked at Jo as she walked by my table, grabbing her hand for a quick squeeze. We always could transmit novels with a single raised eyebrow, a wink of an eye. I knew she was wondering about Ben, but I did my best to communicate the calm I could already feel slipping away from my grasp. Secrets or not, I didn't want Jo worrying about anything other than missing a dance step right now. This was her and Dave's moment.

The music slowed as they reached the center of the dance floor. Taking her in his arms, Dave whispered a smile into Jo's ear as their first dance began. Time shrank to a crawl as wedding attendees cooed around them. I blinked, and suddenly, I saw myself in Ben's arms. Ray LaMontagne and my husband's blue eyes. My head on his shoulder, so close that I could smell the calla lily in his boutonniere.

"Just look at me," Ben whispered with a smile. "Just look at me."

Another blink, and I was back in the present. The flashback a fading memory, like sand falling through fingers. I tried to smile, let my genuine happiness for my sister show as Dave twirled Jo closer, dipped her low. Our relatives hollered in approval. I wanted to join in the cheer, but my throat was empty. The world started revolving around me, until I heard a whistle that sent shivers down my spine.

In the back of the crowd, Ben had his index fingers in his mouth.

He was here. Again. Standing by the exit, Ben cheered loudly to make up for his distance. It may have been a trick of the sparklers, but I could have sworn he smiled my way. The song ended and the crowd erupted into applause, but just as I made my way toward my husband's side, desperate to reach out and make sure he was really here and not a figment of my imagination, microphone feedback pierced through the atmosphere.

"Aren't they just beautiful?" Riley's voice echoed throughout the patio. "As we let them rest their feet—just for a moment—I've been told that a special someone has asked to say a few words."

The spotlights turned in my direction.

Ben would have to wait longer yet.

"Amy!" Jo whispered, rushing to my side. "What's going on?"

"Slight change of plans, but don't worry." I smiled, grabbing those three-by-five notecards I had tucked away in my purse. "I still owe you a speech."

"But you hate public speaking!"

"But I love you." I squeezed her hand. "And I'm sorry. Let me do this."

Riley winked at me as I walked onto the stage, the yellow haze beaming into my eyes. I had texted him in secret this morning, when I was feeling emboldened by the idea, but now the microphone felt more daunting in my hand than I could have ever dreamed up in my nightmares. The day was finally cooling into night, but my skin felt slick with sweat. I picked at the cards' edge as my public-speaking anxiety surfaced. Just as I was beginning to weigh how embarrassing it would be to fake a stomach bug and run off the stage, I saw Jo's grateful face and my resolve set.

I would do this, for her.

I tapped on the microphone, thinking that was something that dignified speakers did on TV. It only sent a strange thumping sound throughout the space. I winced. "Sorry, I thought that would be cooler." The guests laughed, and I felt my face turn pink. "Sorry again. I totally thought I was saying that just in my head. Off to a great start." I let myself join in on the joke this time. "For those of you who don't know me, my name is Amy Sharp, and I'm Jo's twin sister. Yes, the girl who is barely stringing together a sentence right now is not just related to—but *twins* with—the girl whose vows alone are probably being printed, bound, and sold by her agent as we speak.

"Jo had originally scheduled my toast to be during the rehearsal dinner. But after some very unsisterly mistakes on my part, I wasn't able to make my speech last night. I'm sorry, Jo and Dave. And I'm sorry to all of you now, for what you're about to endure. You were so close to missing my misery! It'll be short, I promise."

Deep breath in, deep breath out. Just like Nina had taught me. I scanned the crowd, my nerves climbing up from my heels. My parents smiled back at me, Jo flashed a thumbs-up for good luck, but it was Ben's gentle, proud grin that calmed me. It was like he had reached out across the room with his soul, taken my hand, and squeezed.

I looked down at the notecards, but I knew then that I couldn't recite any borrowed words. Any copy-and-paste compliments. Not after all that had transpired this week. All I had lost and learned.

Dropping the index cards onto the floor, I took a deep breath and went off script.

"Having a twin is like growing up with a photo album. All you have to do is look over across the dinner table, and it's like falling back in time. Living with your best memories at an arm's length. Inside jokes that span for hours, laughter that can't be explained but still makes you cry. A partner in all pursuits, ready-made from birth.

"I have the best partner in my sister, Jo. Living with a photo album isn't always easy. Those memory-lined pages show plenty of mistakes, too. The wrong words like tattoos on our faces. But with Jo, even the worst of times feel like poetry. Even the saddest moments, beautiful. Ever since we were little, Jo had this stunning—sometimes annoying— tendency to see life through rose-colored glasses. It's like she can see into the soul of everything. Encourage its purpose. It used to drive me crazy. Ben and I—my husband, Ben—we used to tease her about it as kids. How could she be so calm when everyone else wanted to scream?

"Of course, it's that exact trait that's made her the best partner all these years. My perfect counterpoint. Her unending ability to find that joy, that meaning, in each day. When I wanted most to hide, Jo would pull me out and make me look up at the sky. Even in the rain. Seriously, I swear she gave me pneumonia once, we were out there for so long, toes soaking in puddles. Now as a grown-up, struggling to learn how to act like an adult, I spend each day with a little Jo in my ear. I promise, it's less troubling than it sounds. But when I see something sad, something that would otherwise make me want to scream, I think about Jo and how she would probably run up to it and hug it and sprinkle it with her glow. Make it sparkle.

"Dave, I can say with firsthand experience that you

are gaining the world's best partner in my sister. She will take your mistakes, your heartaches, and wear them as her own so that they feel less heavy. And in good times, which I know there will be plenty, she will champion your successes so much that the wins feel magnified. I've watched her do it my whole life. Our photo album is filled with triumphs and tribulations. Each one magic, each one possible, because of her.

"Dave and Jo, I can't wait to watch your photo album unfold. May there always be more smiles than sadness, more candid laughter and funny faces than photobombs or blurry focus. And I'm now realizing this metaphor may have sounded better in my head. So, with that," I said, raising my glass, "here's to the newlyweds. May your snapshots last forever. I love you. I'm so happy for you. And, Dave, I'll do my best to share her."

Jo was up out of her chair, holding me tight before my brain could process that my toast was over. "Thank you," she said in a muffled voice into my ear. I felt Dave's arms on my back, my newly minted brother-in-law joining in.

"Love you guys," I said through a sniffle. As the band started playing, I wiped my face dry. "Now go dance." Dave and Jo led the charge to the dance floor, quickly surrounded by relatives offering congrats in between choreography and lip-syncs. The ensuing block of humans was a beautiful blend, a mixture of families and geographies all united with one purpose. Normally, I positioned myself right in the center of it all, dancing until my feet hurt. But now, I needed to get through the crowd and over to my husband.

Ben stood at the Out's entrance gate, taking in the same blissful mess that I was. He caught my eye and waved. A small gesture that meant everything. I leapt off the stage.

The dance floor felt like quicksand as I tried but failed to move through the crowd. An aunt, an uncle, a family friend grabbing my hand and giving me a twirl. With a smile on my face and a song on my tongue, I worked to push through, to dance my way out. To hide the fact that the very fate of my marriage was hanging in the balance, but yes, sure, one more spin. One more verse.

When Jo saw me out on the dance floor, she grabbed my arm and pulled me closer. "That speech was so beautiful, Amy. Seriously." Her voice was sparkling, a glass already emptied in hand. "But you have to look over there." My eyes followed in the direction of Jo's finger, over toward where Emmett stood, his arm not-so-casually propped against the wall, his eyes wide and attention trained on none other than Paige.

"She owns all of his books!" Jo said. "Who would have thought?"

"Honestly, good for them." We burst out laughing.

"Love is everywhere in this town," Jo said, her head now cocked to the other side of the patio, where Mary and Tyler were dancing close. "Now, it's your turn." She squeezed my hand and then pushed me in the direction of where Ben was still standing. Mr. Watts had made his way over to Ben's side, a drink in his hand and surely talking his ear off about the latest Mets loss. I didn't care. Ben was still here. It was the only sign I needed. I could do this.

Until a loud pop made the entire party crash to a halt.

The music stopped, the dancing frozen. In the darkness, Jo's face glowed pale as a ghost.

The power was out.

CHAPTER

29

"AMY, WHAT DO WE DO?" JO'S VOICE WAS A WHIM-per. Dripping in defeat.

I looked out at the disarray and braced for disaster.

While the electricity cut out, the band had initially remained onstage, fiddling with power buttons and extension cords, but it soon became clear that the solution required more than a simple reboot. They trickled offstage and joined the crowd by the bar, awkwardly sipping beers and cocktails. Everyone waiting for someone to tell them what to do next, that everything would soon be okay. Guests filled the air with whispers, wondering what might be wrong, while secretly relieved it wasn't their own wedding derailed by technical difficulties. My parents were with Riley, trying to assess the source of the damage. I couldn't make out their sentences, but their frustrated expressions and hurried hand movements didn't bode well.

The only reason I was remaining even one-ounce calm was because of Ben. A second after the silence, Ben was right by my side. The string lights were shut off, but his face still shone like the sun, cast in the amber moonlight. "I'll fix this," Ben said, grabbing me by the shoulders. "Tell Jo not to worry." He quickly kissed my cheek and vanished before I could even inquire after his plan. The prospect of apologies, the conversation about our marriage, all fizzled out like the missing voltage.

Ben could fix this. I knew he could.

I wrung my hands together. The minutes ticked, threatening to topple the entire schedule. Food was growing cold, the bride and groom growing restless. Jo looked at me with watering eyes. An electrical mishap of this magnitude would break even the easiest-going of brides.

"Riley said they'll waive our exit time. We can stay all night if we want. No extra charge," my dad said, as our parents joined the family huddle.

"We don't need *more* time if there isn't even music," Jo said, her voice tight.

"We should have hired that psychic. She could have been doing palm readings right now," my mom said. If even she was talking in should-haves and could-haves, we knew something was wrong.

"It's going to be fine," Dave said, but his face wore a frown and his eyes were trained on his own parents, off bickering in a corner.

I took in the sight of my family, the stressed and sorry

expressions that cut right to my core. The patience they had spent on my forgiveness run dry. We had all reached our emotional bandwidths: these were the faces of family members spent.

My eyes darted around for Ben, but I couldn't find him anywhere.

We were running out of time.

"Dave's right," I decided. "It's going to be fine."

Jo's eyes widened as I pivoted away from my family members and strode right toward the now-vacated stage. My blood was racing, my skin shaking as I climbed up the stairs and positioned myself front and center. Anticipating my move, Dave grabbed a cell phone off the nearest table and shone its flashlight toward me. After a deep breath, I opened my mouth.

I sang.

"Oh yeah, I'll tell you something, I think you'll understand," I started, my voice shaky and off-pitch. Jo's jaw may have been on the ground, but the corners of her mouth were edging toward a smile when she realized what illogical stunt I was beginning to perform. "When I say that something—"

"—I want to hold your hand," Dave's voice graciously echoed out from the audience, joining my own for the chorus. I laughed through the notes, grateful for his company.

With each line, more voices layered as phone lights began to glow. My parents threw their arms in the air, waving to the rhythm and inspiring others to join in the growing anthem. Guest by guest, the crowd joined in. Together, we sang about connection, about reaching out and holding hands, in life and love, together. We let our inhibitions free, our voices climbing until we all were belting out the chorus in various keys.

As the faces around her hummed and buzzed, Jo remained too stunned to sing. Her shock amid the song. All this for her? Her face was frozen in marvel. Dave wrapped an arm around her, swaying her shoulders to the rumble of the crowd. Relatives had started stomping their feet, clapping along, making instruments with stemware and table settings. All to our favorite song. It didn't matter that the cacophony of pitches may have had the Beatles clutching their pearls. It was our own Fire Island magic. Intoxicating as the summer wind.

Just as we began the final verse, the lights kicked back on like an illusionist's trick. The microphone onstage picked up my voice and blasted it through the revived speaker system. The broadcasted sound of my singing would normally have sent me into a self-conscious tailspin, but now, I just used it as an excuse to sing even louder. Finally, I felt free.

Jo and Dave, bolstered by the electricity, jumped onstage and grabbed instruments. They dove straight into the strange display of resilience. Laughing, I tossed the microphone to my dad, who was ready to fulfill his lifelong dream of becoming a retired rock star. My mom followed him up and into the bright lights, having taken both Dave's parents by the hand as well. Dave looped guitar straps over Valerie's and Conrad's necks, both only stopping their singing to share a quick hug with their son.

As the song steered toward its final coda, I caught a

glimpse of Ben, once again standing solitarily by the Out's entrance gate. This time, he looked sweaty, with a hint of an oil smear stained atop his forehead. What electrical trick had he pulled off? He tapped his foot along to the music, humble yet triumphant. An engineering degree put to good use in the most unexpected of ways. That was my husband.

I handed the second microphone to Rich Mahogany's front man, who had rather reluctantly tabled the remainder of his drink to join the group of musicians back onstage. They mingled with my family members, teaching Valerie how to strum the proper chord and tutoring my dad with drumsticks. It was a scene from a movie, a memory that only a mistake could have made. Lemons to lemonade, etc. When the professional singer's voice filled the air, much more melodic than my own, the party picked up exactly where it had left off. This time though I wouldn't let Ben stand by himself for one second more.

My feet flew off the ground as I ran toward my husband.

He greeted me with a hug, arms tight around my waist, propelling me up and into the sky. My mind once again flashed back to our own wedding night. As the melody of our first dance trickled through the air, Ben had lifted me so high I could have touched the stars. He was right. In that moment, I paid no mind to the hundreds of eyes watching our every move. My anxieties surrounding the menu, the venue, even my footwear, all washed away.

Ben was always the only thing that mattered.

"I'm so sorry," I whispered now into his ear. "You are everything to me, Ben. Everything. I am so, so sorry."

He held me tight, frozen in time. "Come with me," he finally said, taking my hand and leading me out toward the dock. The music fell faint, but we could still make out the tune of a slow dance filling the air. He pulled me close and moved our bodies to the delicate beat.

My mind rotated through a thousand versions of apologies. The moment was here, but my voice choked. What I said next had the power to change everything. Each syllable so high stakes that it frightened me into silence. When I heard Ben clear his throat, I braced for the worst.

"Amy," Ben started, my head still glued safely onto his shoulder. I vowed not to move from this very spot unless I was being dragged by my feet. "I'm so proud of you."

"What?" I nearly did a spit take.

"Everything you do, you do with such strength. Such spirit. You are the only person I know who makes a plan and actually sticks with it. And when your plans falter, however rarely, well . . ." He placed a finger on my chin and pointed my face up toward his. I could just make out tears forming in his eyes under the moonlight. "This week. This past month. Amy, I don't think I really understood just how sick you've been making yourself. Last night was awful. I can't pretend it didn't crush me. I was so angry it made me nauseated. This morning, well, I just needed some time to process. I'm sorry I missed the photos—"

"Ben, *none* of this is your fault. I ruined everything."

"Still. I've been thinking all day about us. About what happened. And angry or not, all I know is that I want to be with you, Amy. I need to be. Our life, our future—"

"It's the only thing I care about. I swear. You mean everything to me, Ben. I want our future more than anything in the world. Whatever it brings. Ups and downs, I'm ready for it all. I'm ready. I will never do anything to risk it again."

"You scared me this week, Ames."

"I know. I pushed you away. I pushed myself away. I'm so sorry. Forever sorry."

Ben held me close.

"I love you, Bear," I said. "I love our history. Even the losses."

"Especially the losses," he whispered into my hair.

"But what if it happens again?" I finally asked, my voice barely audible. It was the question I'd been afraid to ask him, to ask myself even, ever since the miscarriage. How could we open ourselves up to the risk of heartbreak again?

Ben looked me in the eyes, tears forming. "We'll hold each other even tighter. We'll love even harder. And we'll never let go."

I let myself fall deeper against his arms. My own tears, my own anxieties, all releasing at once. It went unspoken that we would always hold space for what we had lost. We would never forget the loss, the pain. Could never if we tried.

Instead, maybe the pain could push us forward. Living on always, a reminder to cling to what we had. Our roots, our bones. The love that made us feel known.

"We can get through this," I promised. "I know we can."

"We *will*," he said, before kissing me. My heart swelled into my throat. "I love you, Amy. Through everything."

A roaring bang rocked our embrace.

The fireworks were beginning.

"Happy birthday, love." Ben smiled, wrapping his arm around my shoulder and leading me to the dock. Colors exploded along the horizon as we bore witness to hundreds of local firework spectacles along Long Island's edge. Most people subscribe to just one individual show, sitting on a lawn with picnic blankets, leaning back to watch a Starburst or Lady Fingers explode right over their faces. The smoke slipping into their nostrils. The taste of summer.

From Fire Island, we could see all the mainland's fireworks at once. Small against the distance, but mighty in its collective display. Cameras and videos never did the sight justice, so crowds would watch with electronics pocketed away. Settling into the sight, surrounded by my family, ears straining for the explosions' echoes bouncing along the bay's waves. My parents used to say it was the entire world throwing us a birthday party.

Jo and Dave appeared by our side. The wedding guests had followed out onto the dock, everyone itching to soak in the show. A chorus of "Happy Birthday" broke out in the back, as per Fire Island tradition. Ben and Dave molded into our human jigsaw, the four of us with threaded limbs and interwoven fingers, beaming in celebration. Our duo had doubled, but it felt just as natural as when it was just me and Jo, our tiny legs dangling off the dock, our tiny minds dreaming the way fireworks always made us dream.

Alight with love.

SUNDAY

CHAPTER

30

"WE'RE GETTING A DIVORCE."

My hangover pounded through my temples, causing me to question if my eardrums had somehow combusted overnight. Broken amid the party's debauchery. Maybe my ears were just still sleeping, dozing off until sobriety returned.

The knowing faces around the table confirmed the declaration. This was happening.

There was nothing in Fire Island that couldn't be cured by whitefish salad, so I grabbed the bowl and handed it to Valerie with the gentlest eyes I could muster. "I'm so sorry."

"Don't be." She shrugged. "It was a long time coming."

"That's for sure," Conrad said from across the room.

"I still don't know why you needed to wait until after the wedding to make your announcement," Dave said, his frustration manifesting in an aggressive cream-cheese spread, attacking an everything bagel like a punching bag.

"That's what I said. Who cares?" Lila said, her mouth full, her eyebrows burrowed, hints of last night's eyeliner stained under the surface.

"We didn't want to hog the spotlight," Valerie said.

"It was your mother's idea," Conrad added, under his breath.

"If that's what your souls need, then I say good. This is exciting, honestly," my mom said, toasting her glass.

"What she means is, we're excited to see what comes next," Jo added with a smile, squeezing Dave's hand ever so slightly under the table.

Valerie and Conrad had never hated Jo. There was never a clandestine plan to kick her out or stop the wedding. The only relationship they were interested in ending was their own.

As Valerie explained over bagels in our kitchen, she and Conrad had been growing apart for years. Their lifestyles had diverged, and the difference was now drastic. While they loved their family and were grateful for their shared past, they both had agreed on a different route for the future. Dave and Lila had picked up on their hints, the forced smiles among permanent frowns, and demanded answers from their parents earlier that week. Valerie and Conrad confessed their truth, their hope for divorce, but insisted on keeping it a secret from the Sharps—Dave was only allowed to tell Jo. Their family had kept it from the rest of us, and all the other wedding guests, until now. The hushed voices, the pained looks. Jo and Dave's heartbroken fights, the private dinners and beach outings all explained away.

How wrong my own contorted fears had been.

Perhaps unsurprisingly, Valerie and Conrad were practically glistening in the morning light. Unburdened of their secret, they had even made a round of mimosas for the group. It wasn't until noon that they at last bolted from the table, an alarm signaling a reminder for their ferry home. The first stop on the ride to their new futures.

"Thank you, Grace, for everything." Valerie's voice was practically singing as she wrapped my own mother in a hug. "It was splendid. Truly."

"What a blast! This island is something else," Conrad chimed in, clapping my father on the back. "Can I come back for Labor Day?"

Hugs exchanged, bags packed, and the Beaumonts left as peculiarly as they had arrived.

"Your parents are awesome, Dave," I said when a calm had once again coated the Summer Wind table. Laughter crashed like the waves. As my dad cleared the kitchen, and Ben and Dave carried the newlyweds' suitcases out to the front steps, Jo pulled me off to the side of the house, in front of the hedges where I'd first panicked about Emmett's entrance. It felt like a year ago, so much had broken since then. So much had healed.

"I've been dying to tell you about Conrad and Valerie, but Dave swore me to secrecy," Jo said now. "I was freaking out. The reminder that relationships are always ending, changing, just as I was about to commit to my own. That, plus the whole Zach thing . . . I'm sorry if I was acting like a strange breed of bridezilla," she said with a wince.

"Are you kidding? *I'm* sorry I couldn't help you through

it more. I wish I could have been there for you, with every-thing." I squeezed my sister's hand. "But if I've learned any-thing this week, it's that you can't compare what you have to anyone else. Not to Dave's parents, not to your twin, not to your past. Ugh, I'm sounding so cheesy again, I can literally taste it." I groaned. "But everyone makes their own path, Jo. And yours is looking pretty perfect to me."

"Yours, too, Ames." This time, my heart agreed. "We did it."

She pulled me into a final hug. "Congratulations," I whispered. "Love you."

"Love you more."

When I realized Jo was also crying, we both burst out laughing.

"You sure we can't squeeze in your luggage?" Ben's voice called out from behind us. Suitcases ready, wagon loaded and strung with its very own "Just Married" sign.

"We'll send you plenty of pictures," Jo said, pulling him into our group hug. Our trio, salvaged.

The new Mr. and Mrs. Beaumont had booked a water taxi and a car service to take them straight to JFK, headed toward their honeymoon in South Africa. Their real celebra-tion just waiting to begin. Two weeks on a safari had sounded heavenly when Jo announced their plan. For months, my own jealous dreams were filled with scenes admiring giraffes and lions, drinking gin and tonics in a stirring bush, sleep-ing under the stars. Now? I felt like I'd had enough of all things wild for a lifetime, and we hadn't even left New York

State. I couldn't wait to curl on my couch, pour a glass of red wine—or three—and enjoy the quiet comfort of our living room with Ben.

The happy couple departed with more hugs and tears, and then more laughter over the fact that we even had tears left to spend. We were all exhausted, but happy exhausted. There was a peace running alongside the current, one that only arrived after the extreme. We had all made it onto the other side of Jo's wedding week.

We were thirty.

We had survived.

The ferry rocked my thoughts into a pleasant murmur as Ben's eyes sparkled against the afternoon sun. After repeatedly offering to stay and help clean the rest of the house, and my parents repeatedly refusing, we packed up our suitcases and departed Summer Wind. On our way to the dock, we stopped by Party of Five to poke our heads inside, but even from the street we could only hear the sound of quiet snores and hungover slumber. The house's lights were off, and we didn't dare wake its inhabitants. I knew I'd see Bobby and Mary soon; we had monthly dinner dates in the city to try new restaurants or see the latest Broadway shows.

As for Emmett, I didn't think I was ready to say goodbye or hello again. Not anytime soon, at least. We weren't so naive to think our paths wouldn't merge one day, with Dave's and Jo's lives now legally cemented. Our social circles were bound to overlap again. I'd cross that bridge whenever it happened, I decided—not every situation needed a plan. A lesson hard learned.

As Ben looked out at the bay's waters from the ferry's upper deck, I slipped my hand into my purse. Wrapping my fingers around the envelope, I pulled out Jo's birthday card. A message saved for a later return. Despite the wind threatening to overtake the piece of paper, the timing now felt just right. I held on tight and steeled my heart for my sister's words.

Dear Amy,

If you're reading this, that means we are thirty. Did we make it? I sure hope so.

I'm writing this one week before our birthday, before we pack our bags and head to Kismet, before the wedding festivities commence. I worried that card writing would get swept to the side amid the pomp and prep sure to come this week, so I wanted to make certain I wrote this free of distraction.

I know things have been strange recently. This year tossed its fair share of changes at us: new addresses, new jobs, new people. Curveballs that hit our heads and left us with migraines, messes. No instruction manuals on how to put back the pieces. But in classic Sharp fashion, I like to think we embraced the changes. Tried our best. The shifts that could have been sad or stressful were celebrated. We found the good. It wasn't always easy. I know you might have felt stuck in the surprise, but I truly believe that by now, we have perfected the pivot.

Thirty is going to be our year. I love you. I love us. I love all that our future inevitably holds—through thick and thin, the messy and the magic. I have the best life because I have you as my ("big") sister. Happy, happy birthday.

Xo Jo

PS—"big" is a joke.
200 seconds don't actually make you older. Xx

My head fell heavy on Ben's shoulder. Kissing my hair, he grabbed my thigh and squeezed.

"Good birthday card?"

"The best."

Together, we watched the island shrink farther away, folding itself into the distant shoreline. The lighthouse, once looming, dwarfed down to just a single, glowing speck. This descent, the departure, usually brought with it a pang of sadness. Leaving the most carefree place, the happiest version of myself, always felt bittersweet no matter how many times we performed the dance. Vacation never lasted forever.

Kismet may have been dwindling in the distance behind us, but this time, my heart breathed easier. Lighter. Taking

Ben's hand in my own, I opened my face to the sun. The rays danced against my cheeks, coated my lashes in gold.

I didn't want to be anywhere else.

I didn't need any more signs. Any more doubts.

Any more journal entries from the past.

I was choosing my own destiny.

The best was yet to come.

Acknowledgments

Amy's story may begin on the Fire Island ferry, but the road to *Kismet* really began on the twenty-seventh floor of 1325 Avenue of the Americas, when Sabrina Taitz and I first met as WME interns. To the incomparable Sabrina, building lockstep careers with you has been a destiny all its own. Thank you for being my agent extraordinaire, my co-assistant for life. (And to Eric and Isla, thank you for sharing her.)

To the brilliant Cassidy Sachs, thank you for taking the chance on my debut, for your keen editorial insight, and for your friendship. I'm beyond lucky to know you.

Thank you to the WME book department, especially Ty Anania, Carolina Beltran (and our mailroom lunch walks), Caitlin Mahony, Sam Birmingham, Suzannah Ball, and Eve Attermann. To Jennifer Rudolph Walsh, Tracy Fisher, Alicia Everett, Claudia Ballard, Alicia Gordon, and Erin Conroy, thank you for your guidance on this path. They say writing a book is a solitary act, but my time working in books has been far from lonely. I'm so very grateful to have started it all at WME.

To my dream imprint, Dutton, and the visionary minds at Penguin Random House, for your support, especially John Parsley, Christine Ball, Stephanie Cooper, Amanda Walker, Susan Schwartz, Ryan Richardson, Alice Dalrymple, Ashley Tucker, and Gina Centrello. This book does not exist without you all, and I still can't quite believe that I get to count myself among your authors. Thank you.

To Alexa Ginsburg, Rebecca Servadio, Sarah Pocklington, and Gracie Salmon, for your early reads and encouragement. To Brittany Schwartz and Zoe Goldberg, for your (desperately needed) design skills and support along the way.

To the exceptionally creative Sunday Night team, for inspiring me to write on Saturday mornings.

To the Kismet community, especially the Mandels and Summer Wind, for always making space for me in your beach circle.

To Debbie, Eddie, Matt, and Craig Schwartz, for welcoming me not just to the magic of Fire Island but into your Party of Five family.

To Sam Chalsen and Katie Aldrin, the greatest big siblings, for your instrumental notes and wisdom. I'm forever looking up to you both.

To my quads, Joanna, Maggie, and Lizzy Chalsen, for all the ways our sisterhood has shaped me. There is no better story than being a quarter of ours. (And to Bobby, Brendan, and Jack, for making it four times sweeter.)

To my parents, Georgine and Chris Chalsen, for building the runway so that I could dream, for giving me a life so blessed that all I had to do was live it. There aren't enough thank-yous in the world.

To Zack, my very own kismet, the cutest boy on the school bus. Here's to our ride.